MAESHOWE
MURDERS

B. K. BRYCE

MAESHOWE MURDERS

FM-N

The area between Skara Brae and Maeshowe

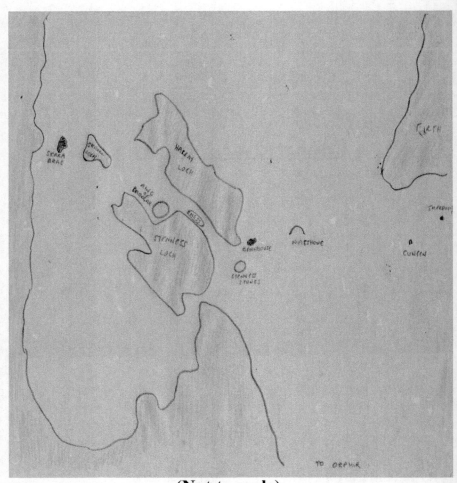

(Not to scale)

Maeshowe Murders

Chapter 1

Joel's body was not the first Marna had seen. Her father, too, had been pulled from the sea, with his pale cheeks swollen and his eyes devoured from their sockets by ravenous fish. That was many summers ago, but the image still haunted Marna. Joel was in a better condition. The men had got to him early and wrenched his bloated body from the clutches of the sea spirits. They were not in time to save the breath escaping from his lips and leaving them a greyish blue like the angry ocean. His empty form was strewn on the sand, swaddled in bladderwrack and mermaid's purses.

'I'll fetch Jona,' Thork said.

'We don't need a priest to tell us he's dead,' Roben sneered.

'No, but the body will need purified and prepared.'

'In good time. Shouldn't someone tell his wife?'

'I can do that,' Marna said. She could see Henjar approaching the beach from the village, carrying little Boda in the folds of her tunic. Marna hurried to reach her friend before she spotted her husband's body. Boda was gabbling his baby talk. He had yet to see a winter in the village. Normally Marna would laugh at the child's attempt to win his mother's eye, but today she couldn't raise even a smile.

'What have the men found?' Henjar strained to look past her. 'Is it a young whale?'

'No, not a whale… Let me take Boda for you,' Marna said, holding out her arms.

'What has happened? Is it a body? Oh no.' She staggered back and Marna reached to support her.

'I'm sorry…' Marna began

'Jo...Jo…' Henjar tried to speak her husband's name, but the word caught in her throat. She raised a quivering hand and pointed.

'Be strong.' Marna unwound the child from her friend's clothing and took him in her arms.

The baby cried as his mother rushed towards the shore, tripping as her feet caught in the sinking sand. Marna bobbed Boda in her arms and made silly faces to soothe him. In the distance she saw Henjar fall to her knees beside Joel's body. Roben put a hand on her shoulder, but she brushed him away.

'Don't stand there like a carved stone. Bring the child indoors before he gets a chill.' Marna's mother was walking towards her from the stone houses. 'There is a wind calling up from the sea. It's no place for a babe.'

Marna took another look at the scene by the shore; Joel lying in the sand, his fingers stirring only with the ripples of the tide. She shuddered and the babe in her arms grumbled.

'Sorry,' she whispered.

Her mother gestured to urge her indoors and she obeyed, meeting her near the entrance to the village. A group of women, old men and children were gathered, their curiosity marked by a nod or a twitch of the shoulder. Marna's mother pushed by them without a word and Marna followed. The usual warmth from the huddle of interlinked houses that made up Skara Brae was gone. In its place was the chilling harshness of life.

'Joel is dead,' Marna said once she was inside their house, warming herself and Boda by the hearth. 'Thork has gone to fetch Jona.'

'It is too late to ask the gods for help,' her mother said. 'It's the child and his mother that need taking care of now. At least it looks like the babe has been fed. Wrap him in a seal fur and lay him in the cot.'

'It's warm here. I don't mind holding him,' Marna rocked the child in one arm, tickling his tummy with the other.

'I imagine not, but there is work to be finished before dark. Thork and the other men will want stew to fill their bellies once they have seen to Joel's body. You could help me with the grinding. My fingers stiffen when the weather turns sour and the wind bites.'

Marna played with the child's thumb, twisting it around her fingers before wrapping him snug and laying him to rest. He began to cry.

'What will Boda do without a father?' she asked. 'Who will provide for Henjar?'

'Henjar is young. She will find another man,' her mother turned away sharply.

'I'm sorry. I didn't mean to remind you of father.'

'A good man drowned at sea – how could I not think of your father?'

'We are lucky to have Thork to hunt for us and bring home meat,' Marna said.

'Thork is a good son, but he will take a wife soon and have children of his own to provide for. It is too much to ask that he feeds us all.'

'I can look after us,' Marna said.

'Can you throw a spear to hit the wild boar or bring down the deer? I know you have been practising, but you don't have Thork's strength.'

'I don't need it. I know how to gather and prepare the plants to make coloured pigments. I can trade my dyes for meat.' Marna had taken the grinding stone from near the hearth and was crushing the rough grain heads into flour. 'We could get a sheep once Thork has left.'

'And let it sleep in his cot?' her mother said.

'Perhaps Thork will take Henjar as his wife,' Marna

pondered. 'Then we could live here together.'

'You know Thork has received Jona's blessing to marry Caran. She will be visiting from Orphir soon, with the basket of bog-iron for Roben. It may be that Thork will ask her then.'

Marna smiled then frowned. 'I like Caran, but she will wish to stay in her own village, with her own people.'

'That is her right,' Marna's mother answered.

'Then Thork would need to move to Orphir,' Marna pounded the grain.

'Not so hard,' her mother warned.

Marna sulked with her head bent towards the quern stone before looking up. 'Do you think Caran will have spare bog-iron? I could mix it with heather and dock leaves to make the dye for Jona's cloak. He wants it red to match his hair.'

'Ask Thork. I'm sure he can persuade Caran to save you some,' her mother said. 'Are you finished now?'

The bere heads were ground to flour. Marna's mother took the stone from her daughter before Marna's enthusiastic pounding reduced the powder to dust. She fingered the mixture to remove the remaining ears then poured the flour into a stone bowl, before adding water to fold the paste into bannocks.

'Don't touch,' she tapped Marna's fingers as she reached to taste the dough. 'Make yourself useful and fetch the honey from the dresser.'

Marna reached for the pot. 'It's empty.'

'Joannet will have some.'

Marna screwed up her face. 'You know what Joannet's like. I won't get away until I've answered all her questions.'

'Then the bannocks will have to do without.'

Marna inspected the pot again, but no honey had mysteriously appeared. She ran a finger round the brim. A dribble of honey stuck to the tip. She was about to lick it off, but Boda gave a cry and she moved to soothe the child by letting him suck her finger. She was humming to Boda when Henjar came to collect him. Her eyes were puffy and stained red from weeping and rubbing.

'Drink this,' Marna's mother handed her a beaker. 'I've heated the ale over the fire.'

Henjar accepted. Her hands shook and Marna moved close to her friend to steady her.

'Joel was a decent man,' Henjar said. 'He caught nets of cod and ling for us – for mother and Sempal too. There are not many men in the village who risk their lives at sea. I told him to take care, but he laughed and said he was always careful on the water. He had the seal bone charm that Wilmer made for him. He told me that seals were the guardians of seafarers, but today I found it on the dresser.'

Henjar was talking to herself, mumbling as she sipped

the drink.

'I have added poppies to comfort her,' Marna's mother whispered to Marna. 'It will make her drowsy.'

It wasn't long before Henjar was lying in the cot with her son. Her eyes drooped and she began snoring. Marna returned to work, preparing dyes for a neighbour.

'I wish you wouldn't do that inside,' her mother complained. 'The smell clings to the furs and lingers.'

'I don't like the workshop,' Marna answered. 'It's too...too...you know.'

Her mother sighed and moved to check on Henjar and Boda. 'The child will need fed again soon.'

Marna stopped her work to move beside her mother. 'Henjar is sleeping so soundly. It is a shame to wake her.'

'You might not mind her grunting and Boda's wailing, but I have sensitive ears.'

Marna leant to shake her friend on the arm. Henjar rolled over. 'Henjar is right,' Marna pondered while she waited on Henjar stirring. 'Joel knew the tides and the winds as well as any sea creature. He is the last person anyone would think of to fall in the water.'

'He may have had an attack of the chest. Joel was older than Henjar. These things can happen. Was anyone with him in the boat?'

'I didn't see the boat,' Marna said, 'Just the body.'

'What did Sempal say?'

'I didn't see Sempal on the beach. He wasn't with Henjar either.'

'If that fool was in the boat with Joel, it would explain everything.'

'Sempal isn't a fool,' Marna protested. Her mother gave a look to suggest otherwise and Marna went back to her work in a huff.

Henjar's brother had been stuck at birth and was born with an over-large head. He hadn't developed as other boys do and although he was a year older than Thork he was smaller than she was. His muscles were puny and he dragged his left leg when walking, but that didn't make him an idiot.

Her mother seemed to read her thoughts. 'There's nothing to be done about it and pounding those plants until you crack the pot won't help.'

'Sorry.'

'Why don't you take a look outside before it gets dark? The men should be on their way back.'

'I haven't finished.'

'You won't tonight. Your mind is not on it. I'll see to Henjar and Boda.'

Marna set the pot of mashed meadow flowers on the top of the dresser and fetched her cloak from the bottom of her bed.

'I won't be long,' she said, bending her head to leave

the hut. She made her way along the covered passageway between the buildings, tiptoeing past Jona's house. She needn't have bothered, because the priest was out. Someone had emptied their pots into the drain and Marna held her cloak over her nose until she was out in the open. The wind blew in her face and she had barely reached the edge of the bere strips that lay between the village and the shore before she spotted Roben. He was being blown by the wind towards her and Marna had to step aside briskly to prevent being bowled over.

'Watch where you're going,' Roben grumbled.

'I'm looking for the others. Will they be long?' Marna asked. She didn't look at his face. The blank socket, where his left eye should have been, made her feel squeamish.

'I imagine not. The task is finished. What do you want with them?'

'Mother has made stew and bannocks.'

'Has she?' Roben licked his lips. 'I have been sent ahead to light a fire in the gathering chamber.'

'Will Jona speak about what has happened?' Marna asked. 'Has he received a message from the other side?' She was more than a little afraid of the priest when he donned his head-dress, raised his staff and spoke in riddles.

'He may or he may not have. Either way, we shall hold a remembrance for Joel. Walf will kill one of his sheep. We'll need ale. It may be a long night.'

'Of course,' Marna bowed her head. Remembrances were sad events. The villagers would eat together, but their faces would be grave. Thork would beat his drum, but there would be little music and no dancing. That would come in later months, once Joel's being was reduced to whitened bones which they could lay to rest in the burial cairn with suitable feasting and celebration.

'Perhaps Sempal will tell us a story,' Marna spoke her thoughts aloud. Her mother and the others thought Sempal a fool, but when it came to storytelling he could capture an audience with the tone of his voice, or a simple hand gesture, better than Jona with his messages from the gods or Roben with his fire tricks.

Roben grunted. 'A remembrance is no place for tales. Besides, Sempal is under suspicion. Jona will demand to know what happened in the bay. That is, if the boy can be found. He hasn't shown his face since the body was brought ashore.'

'What do you mean?'

Roben didn't answer. He glowered then pushed her aside to stumble towards the village entrance. She watched him bend to enter. The top of his head was bald and burnt a dark, shiny pink. She should feel sorry for him because of his accident, but she couldn't help being repulsed. His temper had been short before the flames took his eye and half the skin from his head, but since then it took only one false word, or a misguided look, and he would flare up like the fires he stirred. With the colder weather approaching, she would be forced to see him more often. Her mother or Thork would call on his services. They needed fire for warmth as well as cooked meat.

'I know how to light fires too,' Marna muttered into the wind as she watched him disappear.

That wasn't true, but she had seen how Roben prepared the kindling and rubbed the stones to entice a spark. If she had his black stones, she believed she too could light a fire – with a little practise. Roben wrapped his black stones in a cloth made from nettle fibres and kept in a sealskin bag attached to his belt. He never took his belt off.

Marna stood for a moment, waiting on the others. The sky had darkened and the rain arrived before the villagers. The wind thrust drops at her face. The others would quicken their pace if a storm was brewing. Marna thought of Sempal. If he wasn't with the others, as Roben said, she would have to find him. Henjar would have enough to worry about without her brother being lost in a storm. Besides, she was keen to hear what he had to say, before Jona and the village elders began their interrogation. Sempal would get flustered and tongue-tied, especially if Jona raised his voice. He would need her help to stay calm.

Marna guessed Sempal would be walking along the cliff path from the shore. It was where he went when he wanted to be alone. He enjoyed watching the patterns of the waves breaking against the rocks or studying the sea birds in flight.

'One day we will take to the skies like the birds,' Sempal told her with outstretched arms.

'Then we could fly up to the gods and give them a piece of our minds,' Marna joked, but Sempal was serious.

'Would you like to travel across the sea?' he asked.

'I like meeting different people,' Marna said. 'I love hearing their strange voices and admiring their colourful clothes. The traders tell wonderful stories of fabulous lands with stone pyramids and armies of men, of amazing creatures and coloured rocks and jewels not found here.' Marna paused for a moment. 'I'm not so fond of their water gods and sea monsters though. I think I prefer that traders come to our shores rather than us going to their lands.'

'I would like to travel,' Sempal told her. With his disability, she couldn't see him fighting against krakens or giant sea serpents. He struggled to haul in the small fish caught in the fresh water lochs, but she didn't argue.

She skirted the bere plots and headed south towards the rocks before spotting Sempal at the top of the cliff. She recognised the dash of blue on his cloak. She had dyed it for him the previous summer using wild sorrel. She jumped and waved, trying to get his attention. Her words were lost in the howl of the wind. The figure wavered and staggered towards the cliff face. Marna feared her friend would be blown over the edge. She put out her arms as if to save him and jumped as she felt a tap on her shoulders.

'What are you doing out here in weather like this?'

She turned. The wind had swept his hair over his face, but there was no mistaking Sempal.

'I thought...' Marna began. She swung round to look back up the cliff. The figure she had seen was gone. 'You were up there.' She turned back to stare at Sempal, as if searching for the wings that had brought him down so quickly. 'Are you hurt?' She reached to feel his face with her fingertips.

'Why should I be hurt?' Sempal asked.

'You didn't fall...?'

'What are you talking about?'

'I saw you on the cliff. I recognised your cloak.'

'I was walking on the shore,' Sempal answered.

Marna was about to protest, but she spotted a line of footprints across the wet sand. 'They said you were in the boat with Joel,' she said instead.

'I was this morning, although we didn't catch more than a couple of flounders. In the afternoon my stomach was upset, so I didn't go out.'

'Joel set sail alone?'

'I think so, although he mentioned a friend wanting to go with him. The weather is turning and it's getting dark.

He should be back soon. I have been carving a toy for Boda. Do you like it?' He raised his right hand and opened the palm to show Marna a wooden figure of an eagle.

'Oh no,'

'I don't have Wilmer's skills, but it isn't that bad.'

'You haven't heard.' Marna covered her mouth.

'Heard what? You are a strange one today Marna.'

Sempal twiddled the wooden eagle between his fingers as Marna blurted out how Thork had found Joel's body face down in the shallow water near the shore. It took several tellings before Sempal understood. When she finished he snapped the wings off the carved eagle and tossed the figure into the sea.

'You shouldn't have done that,' Marna said. 'It was a beautiful carving. Boda would have loved it.'

'What use is a toy when you have no father to protect you?' Sempal said.

'The village folk will rally round.'

Sempal didn't reply. He turned away from Marna and strode towards the incoming waves. Marna feared he wouldn't stop and walk straight into the water.

'The elders are expecting you,' she called after him. 'They need to know what happened.'

'Why ask me? I can't help.' Sempal didn't look back. He reached the water's edge and paused before walking along the tide line, kicking at the water.

Marna watched his figure get smaller. There was no point chasing him. He was almost out of sight when she heard the chatter of the others returning from the dunes, where they would have laid out Joel's body. There was no mistaking her brother. Thork's voice was twice as loud as the others and he was never short of an opinion.

'Someone will know where Sempal is,' he shouted.

Marna decided it was best not to meet up with them. She made her way to the village through the bere, where the stalks were tall enough to hide her. When she arrived home Henjar was awake and feeding Boda.

'Where have you been?' Henjar asked.

'Nowhere.'

Her mother entered the hut carrying bannocks arranged on a stone slab. 'Good, you're back. Take these to the workshop while I see to the stew.'

The workshop doubled as the village meeting area. Marna made her way with care, not wanting to drop the bannocks. Roben was kneeling in the centre of the room, stoking his fire.

'These bannocks need warmed,' she said, laying the stone beside the hearth.

Roben looked up and scowled. 'Don't touch that.'

Marna had picked up one of his black stones. The smooth surface was hot. Her fingers tingled. Roben snatched at it, but Marna slipped her hand away.

'Give it back at once.'

'Or what?' Marna teased. Roben twisted his face into a scowl and Marna handed him his stone. She walked across the room to move pottery items and tools, making space for the villagers to gather. 'You should teach someone how to use them.'

'When I have a son, I'll teach him.'

'If you had a son tonight, it would be years before he was old enough to learn. Something might happen to you. Thork says Barnhouse has been without a fire-maker for weeks. Hector died after being gored by a stag and his wounds festered.'

'Hector was a fool and now the villagers from Barnhouse have to pay dearly, but I have endured the fire's test and survived,' Roben pointed to his missing eye. 'What else can harm me?'

Chapter 2

Winters were never easy in the village. The gods needed the daylight and Jona had a hard time persuading them to spare a little. The seas were too angry for the fishermen to venture out and even the lochs were unwilling to provide fish. The stores of grain were reduced to a few tired ears and the wild plants folded their leaves to sleep until spring.

The wild geese arrived late, taking over the land east of the village and waking sleepers with their gaggling. Thork was an expert at catching the birds. He and his friend Albar knew how to circle the birds without a sound and throw a net over them before they flew off. They trapped enough birds for everyone in the village, but after three weeks, Marna wished for the earthy savour of hare or deer.

'There's no pleasing some people,' Thork huffed. 'Still, if you don't want any goose, I can devote my time to polishing the mace head I got from Albar.'

'That's more useful than carving stone balls to toss around the place,' his mother muttered.

'I'm a champion thrower,' Thork boasted.

When the storms bit they blew anyone who ventured from the village off their feet. Stuck indoors with a rumbling stomach, Marna chewed on dried hazelnuts and wished she hadn't complained about the geese.

A day after the midwinter solstice a whale was washed up on the shore.

The winds and rain died down for a few hours and Marna took the chance to go outside. The close-knit houses were stuffy and it was good to escape.

'I'll fetch seaweed and shellfish from the shore,' she told her mother.

Sempal spotted her as she made her way along the passageway to the exit. 'Do you want company?'

'Only if you tell me a story,' Marna answered.

Sempal was the first to spot the whale. He was recounting a tale about a mysterious sea creature that swallowed boats whole when he pointed at a blob on the sand. The creature was twice his size and several times his weight, but when he reached it, he tried to shove the beached body back into the sea.

'It's too late,' Marna said. 'Its spirit has left its body.'

Sempal kicked the sand at his feet in frustration.

'Its body will help us survive,' Marna said. 'We'll need to tell the others and get help carving the meat and gathering the blubber, oil and bones.'

'You do that,' Sempal said. His face was a pale shade of green and he held a hand over his mouth as Marna described the dissection process. She heard him retch as she turned to hurry back to the village.

Roben's was the first house she reached, but the fire-maker didn't answer her call. She heard voices in the house where Sempal lived with his mother, Henjar and Boda.

'We've found a whale washed on the beach,' she said, stepping into the circular room. There was no-one there, despite the voices. Boda's cot was empty and the fire had burnt out. She was about to leave, but heard rustling from behind the stone dresser. 'Hello.'

Henjar stepped out, her face red. 'I was just...' she pushed a strand of hair from her eyes. 'A whale, you said? Are you sure?'

'I know what a whale looks like,' Marna replied. 'Sempal spotted it first.'

'Then it is more likely a rotten fishing boat,' Roben said, appearing from behind the dresser. He stood beside Henjar, with an arm round her waist.

'It is a whale. If you don't want to come, I'll find Thork and Albar. They will know what to do.'

'What's this commotion? Did someone mention a whale?' Jona's house was opposite Henjar's and he came out to see what was going on. Marna saw her brother and a few others appear beside him.

'A whale has been washed up on the beach,' Roben answered before Marna could speak. 'Henjar is about to fetch pots while I sharpen my knife.'

'You didn't think to let the others know?' Jona accused.

'Marna was about to,' Roben scowled at her. Perhaps it was meant as a smile. Either way he was showing her who was in charge.

'Sempal spotted it first,' she repeated.

'This is a gift for the whole village,' Jona declared. 'The gods be praised.'

The villagers showed their appreciation with a cheer. Young and old were roused from their dwellings. Tools were brought and tested for their sharpness. Every stone pot, wooden box, nettle fibre bag and sheep or sealskin in the village was carried to the shore. The tidal water was lapping around the lifeless beast, threatening to steal the body back. Marna looked for Sempal, but he was gone.

'Where is that useless brother of yours?' Marna heard Roben ask Henjar as they set to work on the carcass, reducing it to oil, blubber, bones and meat.

'He's sensitive,' Marna answered.

Roben gave a laugh. 'You mean he's behind the dunes spewing his guts up. And he calls himself a man.'

Marna wanted to give a suitable retort, but she couldn't think of anything.

'Give us a hand,' Thork called.

Marna made a face at Roben behind his back as she joined her brother. The villagers worked quickly, but the daylight hours were short and the weather was turning. Before the sun set behind the hills they dragged the remains further up the shore, singing as they heaved it onto the stones. Marna was glad to get indoors. She helped her mother prepare a whale meat stew, adding in the last barley grain that was left in their store. There was enough for half the village and Marna's mother invited the neighbours to share. Sempal returned and Marna invited him too.

'There is hardly room to squeeze in a pup,' Sempal objected, but the aroma of the stew was sufficient to entice him in. Marna handed him a bowl.

'Our sensitive storyteller has arrived home. You have no qualms about eating the meat,' Roben challenged him. Sempal tried to put his bowl down, but there was nowhere to set it. He looked Roben in the eye.

'How will you provide for your mother and sister if you are squeamish about butchery?' Roben taunted.

'Don't you worry, I'll do what I have to,' Sempal answered.

'Little recompense,' Roben nudged his neighbour, hoping to get the man to support him.

'What do you mean?' Sempal stepped towards the fire-maker. He gripped his bowl with his left hand, but his right fist was clenched.

'You needn't wave your fist at me, boy. I may only have one eye, but I can see perfectly well with it. There were two people in Joel's boat when I looked out to sea from the dunes.'

'I have told the elders, I did not go out with Joel in the afternoon. Are you saying I am lying?'

'You are good at making up stories,' Roben said. 'Nadea and Eada swooned when you described the horned monsters with armoured hide that can gore men to death. Nadea now fears leaving the village on her own. You say you were walking on the cliffs. Why shouldn't that be another of your tales? Nobody saw you. Joel's boat has not been found. You could have steered the boat into a bay along the coast, buried it in the dunes then walked back along the cliffs.'

Sempal shook his head. His body twitched. 'Why would I kill Joel?' He spluttered a denial.

'I didn't say it was deliberate. We all know how cack-handed you are.'

Marna wanted to scream at Roben, but it was Henjar who stepped in.

'Stop arguing. You're giving me a headache.'

'When we are coupled, he will have to find somewhere else to live,' Roben insisted.

'You will never marry my sister,' Sempal spat.

'That is not up to you, little boy,' Roben smirked.

Sempal looked from Roben to Henjar. Marna moved to put a hand on his arm.

'Thanks for the stew,' Sempal handed Marna his half full bowl. 'I should be going.' He pushed past her mother and Joannet on the way out. She would have followed, but Joannet was complaining and she had no wish to upset her by asking her to move aside. Instead she busied herself collecting empty bowls and refilling ale beakers until everyone departed.

The whale carcass was disposed off the following day and Jona organised a ceremony to thank the gods for the gift. Thork was given instructions for his mother to bake bannocks.

'What does Jona want me to do?' Marna asked. She knew the priest would have assigned everyone a role.

'You've to dye the cloth for Henjar to sew into costumes.'

'That makes a change from cleaning up afterwards.'

'You'll be asked to do that too,' Thork admitted.

Marna was busy that day and the next, dyeing and drying the skins and woven fibres.

'Jona doesn't realise how long it takes,' she moaned to her mother. 'He thinks he can snap his fingers and get what he wants.'

'He usually does,' her mother answered.

Henjar came to collect the material. Marna wanted to ask her about Sempal and Roben, but the matter was delicate. She hadn't seen Sempal since the argument. He wasn't doing his part in the preparations for the feast and Roben was quick to bring this to Jona's attention. Marna heard them talking in Jona's house, as she poured the waste water into the communal drain.

'The lad has his part to play in the drama of life,' Jona said. 'It would do certain people no harm to mind their own business rather than that of their neighbours.'

Marna stopped herself laughing when Roben stomped out. The fire-maker was not happy and she heard him mumbling complaints about Jona to whoever would listen. It wasn't long before others were finding fault with the priest's judgements.

'He drinks too much strong ale,' Henjar told Marna. 'Roben has seen him chew on roots that send his eyes circling into his head.'

'Thork says it helps him to communicate with the gods,' Marna replied. 'Jona is a wise man.'

'Mmm.'

'Have you seen Sempal?' Marna changed the subject.

'That fool is more often wandering off on his own, than supporting his family. He has stupid ideas about travelling.' Henjar made a crazy face.

'You shouldn't speak of your brother like that.'

'Why not? Roben does, and soon we will be wed.'

'What? Marry Roben? But he is…I mean, so soon after…? Don't you think…? I have to go.'

Marna was anxious to speak with Sempal, but he wasn't at the celebration. Later, when she visited Henjar's house, Roben was there, so she pretended she had come to see Boda.

'I thought I would take advantage of the milder weather to gather shells to decorate my storage box. I could take Boda with me.'

'You need a child of your own to tend,' Henjar said.

'Boda enjoys Marna's company,' Roben said, 'and it gives us more time together.'

Marna wasn't happy at being used as a baby minder by Roben, but she enjoyed playing with the boy.

There was no trace of the whale left on the beach. The wind had died and Marna was playing on the sand with Boda when she spotted Sempal coming down from the cliff. She gathered the baby in her arms and walked to meet him. Boda began laughing when Sempal spoke.

'I'm surprised he still recognises his uncle,' Marna chided. 'Why are you never in the village?'

'My sister is to marry Roben,' Sempal said coldly.

'And you are not happy for her?'

'He pretends to play with Boda, but I've seen him slap the babe when he cries. Henjar won't listen, because Roben brings her gifts. Last week he gave her two new pots and this week a carved whale tooth comb Wilmer made.'

'A carved whale tooth comb?' Marna was envious.

'A bauble. Henjar is blind to his true nature.'

'Of course, if Roben is cruel to Boda, Henjar must have nothing to do with him,' Marna agreed, bouncing Boda in her arms.

'Will you speak to Henjar? She might listen to you.'

'I can speak with her, but I can't promise she will listen. She thinks I am biased against Roben.'

'You dislike him too?'

'Before the winter set in, I dyed a cloak for him. He promised me three clay pots, but he didn't pay. Every time I remind him, he brushes me aside with some excuse or other. Why all the fuss about three pots, he says, but it isn't the first time. Last spring I dyed a tunic in exchange for him showing me how to use his fire stones.'

'Roben would never show anyone how to do that,' Sempal said.

' I know. It was stupid of me to believe him when he swore that he would. He came towards me with a growl like a wild animal when I asked him to honour his agreement. He accused me of dying his tunic the wrong colour. He said he asked for sky blue, but I gave him a tunic darker than the winter sea. I showed him a sample before I dyed the tunic and he was happy with the colour.'

'What did Thork say?'

'He promised to speak with Roben, but you know what he's like. He has put off asking Caran to marry him five times. Confronting Roben is not at the front of his mind.'

'Roben has no right to treat you like that. Someone should tell Jona. He would deal with him.'

'Forget it. Tell me one of your stories - the one where a full grown man was eaten by a whale.'

'I wouldn't want to frighten Boda.'

'He is too young to understand, but he enjoys hearing your voice.'

Sempal didn't need much coaxing to start a tale. He liked to mimic accents and take on the guise of the people he spoke about. If the story was about an old man he would bend his back and speak with a croaky voice, if it was about a stag he would hold tree branches against his forehead.

'I shall tell you a story I heard from traders last summer about the faerie folk that cause mischief in Ireland. Depending on their whims, crops can fail, storms can devastate villages, or babies can be born with two heads.'

'Two heads,' Marna mused. She stroked Boda's fair hair. 'I'm glad Thork has only one. His is big enough.'

'This is a serious tale, Marna,' Sempal pretended to scold her. 'If you won't heed the warning of the faerie folk I shall have to keep my story for those who will.'

'No, I'm sorry. Go on,' Marna apologised.

Sempal began his story, but stopped at the part where the hero was faced with a critical choice.

'What did he do?' Marna was hooked on the tale.

'You'll have to wait until tomorrow to find out.'

Marna wanted to punch him, but she had to wait.

The winter passed with Sempal beginning stories that

panned out over several nights, the hero becoming involved in ever more vivid adventures. The year turned and the days became lighter. Plants budded, flowered and produced berries. The cows gave birth to calves and lambs were born to the ewes. The weather was fine for hunting and the sea calmed for the fishermen to return to their boats.

Jona left the village to consult the gods and thank them for the safe passage through the winter months. When he returned, he called a gathering. That meant ale and bannocks, and Marna's mother was one of the women called upon to prepare the food and drink.

'What do you think he wants to say?' Marna asked her mother as she helped knead the dough on the morning of the gathering.

'He will tell us how our neighbours have faired during the winter. We were able to spare oil and meat from the whale to help them. They may wish to repay us in some way.'

Marna pushed out her lips. 'Will that be all?'

'You will find out soon enough. Was there something on your mind?'

'I was thinking about Joel. His bones have not been taken to their place of rest yet. Henjar wants to marry Roben, but is unwilling to do so until she knows Joel is safely on his journey.'

'If I were Henjar, I would not rush to marry Roben,'

her mother answered, 'but I am not Henjar. I imagine Jona will say something in good time.'

Her mother's reply didn't satisfy Marna, but there was little she could do. That evening, thirty of the villagers crushed into the workshop. Ale was passed round and the people gossiped until Thork beat his drum and Jona entered, dressed in his ceremonial robe. The villagers made way and he took up his position on a boulder in the centre of the room, next to the fire. It was placed to raise him above the others and the flames gave gravity to his words.

'The gods be praised,' he began, lifting his staff. The villagers muttered words of approval. Jona gave a report on the neighbourhood. Barnhouse had a new fire-maker, the stone circle at Brodgar was progressing well although more help was needed and they were warned of a cattle fever coming from the east. The villagers were forbidden to bring in new cattle until the danger was over.

'Finally,' Jona said after swallowing the contents of a mug of ale, 'It is time to place the bones of our friend Joel in the chambered cairn of our ancestors at Cuween.'

Cuween, why there?

Grumbling broke out among the villagers. Henjar shivered and Roben put an arm around her shoulders.

Sempal was the first to speak out. 'There are cairns nearer the village that can be visited with greater ease, should my sister wish.'

A number of people agreed with Sempal. Jona held his arms aloft to quieten them.

'It is true, there are cairns on the route, but do we rest the bones of our dead in cairns to please their families or to obey the gods?' He glowered round, but nobody answered. 'I have received a message from above. While hunting this morning, my hound became trapped in a thorn bush. I bent to untangle it and a voice spoke from the bush, telling me that the cairn at Cuween was in need of bones.'

'Aye, dog bones,' someone called.

'No, the bones of men,' Jona answered.

Marna wondered how he could make out the voice of a god speaking over the howling of his dog, but the others bent their heads in awe. Henjar seemed upset. She whispered to Roben and he took a step forward to speak.

'When shall the ceremony take place?'

'When the moon is full,' Jona replied, rolling his eyes towards the roof of the hut.

The moon was full three nights ago. Marna calculated there would be another twenty five sunrises until it was full again. She edged towards Henjar. 'There is time for the gods to speak again,' she whispered. 'They are a fickle lot. With a suitable gift, they may change their minds.'

Henjar felt the whale bone comb she kept on her belt and smiled.

'That was a gift from Roben,' Marna said. She didn't

feel it was right to offer it to the gods to get a favourable decision on Joel.

'Wilmer can make me another one,' Henjar answered.

'Wilmer has other things to do apart from make you combs. He is the senior elder in Barnhouse. Jona told us the people there are struggling because of the storms.'

'Roben says it's their own fault. They should link their houses like we do here. It is un-neighbourly to live in stand alone houses. They are a strange lot in Barnhouse. It's because the village is too near the standing stones.'

'Did Roben say that too?' Marna couldn't prevent a snide tone. Henjar folded her arms and turned away.

Jona had finished speaking and he stepped down from the boulder. The squashed villagers moved closer to allow him to pass. The meeting was over. The cakes and ale were finished and the villagers were glad to return to their houses. Nobody felt like lingering. Only Roben stayed to tend the fire. Marna was intrigued. She pretended to leave, but sneaked back and hid behind the wall to watch him.

'How did you get here?' Roben called out.

Marna trembled, assuming he had spotted her. Before she could answer she heard Jona's voice.

Surely he had left first? How had he managed to return without her seeing him?

Jona sounded angry. He slammed his fist against the wall, drowning the sound of his words. Marna thought she heard him mention Henjar's name.

'That is no business of yours,' Roben replied.

'I have authority from the gods.'

'So you say,' Roben laughed. 'Why should we believe the gods speak to you? You make up more tales than that useless brother of Henjar's and they are twice as dangerous.'

'You mock the gods and their wisdom?' Jona answered. His voice shook the room and Marna gripped the stone to steady herself. 'Beware what you say.'

'Or what? The gods will be annoyed? Maybe then they will show themselves to me as well as you.'

'I will not listen to this,' Jona roared. Marna had no time to conceal herself before he strode from the room and caught sight of her cowering. His face was as prickly purple as the sea urchins' shells and when he scowled his eyes burnt wilder than Roben's fire.

'What the...?' He was about to say something, but with a look back at Roben, he grunted and marched off.

Marna leaned close against the wall. Roben was still in the workshop. She heard hissing as the final flames died. Roben was dowsing them with his urine. When the dripping stopped she caught her breath and pressed her body into a recess, before Roben trudged out of the workshop and headed towards Henjar's hut.

Marna waited until she was sure she was alone then

peeped inside the workshop. The room was dark, but there beside the glowing ashes was one of Roben's black stones. He had been too angry with Jona to take proper care and return both stones to his bag.

Marna made sure no-one was watching then crept in. She darted to the fire and snatched the stone. It was warm and her fingers tingled. She knew one stone was useless. It took the rubbing of both stones to create a spark, but if she couldn't make a fire with one stone, neither could Roben. That was something she could bargain with for her pots. She slipped the stone into the pocket of her tunic and left.

Over the next few days the stone grew heavier in her pocket. She felt her face redden whenever a neighbour grumbled that their fire had gone out. It wasn't just that one of his stones was missing. Roben himself was absent.

Marna thought he was searching for the missing stone then she assumed he had journeyed to the dark island lying to the south to trade for another stone. Days passed and he didn't return. Every evening Henjar came round to ask Marna if she had seen him.

'What will I do if he doesn't come back? Is it my fault? Did I say the wrong thing? Perhaps Boda upset him.'

'If he is upset by a baby, then good riddance to him,' Marna said. Henjar was not appeased. 'When did you last speak with him?'

Henjar took a moment to think. 'Three days ago. No,

it was the morning after the gathering. He was angry and I told him Joel wouldn't mind Cuween. You can see the sea from the top of the hill.'

'He was angry at Jona's choice?' Marna queried.

'He said something about losing one of his fire stones. He accused Boda of playing with it. Do you think he has left the village for good?'

'I shouldn't think so,' Marna answered. 'Where would he go?'

'He wanted rid of my brother, but Sempal hung around to annoy him. If Roben has left the village because of my brother, I'll...I'll... I should have gone with Roben.'

'You have Boda to care for.'

'I could have taken him too. The babe takes less looking after than Roben,' Henjar said, then held her mouth as if trying to take her words back. 'You know what I mean. Roben has a temper if others upset him.'

'He is easily upset,' Marna agreed.

'Misunderstood,' Henjar corrected. 'I often have to step in when people fail to grasp his meaning. He argued with Thork before the meeting, something about Roben not paying his dues. Later he quarrelled with Jona, but he was more worried about finding his stone. He muttered something about it being in the workshop. He went to collect it the following morning, while I arranged Boda's cot. That's the last time I saw him. How could I know he intended leaving the village without me?'

Marna felt the stone in her pocket. It jumped around the fabric like an agitated toad. Her fingers tightened round it. She would have to confess her deed to Henjar.

'What is worse,' Henjar continued before Marna could speak, 'My beautiful carved comb is missing too.'

'That's impossible. No-one could have removed it from your belt without you knowing. When did it happen?'

'I don't know. Oh Marna, I'm afraid. Roben has gone; his stone is missing and the comb too. It is an omen. Bad things are about to happen.'

Chapter 3

'Tell mother I'm off to the loch to spear fish for supper.'

Marna was sorting her dyes and didn't look up. Thork prodded the nearest pot to make sure she heard. She grabbed her pot to stop it tumbling over.

'I don't doubt you can bring down the running deer and I've seen you stop wild boars in their tracks, but when have you ever outsmarted fish?'

'Want to come and watch?'

'And help you when you fall in the loch? You can't work out the distortion the water causes.' She was about to add '*you don't have the brains,*' but thought it wiser not to, if she wanted her dyes unspoilt.

'Remind me not to give you any fish,' Thork huffed.

'I am short of bog myrtle. I'll gather flowers and mosses by the water's edge while you make a fool of yourself. I wouldn't want you to bang your head on the river bed and drown, or catch a chill and be stuck in the house complaining of ills for days.'

'Thanks, sister.'

Marna collected her shawl and basket. The loch was a short walk from the village, along the road to the stone circle. It wasn't as large as the lochs beside Barnhouse, but it provided the villagers with fresh water, fish, duck eggs and ducks, when they could catch them. The banks were rich in plants and Marna's basket was full before Thork caught a glimmer of shiny scales beneath his feet.

'This one won't get away,' he called.

He raised his spear and Marna watched him catch his foot on a reed and tumble head first into the shallow water. She waited until he stood up, unharmed, before laughing.

'We should go back,' she said. 'It's almost sunset.'

The sky was a glorious mixture of orange, blue and gold that Marna never tired of watching.

'One more shot. There's a trout hiding in the reeds.' Thork gathered his spear and waded up to his thighs. 'You go home. I can't go back with nothing to show. I'll stay until morning if I have to.'

'Perhaps you should ask Jona for tips,' Marna said, spotting a small raft in the middle of the loch. It bobbed with the swell, but Jona was easy to identify with his flaming red hair and beard. He was balancing on the wood, spear in hand, stabbing at the water. Marna saw him bring his spear to the surface with a fish twitching on the end.

'What does Jona know of fishing?' Thork said. 'He is a herdsman.' He pushed through the water to reach his sister.

'The gods must have shown him,' Marna answered.

Thork glanced at Jona. 'He's got a boat. He can reach the deeper water where there are more fish.'

'I would hardly call it a boat,' Marna said, trying to keep her face straight. 'There's a fallen branch beside these curlews. You could make a boat too.'

Thork grunted. 'Here, help me out.' He held out his arm for Marna to pull.

'Look,' she pointed instead. Jona had stopped fishing and stood with his head bent upwards, his feet wide apart and his arms outstretched, reaching for the fading sun. 'What's he doing? If he isn't careful the raft will topple and he'll fall in the water and drown.'

'Hush,' Thork instructed. He stepped out of the loch and stood next to Marna, dripping water into her basket of plants. 'He is receiving a message.'

Why can't we hear? Do the gods speak in whispers?

Marna heard the serious tone to her brother's voice and didn't give the scathing reply that was on her tongue. 'Perhaps the gods have changed their mind over Joel's burial site,' she said

'The procession is tomorrow,' Thork reminded her. 'The hillside tomb has been opened and prepared.'

'Henjar has been praying for Joel's bones to be buried nearer home,' Marna said. 'Why shouldn't the gods listen to her?'

Thork screwed his face until it turned purple. 'The gods choose who they speak to from the most devout of their servants. They don't listen to requests from girls who change their minds when they see stars in the sky.'

Marna was about to remind Thork it wasn't only the village girls who looked to the sky for answers, but a splash from the middle of the lake grabbed her attention.

The boat was empty. Jona had either jumped or fallen in the water. He was near the raft, struggling with arms and legs flailing. His head sank beneath the surface.

'Watch my spear,' Thork thrust his weapon at Marna, ready to rush to Jona's aid. He had taken one step into the water when Jona rose from the loch as if a giant hand was holding him in his palm. Marna reached for Thork's hand, her heart racing and her throat dry. Her brother stood gazing as if in a trance. As Jona made his way to the shore, floating on the ripples, Thork bowed his head.

'He's coming this way,' Marna croaked.

The priest strode from the loch and passed a few strides from Marna. She gulped, but he didn't acknowledge her presence. Thork fell to his knees in the shallow water. Jona's face glowed and his eyes were lit up. Marna told Sempal later they sparkled like the stars.

'Where do you think he is going?' Marna whispered to Thork. 'The village is in the opposite direction.'

Thork knelt in the water, but didn't answer.

'Should we follow him?' She gave Thork a nudge. He lost his balance and fell in the water like a severed branch. The splash brought him to his senses.

'Hey,' he shook water at Marna as he rose. She put her basket of plants down and reached out to give him a hand. 'Thanks, sis.' He took hold of her fingers and yanked her in. 'Serves you right.'

By the time they soaked each other and pulled themselves from the loch, Jona was gone.

'We've lost him,' Marna said. 'That's your fault.'

'You're the one who started it.'

She stuck out her tongue.

'I haven't seen Jona receiving a message from the other side before,' Thork admitted.

'I didn't see anyone on the other side,' Marna said, shielding her eyes from the setting sun.

'The other side, not the opposite…'

Marna laughed. Her brother couldn't tell when she was joking. 'Come on, there's no way you are going to catch a fish even if you wait here until mid-summer. Let's go back to the village and get dried. Jona will tell the village what he heard or saw in due course.' She picked up her basket.

'Where's my spear?' Thork asked.

'Ah.'

'It's in the water. You dropped my best spear in the loch.' Thork knelt and began grabbling among the reeds.

'It's dark, come back and find it tomorrow. If it's stuck in the reeds it won't go far.'

'The water will rot the wood,' Thork argued, 'If someone from Barnhouse doesn't find it first.'

'Come on,' Marna pulled her brother's sleeve. As she did, she glanced past him across the water. For a second she was sure she saw a flash of blue among the rushes. An image flashed in her head. It was the same blue cloak she had seen on the cliff the day of Joel's accident.

'What are you gawking at?' Thork asked.

Marna pointed, but whatever she thought she saw had disappeared. 'Nothing, it must have been the light.'

'Give me a hand. The reeds have twisted round my spear.' Thork was pulling at the shaft, but the harder he tugged, the more the reeds held.

Marna knelt to unwind the fibres, taking care not to damage the wood. 'Free,' she lifted it from the water. As she did, she spotted a chubby fish hiding in the shadow. She could have caught it with her fingers, but being outwitted by his sister would be too much for Thork.

They made their way back to the village. With his spear restored, Thork was in a better mood and talked about the arrangements for the following day.

'I'm the chief drummer, now Weyla is too old for the march.'

'I know, you've told us several times,' Marna answered. She had dyed the seal fur apron he wore to protect his thighs and legs from the chaffing of the drum. It was now a striking red with gold stripes, to show his elevated position.

'The chief drummer has the responsibility of leading the band of musicians.'

'Does he?' Marna pretended to yawn.

'We march behind Jona. There are several villages on the way to Cuween cairn.'

'Everyone will come out to admire your drumming,' Marna flattered him. 'And see your wonderful apron.' Thork grunted. 'Will Caran be coming?'

The question didn't have the expected response. Thork's good humour died. 'I don't understand that girl. She says she loves me. She knows I am the best hunter in the district. I can provide for her and her aging father, yet she won't marry me.'

'Maybe she likes fish,' Marna suggested with a grin.

'I am respected in the village and will be elected an elder. Jona is getting old and seeks an apprentice.'

'Perhaps that is the problem. Caran will want to stay in Orphir. But it is the gods who choose their apprentices, not Jona,' Marna said.

Thork kicked a stone in his path. 'What other man in the village is capable?'

'What about a woman?' Marna teased. 'Why can't we have a priestess? It is not unheard of.'

'In ancient stories. You have been listening to too many of Sempal's sea-faring tales. The fool talks of pyramids and lighthouses as if he'd seen them. With his weak legs he can barely wander far from the village.'

'That isn't his fault,' Marna said, but Thork's words

filled her with relief. With the chatter in the village about who was or wasn't in Joel's boat, she was having doubts about Sempal. She hadn't told the elders about the figure in blue she spotted on the cliff, but she had suspected her friend. Now she knew she was being stupid. With his deformity, Sempal couldn't have got from the cliff top to the shore in such a short time. And he couldn't have been hiding in the bulrushes to make signs at Jona. Not without stumbling into the water.

'I don't intend to rest at being the village priest,' Thork continued his musing. 'The religious leaders at the Ness will have to take note of me.'

Marna didn't understand his reasoning, but she didn't argue. They had reached the village and Thork left to find his friends. Marna returned to their house. The stone door slab was across the entrance, held in place by a wooden bar. Marna had to raise her voice before her mother let her in.

'Careful,' her mother scolded as Marna swung her basket to the floor. The small fire in the centre of the room was about to go out. The flame flickered with the draught.

'Just as well you are home,' her mother said. 'I've been tending the fire, but I don't have your skill. Without Roben, we would have to wait until the fire-maker came from Barnhouse, should it go out.'

'That's why you closed the door.' Marna moved to the hearth to coax the embers into flames. 'It needs more fanning,' she said, blowing on the heated moss. There was a crackle and a small flame licked up. She positioned dead branches over it and waited until they caught. 'There.'

Saving fires was one thing, but starting them was another. Marna had tried making fire with Roben's stone when she was alone on the heather hillside, but she needed another stone.

Thork returned home minus his spear, but with a reasonably sized trout.

'How did you get that?' Marna winked.

'Why can't you be grateful for once?' Her mother took the fish while Thork warmed himself by the fire.

Baked trout with red berries made a delicious supper, but afterwards Marna was in no mood to listen to her mother's complaints about village life. She nestled in her heather-lined box bed, covered herself with skins and shut out the sound of her brother boasting until she fell asleep.

Chapter 4

Marna woke to the pounding of drums splitting her head. She rolled over and hid her ears in the heather, but the noise continued. She sat up. Thork and his friend Albar were at the side of the room, practising drumming.

'Can't you do that outside?' Marna moaned, rubbing her head.

'About time you were up, lazy bones,' Thork answered. He grinned at his friend, expecting Albar to laugh. 'There's food to be prepared before dawn, or do you want us to starve before we reach the cairn?'

'If the sun is not out of bed yet, why should I be?' Marna lay back and pulled the skins over her head. Thork pulled them off. Grumbling, she got up. 'Where's mother? Couldn't she stand the noise either?'

'She's gone to fetch fresh water,' Thork answered.

'Any excuse to escape your awful drumming.'

Thork made a face. 'How about making us breakfast instead of moaning?' he said.

'You'll have to wait. I'm going to find mother.'

The door to their neighbour's house was open and she spotted her mother talking to Henjar. Boda was crawling on the floor towards the fire.

'No you don't,' Marna stepped in to pick the baby up.

'Thanks,' Henjar said with a yawn.

'You're up early. Has Boda been restless?'

'Jona woke me just before your mother came. He has called another meeting. I don't believe he will ever allow Joel a proper passage to the next world.'

Marna shivered as she pictured the pile of whitened bones they had gathered; the flesh around them rotted by the weather and pecked clean by the carrion birds. Joel was a large man, but there was little of him left. If he intended a journey to another world, he had better get going soon, before there was nothing remaining.

'Perhaps the gods have given Jona good news,' she answered. She was about to tell her friend what she and Thork had seen the previous evening, but Boda began to cry. Henjar took him from Marna.

'Jona never hears good news from the gods,' Marna's mother grumbled. 'It will be better when we have a new priest.'

'A new priest?' Marna queried. 'Is Jona ill?'

'There are rumours…' her mother began, but hearing Thork and Albar emerge from the hut and make their way across to Henjar's house, she didn't continue.

'Are you going to the meeting?' Henjar asked.

'What meeting?' Thork looked blank. 'I came to find Marna to get breakfast.'

'Jona has called a gathering,' his mother said. 'You should be with him.'

Thork gave Albar a light punch and the two of them

hurried to the workshop.

'I'll take Boda, you and Marna go with them,' Marna's mother said to Henjar.

There was a crowd gathered round Jona in the workshop. The priest raised his carved willow stick in the air and the murmurs faded to silence. Jona rolled his eyes towards the roof.

'Hear me. The gods have spoken.' The grumbling started and Jona banged his stick on the ground. Marna jumped. 'They say that Joel's bones must be laid in the cairn at Maeshowe.'

Henjar grabbed hold of Marna's hands and jumped on the spot. Maeshowe was nearer the village and close to the healing stones at Stenness.

'We have opened the cairn at Cuween as you instructed,' someone complained. 'Now you want us to close it and open the tomb at Maeshowe.'

'The tomb at Maeshowe is prepared.'

'Impossible. It would take two men at least to open the cairn. Strong ones at that.'

'Nothing is impossible for the gods,' Jona declared. 'The tomb is open and ready for Joel's bones. The procession will begin when the sun is full in the sky.'

'Marna, you were right,' Henjar was crying with relief. 'You are brilliant at knowing the future.'

Jona was preparing to leave the room. He signalled to

Thork to drum him out. Thork obliged, beating a steady rhythm as the crowd parted. Walf, Horen and the village elders followed after Jona then the rest of the gathering departed. There was shoving to get through the narrow doorway and Marna waited. Her mother was standing outside the workshop. Once the doorway was clear she came in, bouncing a crying Boda in her arms. Henjar took her son and told Marna's mother the news.

'If we've to start at noon, you'd better come with me, Marna. There's work to be done.'

Her mother hadn't managed to fetch the water before stopping to talk to Henjar. Marna was sent to the loch to gather it. She made several trips, drawing up enough to pour into jugs that would keep the singers refreshed as they marched. Afterwards her mother needed help packing the bere bannocks into willow baskets – gifts to lay in the tomb with Joel's bones. Marna hadn't eaten breakfast and was tempted to try one, just in case they weren't good enough for the afterlife. Her mother smacked her fingers.

'Don't be in such a hurry to taste the food of the dead, my girl,' she warned.

Everyone from the village chipped in and preparations were ready in good time. The villagers dressed in their best for the march. Thork and Albar strode out, beating their instruments and startling the watching gulls. Behind them, Jona was carried out on a wooden stretcher, supported by poles held by four villagers. One of the men at the back struggled to bear the weight and the stretcher dipped. Jona had to lean awkwardly to prevent the embarrassment of falling off. He was dressed in his priestly finery of dyed skins and bone jewellery. The headdress of seabird feathers had been made years previously. Jona's skull had shrunk since then and the headdress was in constant danger of slipping round his neck. To stop this happening, he used bone clips to hold the band in place, but they detracted from the otherworldly image he was trying to establish. The village children failed to stifle their sniggers.

Jona raised his carved staff and the stretcher tilted in the opposite direction. Albar dropped his drum and rushed to support the struggling bearer in time to prevent Jona landing on his backside. Thork rattled a roll on his drum to distract attention from the scene.

'Bring forth the bones,' Jona ordered.

A sledge was pulled from a wooden hut near the wall of the village. It held a stone urn with Joel's bones and was pulled by Joel's two brothers. Walf and Seth took a handle each. The crowd hushed and fell into an orderly line behind the sledge. Realising his bearers were unable to cope with the march, Jona instructed them to lower his stretcher. He strode from it in a dignified manner and marched to the front of the parade, signalling Henjar to fall in behind him. Boda was left with Henjar's mother, who complained her bones were too stiff for the trek.

'She never liked Joel,' Henjar confided to Marna before taking her place. 'She said he stank of fish. Before we married she wouldn't let him in the house. Now she is more concerned with the missing boat than poor Joel.'

The march began, with Marna keeping near the back to check on the less able walkers. As they passed the edge of the loch where Jona received his vision, she swept her eyes along the bank, searching for the glimpse of blue she saw the previous evening.

'What do you see, Marna?' Joannet was at her shoulder, glancing over the loch.

'Nothing.'

Jona kept a brisk pace. He allowed stops for refreshments, but there were rough throats, rumbling stomachs and blistered soles by the time they reached the site of the new stone circle. The massive upright stones, looking in on one another and casting long shadows in the sunlight made Marna shiver. She edged closer to Jona as he stopped in front of the largest stone and raised his staff. Thork banged on his drum and the singers wailed their tune.

'Stop that racket before you deafen me,' Jona grumbled.

Thork moaned, but the other drummers were happy to set their instruments down, mingle with their friends and take drinks. The dancers rubbed their feet and splashed them in the nearby loch.

'Which stone did you help transport and erect?' Marna asked her brother. Thork was keen to point it out.

'It isn't very big,' Marna said without thinking. Thork made a face.

'Size isn't everything,' their mother tried to appease Thork.

'At least I did my bit,' Thork raised his voice as he spotted Sempal approaching.

'What's that?' Sempal caught the end of the conversation.

'I bet they don't have stones like those in the far off lands you talk about.'

'Bet they do,' Sempal countered. 'I've heard of massive tombs for the dead...'

'Why is everything bigger and better somewhere else?' Thork protested.

Marna left them to their argument and went in search of Joannet, who was in charge of the bread basket. It was soon time to begin the march again and they would be passing the settlement at Ness. Marna felt fluttering in her stomach. The priests at the Ness used the land between the two lochs for their rituals and she imagined she could smell the blood, sweat and fear in the air. There was definitely an aroma of burning and incense.

Jona brought the parade to a halt when they reached

the thick walls surrounding the buildings. Marna knew they would have to get permission from the priests or the funeral procession would not be allowed to pass.

Two shaven-headed men, with painted red beards straggling onto their chest, advanced towards them from the entrance gate. Their coloured tunics and sealskin cloaks proved they were important people. The older man held a flint axe in front of him, with both hands.

'Greetings Patro of the Ness,' Jona bowed his head, but Marna saw the glare of defiance in his eyes.

Patro surveyed the weary travellers gathered round their priest. His eyes settled on the sledge.

'We are marching to the tomb at Maeshowe to inter the bones of our friend, the fisherman Joel,' Jona said.

'I know of the accident,' Patro answered. His voice was cold.

'We have brought a yearling calf as a gift.'

The crowd parted to allow Walf to bring forward the calf. Marna was distracted by Henjar flagging at the side of the group. She went to help and didn't hear the rest of the conversation between Jona and Patro. Whatever they were saying was taking time.

'Tired?' Albar came across to speak with them.

'Hot,' Marna answered. 'Henjar isn't coping.'

'Several of the villagers are struggling,' Albar agreed. 'The calf has been accepted and the negotiations are done.

We can rest at Barnhouse before we reach the chambered tomb. Wilmer is expecting us.'

The village of Barnhouse was smaller than their own. The houses were separated, not joined by tunnels as in Skara Brae. It made Marna suspect that nobody got on with their neighbours. She knew most of the people there, but didn't consider them friends, apart from Wilmer the jeweller. He liked to joke that he was more at home in Skara Brae than in Barnhouse and he visited often, bringing honey and telling funny tales.

Marna spotted him as he came out to greet the procession. She waved and he waved back with a smile that changed to a serious look when he spotted Jona.

'I was truly sorry to hear of Joel's accident,' he bowed his head. 'His passing is a great loss. There are few men with the knowledge of the sea that Joel possessed, but more than that, he was a man of sense and patience.'

'Yes,' Henjar answered.

Wilmer put a comforting arm around her shoulder. 'You must rest in my house before the final parting. There is a private chamber at the side. I have beer and bannocks with cooked fish.'

Henjar gave a small groan. She was fond of fish, but had refused to look at one since her husband drowned.

'Or perhaps you would prefer duck from the loch,' Wilmer was quick to catch her displeasure.

'Thank you.' Henjar opened her mouth, sucked in her words then decided to ask the question on her lips. 'I don't suppose anyone here has news of Roben.'

'The fire-maker?'

'He left our village days ago,' Marna added.

'I'm afraid he hasn't been here lately,' Wilmer answered. 'Certainly, last autumn we needed his help when our fire-maker Hector passed on, but we have young Rawdric now.'

Henjar leaned on Wilmer for support. 'I would like to lie down.'

'Perhaps, Marna, you would like to take Henjar to my house while I speak with Jona.'

'Of course.' She reached for Henjar's hand.

'I have made a neck band of stone beads which you may place in the tomb with Joel,' Wilmer said, freeing himself from Henjar's grasp.

'That was kind of you,' Marna answered for her friend. She took Henjar's hand and led her towards the largest hut.

The Barnhouse villagers invited the newcomers into their workroom where they laid out mugs of beer and bowls of heather tea. Stone slabs held wild fennel bannocks and samphire stalks gathered from the nearby marshlands and boiled in loch water. A beef stew was simmering in a pot over a fire. Marna licked her lips as the smell drifted to her when she entered the building. Henjar was quick to fall asleep in Wilmer's house and she thought it safe to enjoy the feast with the others.

'I'm so thirsty I could drain your loch,' Thork said to one of the men offering him a jug of beer.

'Playing a drum is hard work,' the man mocked.

Marna could tell Thork was about to launch into a full length explanation of the difficulties of drumming and marching. She had heard his lecture many times and wasn't keen to listen again. Despite her feet being tired and blistered, she decided to take a stroll across the meadow to the ring of stones at Stenness.

Compared to the giant ring the men were erecting at Brodgar, these could have been raised for children, but Marna felt an affinity with them. No-one knew how long they had stood there, looking out to the loch. They had a reputation as healing stones. Marna saw them as feminine compared to the brash masculinity of the new circle.

She hoped to be alone as she walked among them, but as she neared the edge of the ring she saw Jona on his knees before the largest stone. He had removed his headdress and his hair was reflected in the sunlight, like burning branches on top of his head. Jona lifted his head and looked round before she could slip away.

'I'm sorry, I didn't mean to disturb you,' she said, fearful of which Jona she was talking to. He was a puzzle to her. Although he was a large man, he was as gentle as a puppy when encouraging his cattle to give milk, or rescuing a calf from a ditch. It was when he was being a priest that Marna feared him. His eyes became glazed, he waved his arms and his voice could drown out thunder.

'Who is there?' Jona asked.

'It's me, Marna.'

'Marna?' he said, as if he was having trouble recognising her. 'Thork's sister? Is Thork with you?'

'No, I'm alone.'

Jona stood up. He gave a nod before glancing back at the stone. 'These are healing stones.'

'Yes, that's what my mother says,' Marna agreed.

'Your mother is a wise woman.' Jona stood with his head bowed. Marna felt he wanted to tell her something, but couldn't find the words. She moved closer. 'Aye, healing stones,' he repeated.

'There is beer in the workshop,' Marna said, thinking Jona was in need of fluid. His mind seemed confused.

'That heals too, in its own way.' He smiled and there was a twinkle in his eyes. 'The time for drinking is over. We must attend to the ceremony at the tomb or it will be dark before we march home. Marna, find your brother and tell him to sound the drum.'

Marna knew Thork would be worse the wear for drink and in no state to drum for an internment, but she nodded. Jona retrieved his headdress from behind a gorse bush.

'Fetch the drummer, girl. What are you waiting for?'

Marna turned and ran. She found Thork stuffing his face with fish slices while telling a pretty girl how he had single-handedly brought down a stag. The girl was listening with awe. Marna waited for him to pause, but it didn't look like he was going to.

'Jona wants to leave now,' Marna blurted out.

The girl stared at her, annoyed by the interruption. Thork burped.

'He needs you to lead the drumming.'

Thork wiped his mouth. 'Where's my drum?'

The girl rushed to fetch it from the corner.

'I need my sticks.'

Marna watched as the girl searched the room.

'They're in your belt,' she pointed out before the girl panicked at not finding them.

Thork's playing wasn't quite to rhythm, but as he got into his stride the more able villagers from Skara Brae heard and emerged from the workshop and houses. They shuffled into a wavy line, waiting on Jona. The priest appeared carrying a flaming torch that he got from Rawdric, the fire-maker. Sempal was with him.

'Where is Henjar?' Jona boomed.

'She's resting. I'll fetch her,' Marna answered.

Henjar was drowsy, but Marna managed to rouse her. When she saw the sledge with Joel's bones she began to cry again. Sempal put his arms around her and led her to the front of the line. Marna fell in behind the sledge and soon a depleted parade was back on the road. The march was slow and disordered, not helped by erratic drumming from Thork and Albar, but it wasn't far to the tomb.

The covered mound stood out in the flat land, in line with the standing stones and in tune with the heavens. The entrance stone was rolled to the side, revealing the enclosed passageway into the chambers. Walf and Seth, who had been pulling the sledge, let it rest on the ground and rubbed their palms. The sledge was too wide to pass through the entrance and the brothers squabbled over who would bear the bones inside.

'Joel's bones shall be placed in the left hand chamber,' Jona announced.

Sempal moved to stand next to Marna. He looked at his hands and Marna touched the left one.

The villagers stood round as Jona bent his head to enter the passage, lighting his way with the torch. Walf removed the pot of bones from the sledge and followed Jona. Seth was close behind carrying the gifts to be laid beside Joel. Thork continued drumming and the villagers hummed a low tune. There wasn't room in the central chamber for everyone, but not everybody was keen in any case. Marna had never been inside a tomb during an internment and was curious to experience the feeling, but she felt a lump in her throat.

Henjar and Sempal walked to the entrance. Henjar took a step back and shivered. Sempal gave his sister's hand a squeeze and she ducked to enter the tomb before him. Sempal banged his head on the stone lintel and stood up to rub it. Marna saw Thork grin and frowned.

Three other men and two women stepped up and entered the tomb. Marna clenched her fists.

'Will anyone else go inside?' Thork asked.

Marna's feet were stuck in the mud. Thork secured his drum sticks in his belt and stepped towards the tomb.

'I'll go,' the words came out without her thinking.

'Why does she want to go in?' Marna heard Joannet mutter to her neighbour. That persuaded her and she pushed her shoulders back and stepped towards the entrance. Thork moved aside.

'Mind your head,' he advised with a grin.

Marna ducked and scrambled along the stone corridor. The flames from Jona's torch threw shadows on the damp walls and she imagined the spirits of the dead dancing their way on their final journeys. At the end of the tunnel she stood up and pulled her shawl close. It took a moment for her eyes to adjust. Sempal was standing near her, shaking. Nobody was watching him, so Marna moved to take hold of his hand. Jona was swaying and Seth had thought it wiser to take the torch from him. The humming from the mourners inside the tomb swirled round the walls and echoed off the stones and into Marna's head. She could tell it was affecting Sempal.

'There's nothing to be afraid of,' she whispered. 'There are only bones in the chambers.'

'That's nothing to be afraid of?' Sempal whispered back.

In the chamber, even whispers echoed. The call of 'afraid, afraid' circled the chamber. Marna let go of Sempal's hand to hold her ears, but jumped as a thud shook the roof. Thork had crawled through the tunnel into the chamber and was beating his drum. The sound was echoed by Albar, drumming from outside the tomb.

Jona required space to light a fire in the central hearth. He snatched the torch from Seth and staggered towards the pile of wood, dried heather and aromatic plants, prepared when the entrance stone was removed. He struggled to get them to light and his curses could be heard over Thork's playing. Marna had to stop herself from stepping forward to help. The air in the tomb was heavy and she wanted to blow on the heather for the flames to rise.

Smoke eventually began to swirl round the chamber, mixed with the sweet smell of poppies and celandine. Marna closed her eyes to stop them burning. The noise from the crackling twigs, the beat of the drum and the incessant humming reverberated in Marna's ears like the wind that blew the waves against the cliffs. The air was warm, but she felt a chill, starting at her neck and creeping down her back, as if the spirits from the other worlds were speaking in a mystic language. It wasn't the solstice, when the setting sun shone along the entrance passage to open the window between the worlds, but she sensed a gateway was there and it was a fragile one.

She felt for Sempal's hand. Jona tossed the torch into the fire then raised his arms and threw his head back.

'Hear me,' he roared. He was holding pieces of quartz and the stones glowed in response.

Marna shuddered. She heard a gasp from the woman behind her. Jona began reciting an incantation and Walf brought forward Joel's bones. Marna let go of Sempal's hand and shuffled to the side to allow him access to the burial vault. Jona signalled for the others to do likewise. Henjar had been leaning against the side wall, her head bowed to hide her tears.

'Henjar, you must come forward,' Walf said.

Henjar didn't move.

'I'll take your hand,' Marna re-assured her. She stepped over and helped Henjar across the chamber.

'Go in peace brother Joel,' Jona's voice echoed around the chamber.

Joel, Joel, Joel.

Thork beat his drum louder. A slither of light lit up the

chamber from along the entrance. Shadows grew in the semi-dark. Marna felt light-headed. She wasn't sure if she was supporting Henjar, or her friend was supporting her. The drumming seemed to beat louder until it took over the chamber.

'Aargh.'

A hair curling screech rang round the cairn. Jona stopped reciting and dropped the quartz. Everybody turned to stare at Sempal. He was on his knees, quivering. His shaking hand was pointing towards the chamber on the right. The light from the hearth fire flickered into the opening and Marna spotted two sandal-less feet, stained with blood, poking from the tomb.

Chapter 5

Marna reached to soothe Sempal while the others pushed into one another, trying to see what was in the tomb.

'There should only be bones,' Jona lamented, clearly feeling a whole body was tantamount to blasphemy.

Henjar gave an exaggerated cry, but when the light from the fire caught her face, Marna could see from the glint in her eyes that she was as curious as the others. Seth and Walf stepped forwards and grabbed a leg each.

'Move aside,' Walf warned as they dragged the body into the central chamber. The belt stuck in a groove in the flagstones, but Seth and Walf were strong men and heaved it free. The click echoed round the domed chamber walls. The flames flickered as the body landed on the floor next to the hearth and Marna felt a shiver. Seth tore a strip from his tunic and wound it round his hand before grabbing a lighted branch from the fire. He held the torch above the body, so they could see the face. The single eye was open, but glazed.

It took a moment for Marna to realise what she was seeing, but before the gasp was out of her mouth, Henjar fainted on top of her. Marna fell sideways onto Sempal, who struggled to stay on his feet to prevent Henjar banging her head against the stone wall.

'It is Roben, the fire-maker,' Jona announced. 'What is he doing here?'

'He's dead,' Walf said.

'I can see that,' Jona answered.

'He couldn't have put himself in the tomb,' Marna said. 'Could he?' She left Henjar sitting with her back to the wall and edged forwards to get a better look.

Mumbling reverberated round the chamber.

'He's been murdered,' Sempal said. The others turned to stare. They hadn't expected him to speak, but he had regained his senses and was kneeling beside the body. 'There's dried blood on his head and the bone is showing through. The skull has been cracked open,' Sempal pointed to the wound. Marna felt sick. She needed air. There was a strange, unpleasant smell of death choking her throat. Jona smelt it too. He was holding his arm against his face.

'The tomb was only opened yesterday morning,' Walf said. 'It took three strong men. The body must have been brought here some time between then and now.'

'But Roben has been dead for longer,' Jona said. 'I have seen many dead bodies, of men, women, children and animals. Roben has been dead for several days.'

'It has been two weeks since anyone saw him in our village,' Thork said. 'Perhaps he was killed shortly after leaving.'

'Or before,' another man ventured.

Marna shivered at the thought.

'Impossible. Not in our village,' a woman said.

'This is not the place to discuss the matter,' Jona took control. 'Let us place Joel's bones in the allotted tomb with dignity. Afterwards we can bring Roben's body out to examine it in the light.'

Henjar was leaning against the wall of the cairn with her head in her hands. She gave a loud wail. 'My poor Joel, why this? And Roben... it's awful.'

To Marna, her complaint seemed planned to gain attention, but Walf moved to put his arm around his sister-in-law's shoulder and she rested her head on his chest. Seth handed Jona the torch before placing Joel's bones into the chamber on the left. Jona muttered a few words. Thork beat a slow rhythm on his drum and the others began to hum. Sempal and Marna stood in silence. There was little room in the tomb and they were close together. Marna could hear Sempal's heart beat. It was faster than a running deer's. She touched his hand. It felt clammy. She didn't want to hold it.

.'..And protect Joel on his passage to the afterlife,' Jona finished. Thork beat a roll on the stretched skin of his instrument. He was about to begin a new tune, but a grunt from Jona stopped him.

'It is time to leave,' Jona said, glancing at Roben's dull eye before heading for the exit passageway. Marna suspected the priest had prepared a longer speech for Joel, but under the circumstances everyone was glad to be free of the tomb.

Marna and Sempal helped Henjar out while Seth pushed and Walf pulled Roben's body through the narrow tunnel. The others crawled out with ashen faces. Thork scrambled out last, ready to beat a tune for the dead.

The villagers were waiting. Albar began drumming and the singers took deep breaths ready for another chorus. Then they saw the body. The drumming stopped and the questions started.

Is it a stranger? No it's Roben. Is he dead? How did he die? Why was he in the tomb? When did it happen? Who was to blame? What will happen next?

Jona seemed in a trance. Thork and Seth approached, but he waved them away.

'We must get home,' Thork said. 'It will be dark soon.'

'What should we do with Roben's body? Leave it here or take it back with us?' Seth asked.

Everyone waited for Jona's decision. They waited and they waited. It was the first time Marna had seen Jona lost for answers and it frightened her. The priest didn't seem aware of the questions or the people round him. Jona hadn't been a friend of Roben's. It didn't make sense that the fire-maker's death should affect him in such a way. Whatever the reason for his behaviour, Jona was unable to control the situation. There was an atmosphere of unrest and anger.

'We could stay the night at Barnhouse,' Sempal suggested.

'We can't all stay there,' Seth countered. 'There are too many of us.'

The crowd began agreeing or disagreeing. Thork banged on his drum and stood on a boulder to speak. 'The youngsters and older folk should rest in Barnhouse and return home tomorrow, while the fitter ones should return home tonight.'

Marna saw Sempal shuffle his feet in the grass. She guessed he didn't fancy the walk back with his bad leg, but he wouldn't want to be put with the youngsters or old folk.

'We women should stay,' an older woman shouted.

'No, the women are needed at home,' a man called.

'The priest should stay to guard Roben's body.'

'Roben's body should be brought back tonight.'

'The Barnhouse villagers can see to it.'

'You are forgetting he was a man, not an animal. Roben was one of us and should be treated as such,' Horen raised his voice above the uproar.

Everyone had a different view.

'Jona must decide,' Seth said. The crowd hushed.

'Where has he gone?' Thork asked.

Jona was no longer among them. Marna guessed he had wandered to the stone ring, but didn't say this. The situation was ridiculous enough, without Thork organising a search party for their leader. An argument threatened to break out over who should take charge until Wilmer strolled towards them across the meadow.

'It is getting late, what is keeping you?' he asked cheerfully, then spotted Roben's body lying where Seth and Walf had dragged it. 'Ah.' He moved to take a closer look then held his hand over his chest. His face drained of its colour.

'It is Roben, our fire-maker,' Seth said. 'He has been absent from our village for days.'

Henjar was standing beside Seth and at the mention of Roben's name she began crying again. Wilmer moved to her side and she let him comfort her.

'I knew Roben well. He was a skilled fire-maker and a better ball thrower with one eye than anyone with two,' Wilmer said. 'Why would anyone harm him?'

Marna had felt like harming him several times.

'I didn't like him,' Sempal said. 'I'm glad he's dead and I don't think I'm the only one.' His voice was low. Luckily only Marna heard.

'What does Jona have to say?' Wilmer asked. He made a show of looking for the priest although Marna realised he knew Jona wasn't there.

'He has wandered off and left us,' Seth said.

'Wandered off?' Wilmer queried in a voice that made Marna suspect he knew where Jona was.

'He has gone to ask the gods for help,' Thork said.

'Aye,' Seth wasn't convinced.

'I don't want to rush the gods, but a decision has to be made,' Walf spoke up. 'Do we stay here or return to our village? If we return, do we take Roben's body with us?'

'If I could make a suggestion,' Wilmer raised his voice so everyone could hear, but his tone was calm. 'The people left in your village will be concerned if no-one returns tonight. Why don't two or three of the fitter young men return to Skara Brae to re-assure them that everything is under control? The others can stay with us in Barnhouse and put to rights the rumours that we are inhospitable to travellers. There will be beds and supper for everyone. We mourn the loss of Roben, but we should celebrate Joel's passage into his new life.'

Henjar gave an exaggerated cry at the mention of the names, but there were murmurs of approval from the others.

'I hope you have plenty of ale,' Seth said, slapping Wilmer on the back.

'I have heard the people of Skara Brae are experts at downing liquor,' Wilmer replied, forcing a smile.

'We need volunteers to return to Skara Brae,' Seth turned to his fellow men.

'I'll go,' Thork said. 'I can be there by nightfall.'

'Good,' Wilmer said, 'but you can't go alone.'

'I'll look after him,' Albar said.

'I'll go too,' Walf said. 'My wife is expecting our first child.'

Beer, bannocks and honey were brought for the three men before they began their trek.

'We aren't travelling to the other side of the world,' Thork objected. 'We don't need supplies.'

The food was thrust upon them and Thork stuffed a loaf under his tunic. 'I won't be able to play my drum with any more.'

'Drumming will slow our pace,' Walf said. 'We want back before the moon and sun change place.'

'They won't be back before the moon rises,' Marna whispered to Sempal.

'Walf is making excuses. He hates drumming.'

'You can leave your drum with me,' Marna said to Thork. 'I'll make sure nothing happens to it.'

'It had better not.' Thork relinquished his drum and the three men set off.

The others separated into groups to be welcomed into homes. Marna found Henjar, who was fretting about Boda.

'He is over a year old. He can eat soft food without need for your milk,' Marna said. 'Your mother knows how to look after him.'

'She looks after him too well, spoiling him with honey and sweet water,' Henjar answered.

One of the women from Barnhouse was listening and stepped in to offer Henjar a warm drink that smelt of tangleweed. 'You need to rest. Today has been stressful. I know what it is like to lose a husband before his time.'

Henjar accepted the mug. Strips of seaweed floated on the surface. She hesitated before drinking, but finished it and yawned.

'My name is Freya,' the woman said, taking the empty mug. 'You must stay with my family tonight.'

A bed of heather was prepared for Henjar and Marna in the corner of the woman's hut and they settled, wrapped snugly in skins. One of their host's daughters was a talented singer and she sang for them.

'Not that song,' her mother said. 'It is too sad. Sing something cheerful.'

The girl sang about a cheeky goose that couldn't find a mate. The words didn't make sense, but Marna enjoyed listening to the melody, even with Henjar snoring. She clapped in time to the music, but it wasn't long before her eyes closed and she nodded off.

She woke the following morning to cold feet and the sound of raised voices outside the hut. One of them sounded like Jona's. Henjar was still asleep, with her legs kicking against Marna. She had managed to pull all the sheepskins over to her side. Marna rose and straightened her hair. The other occupants of the house had left. The fire in the centre was out, but the ashes glowed with flashes of orange. Marna was tempted to rekindle it, but she was curious to know what was going on. She stepped outside. A crowd of about twenty people had gathered with Jona at the centre. Marna recognised people from Skara Brae, but there were also on-lookers from Barnhouse.

'Roben's body must be taken to the complex at the Ness,' Jona declared. His voice was sharp and Marna guessed there was some disagreement.

'Roben belonged to our village,' Seth answered. 'We will not allow his body to be cut open by self-important priests in some unnatural ritual. They may do what they will with their cattle, but not with our people. We will take Roben home to lay him out. When it is time, we will inter his bones as is proper.'

The others cheered Seth's words. Marna could see Jona's face turn from bright red to grey.

'What is this nonsense about cutting open bodies? Who put such ridiculous ideas into your head? The priests at the Ness are our kinsfolk. Our customs are their customs,' Jona protested.

'Why do they need such a thick wall, if not to hide their activities from decent folk?' Seth argued.

The crowd sided with Seth. Jona spluttered words that nobody could make out. It was obvious he wouldn't get his way, not without divine help. He raised his arms in the air and looked up to the sky. A dark cloud passed overhead.

'You wish to challenge the gods? Hasn't our village seen enough hardship?' Jona cried. 'We have lost a good fisherman and now our fire-maker. Who will be next if we disobey?'

Some of the men moved towards Jona with their fists raised. Others stepped across to protect the priest.

'You have gone too far,' Seth said.

Marna could feel the tension and feared they were going to fight. Fortunately, Wilmer appeared from his hut. He had a comical way of walking, wobbling from side to side like a duck on the shore desperate to reach the water. That, and his broad grin, made everyone feel at ease.

'Jona, it is good to have you back. Now, did someone mention a fire-maker?'

Jona looked away. The men who challenged him shuffled their feet. Seth gave a snort, but didn't reply. Wilmer looked around for an answer.

'We don't have one in our village,' Marna stepped forwards. 'Roben didn't have an apprentice. He guarded his knowledge like he did his stones.'

'Marna is right,' Seth agreed. 'We can choose someone and send them out to learn from the neighbouring fire-makers, but that will take time.'

'Here at Barnhouse we know what a hardship that is,' Wilmer chewed his bottom lip, waiting for Jona to speak. The priest glowered, but remained silent. 'Perhaps I can help,' Wilmer offered.

'How?' Jona turned on him. 'Making buckles and pins

from bone will not keep us warm or cook our food.'

'I have gained instruction on making fire using flints from Rawdric, our new fire-maker. I can't pretend to be as proficient as Roben, but I can tide things over until your apprentice returns or another fire-maker arrives.'

'You will come to Skara Brae?' Seth asked.

'Unless you have a better solution.'

Everyone turned to their neighbour to give an opinion, but no-one came up with a workable alternative.

'Very well, we have a new fire-maker,' Jona said. 'You are welcome to stay in my house while you are with us. I shall send my son Kali to learn the skills from the fire-makers in the Ness. However that doesn't solve our current dispute – what to do with Roben's body.'

'There is no dispute,' Seth said. 'We take the body back to our village.' He turned to address the gathering. 'Does anyone disagree?'

In the silence, Marna could hear the bitterns booming from the reeds. Jona knew he was beaten. 'So be it. I will prepare the body with herbs to keep it fresh on the journey. We will need volunteers to pull the sledge. This task cannot be left to beasts of burden.'

Roben was not popular and Marna wondered who would volunteer for the back breaking task. She could see a smile cross Jona's face as no-one stepped forward.

'I will volunteer,' Seth said.

'Roben owed me pots, but I will not hold it against him in death,' Horen said. 'I also will volunteer.'

Four other men and women raised their hands to help when Seth and Horen tired.

'We will leave when Jona has finished dressing the body,' Seth declared.

'We will leave when the gods allow,' Jona corrected. Seth glowered.

'The gift of a gem stone ring may persuade the gods to give their permission,' Wilmer tried to pacify Jona. He took the ring from his finger and handed it to the priest before going to collect the possessions he needed for his stay in Skara Brae. The villagers readied themselves for another march. Jona saw to Roben's body and Marna helped gather the plants he needed.

'You are skilled with plants,' Jona observed. 'You will be a wise woman one day.'

Marna wanted to say that she already was, but knew Jona wouldn't appreciate the joke. 'I learned from my mother,' she answered.

'It is a wise girl who listens to her parents,' Jona agreed. Marna guessed he was thinking of his daughter Fara, who had married a farmer from Eynhallow and left to live on the remote island. She was about to say something, but before she could Wilmer appeared, tripping as he carried a pile of skins.

'I was keeping them for when I got married,' he joked, 'but that doesn't look imminent.'

Marna wondered why Wilmer hadn't married. He was well off and respected, but she knew it wouldn't be right to ask.

The journey back was a solemn one. There was no singing or drumming to ease tired feet. The folk from Barnhouse had used their supplies the night before and there was little to spare. They would be home before anyone starved, but chewing on bread or strips of dried meat helped speed the journey. Luckily they could gather water from the loch to prevent flagging.

Wilmer brought his own sledge, a sophisticated wooden platform attached to runners and pulled by a cream coated ox. There was room for the less able villagers. Henjar sat beside Wilmer at the front. Marna deposited Thork's drum on the sledge, but chose to walk beside the ox, stroking the rough hair on its forehead. Whatever Wilmer was saying to Henjar, it seemed to cheer her and Marna heard her laughing.

'There's space for you too, Marna,' Wilmer said. 'Jump up and amuse us with your stories. Perhaps they will make the journey pass faster or end sooner.'

Her feet ached, but Marna was too proud to accept the lift. 'Someone needs to soothe your ox,' she said, rubbing the animal's ear.

When they reached the loch near the village the pace quickened with the anticipation of supper and bed.

'I can smell fresh bread,' Henjar sniffed the air.

'I wish I could,' Wilmer joked. 'My nostrils are bunged up with the waste from the ox's backside.'

Thork and Walf were waiting for them as they approached the village. Jona raised his arm to halt the procession. The villagers were keen to disperse to their homes and no-one wanted a long discussion. Seth and Horen laid the sledge down with a thud. Horen was quick to walk away and most of the others followed him. Wilmer pulled on the rope to bring the ox to a stop.

'Don't stand there like a frightened hare, help Seth with the body,' Jona ordered.

Walf moved to help his brother. Realising they were struggling, Marna made a face at Thork and he ambled over. Seth took hold of both arms while Thork and Walf held a leg each. It didn't look dignified and Marna felt sorry for Roben.

'Carry it to the dunes,' Jona instructed.

'Wait,' Wilmer wobbled down from his seat and walked over. He put a hand out to stop Thork and Walf lifting the body. 'Shouldn't someone examine Roben for clues to how he was killed before his body is devoured by the weather and the birds?'

'His skull is smashed. Any fool can see,' Jona said.

'But what weapon was used and why? Who killed him and left his body in the tomb?'

'It seems obvious,' Jona said. 'Sempal had no love for Roben. He didn't want the fire-maker to marry his sister. Leaving a corpse in a tomb meant for bones would mean little to him.'

'That's not true,' Marna blurted out. 'Sempal couldn't kill anyone.'

She assumed Sempal had gone to find Lin, but he appeared, hobbling from behind Wilmer's sledge.

'Did someone call me?' he asked.

'I shall call you when I want to speak with you,' Jona answered.

Sempal appealed to the others, but no-one contradicted Jona. 'Seth? Walf?.. Marna?'

'We'll let you know what is said,' Seth replied.

Sempal turned to walk away.

'It would take a heavy stone to do that damage to a man's skull,' Thork said, pulling back the seal skin to examine the wound. 'I doubt Sempal could lift it.'

'I could so,' Sempal grumbled as he made his way to the huts. Only Marna heard him.

'He may have pushed Roben from behind; taken him by surprise,' Jona suggested.

'But could he have carried Roben's body to Maeshowe and positioned it in the tomb?' Wilmer put in.

'Perhaps he had help.' Jona stared at Marna.

'What does that mean?' Thork was quick to come to his sister's defence.

'Everyone knows your sister quarrelled with Roben over payment.'

'You think Marna would kill somebody for the sake of a few pots?' Thork laughed.

'People have been killed for less.'

'Not in our village,' Thork asserted.

'You could have helped your sister.' Jona was warming to his theory.

'That is ridiculous.'

'I would fight any man who cheated my sister,' Walf said.

'We don't have a sister,' Seth said.

'If we did...'

'If we are accusing those who argued with Roben then you are also under suspicion, Jona,' Marna raised her voice. It was trembling, but she continued. 'Roben didn't think you were fit to be our priest.'

'What are you saying, girl?' Jona took a step towards Marna, but Thork blocked him. The priest shook his fist. 'What stories are you making up?'

'You wanted the tomb at Maeshowe opened,' Marna was thinking fast. 'It had been decided to bury Joel in Cuween. Was that too far away to take the body?'

'You think I would be stupid enough to hide a dead body in a tomb and then lead the whole village to the spot. Or do you think I am mad?'

'You gave instructions for Joel to be placed in the opposite chamber. If Sempal knew his left from his right, Roben's body would have gone undetected,' Seth said.

'I did not kill Roben.'

'Enough,' Wilmer stepped between the men and raised his arms. 'Friends,' he appealed for calm. 'I understand this has been a harrowing time, but there is no need for spats. Please, show respect.'

'Sorry,' Marna bowed her head.

'There is no advantage in accusing anyone without proof,' Wilmer continued. 'You need someone removed from the village to ask questions, give thought to the matter and discover what happened.'

'Who?' Jona asked. Wilmer shrugged.

'Will you be that man?' Walf asked.

'If everyone agrees,' Wilmer answered.

'What do you say, Jona?' Thork asked.

'There has never been a time before when we couldn't settle village matters among ourselves.'

'There has never been a murder in our village before,' Marna said.

'What knowledge does Wilmer have to solve this mystery that we do not?' Jona asked.

'This,' Wilmer reached in the fold of his cloak and removed a piece of haematite.

'That is one of Roben's fire stones,' Thork said.

'As I thought,' Wilmer agreed. 'One of his stones. I found it on the ground at the entrance to the tomb and assumed it fell from his pouch as he was dragged through the passageway. I took the liberty to search for the other stone. It was not on his person. I searched the tomb before it was closed. It was not there either.'

'He could have left it at home,' Thork suggested.

'A fire-maker would not go far without his stones,' Wilmer answered. 'It seems to me that the mystery lies in finding the second stone. Whoever has it knows how Roben died.'

The others were silent, contemplating Wilmer's words.

'It could have been lost at any time,' Marna said, but her words sounded weak. She felt in the pocket of her tunic. Her fingers touched the sleek black stone and she felt her face burn.

Chapter 6

Marna thought it better to keep out of Jona's way for the next few days until tempers cooled and life returned to normal. Wilmer delighted in his role as detective and had scarcely unloaded his possessions in Jona's hut before beginning his investigation. His questions seemed trivial, almost nonsensical, but he had a way of asking, staring through people as he spoke, that made even Henjar feel in part responsible for Roben's death.

'Wilmer has been here all morning,' Henjar confided as Marna teased Boda with a bird she carved from a rowan branch. 'You're not paying attention to me, are you?'

'Of course I am,' Marna lied.

'What did I say then?'

Marna guessed the likeliest thing Henjar would be discussing. 'Albar has strong arms?'

'You weren't listening. I was talking about Wilmer.'

'He doesn't have strong arms,' Marna said.

'He was asking questions about Roben – and stuffing himself with my honey cakes. How am I supposed to remember what Roben ate before he left? I don't remember what I ate yesterday.'

'Wilmer is trying to establish when Roben died.'

'How can knowing what Roben ate tell him that?'

'If the food was still undigested in his stomach...'

'How could he tell if...? Ugh, you don't mean..?'

'I'm afraid so.'

'With a knife? That is gruesome.'

'Wilmer will have treated Roben's body with respect. He has finished his examination and the body has been left out for nature to attend to.'

Henjar bent to stroke her son's hair. 'Wilmer didn't only ask questions about Roben. He talked about fish.'

'What does a jeweller know about fish?'

'More than you would imagine. He wanted to know what fish Joel caught. I told him I enjoyed the flat fish Joel brought home and Wilmer explained how to wrap them in leaves to keep in the flavour. I could taste the plaice. My mouth was drooling when he asked if I had seen my brother on the morning of Joel's accident. I could hardly answer without choking.'

'He was trying to catch you off your guard,' Marna said. 'What did you tell him?'

'I can't remember if I saw Sempal yesterday or the day before, never mind last autumn. Besides, how can Joel's accident have anything to do with Roben's death?'

Tears gathered in Henjar's eyes and she wiped them on her sleeve. Marna moved to comfort her although she wasn't sure if Henjar was crying because she was upset or because she felt she should be.

'Don't worry about Wilmer's questions. He is a good man and a fair one. He believes all events are connected and wants to know the facts before making a judgement.'

'What do you mean?'

'A storm brings the body of a whale to our shores, our farmers can fashion new tools from the bone, the land is turned over and produces good crops, Jona is happy and allows his daughter to marry and move to Eynhallow, taking new blood to the community there.'

'I don't see what you are getting at,' Henjar interrupted Marna's flow. 'Fara would have married Gerk whether the gods sent a whale or a downpour of hailstones. Jona could not have prevented her.'

'That was an example. What I meant was, if Joel hadn't drowned then Roben wouldn't have moved in and Sempal wouldn't have argued with him, so he may not have...' Marna stopped and sucked her lip. There was no tactful way of saying it. 'Oh look, Boda is making the bird fly.'

'Wonderful,' Henjar clapped her hands. Her attention was on her son and she broke into a smile.

'He's such a clever boy,' Marna said.

'He doesn't get his wisdom from me,' Henjar answered. 'Mother says I came out so fast I left mine behind in her womb. Sempal must have found it. He has twice the wisdom of men his age.'

'And four times that of Thork,' Marna laughed. She guessed her friend believed her mother's story and wanted to make light of it. 'Wisdom comes in different forms. You have a way with children.'

'I know. I wish I could have more babies. Boda will need brothers and sisters to play with.'

'There is time,' Marna had been kneeling to play with Boda, but her bones were stiff and she stood up. A thrill ran up her foot and she staggered to stay upright.

'Will you stay for supper?' Henjar asked.

'Thanks, but I have work to do before it gets dark.'

'Outdoor work?' Henjar asked with scorn.

'The sea breeze clears my head,' Marna answered.

'I prefer what is in my head to stay there.'

Marna gave Boda a kiss before leaving Henjar's house. She headed along the tunnel and into the fresh air where she stopped to fill her lungs, clearing away the village smoke.

The day should have been over, but the sky was still light. In the summer months, the sun stayed well into the night, allowing the stars only a few brief hours to dance. She walked towards the cliffs where the gulls were guarding their nests. Her eyes were drawn to specks of blue and she thought about climbing down to gather the eggs. Her mother and Thork would appreciate them for their morning meal, but climbing took time and she wanted to find Sempal. No-one in the village had spoken to him since the return from Maeshowe.

'Running away is a sign of guilt,' Thork said.

'He hasn't run away,' Marna defended him.

'He can't exactly run with his bad leg,' Thork agreed, 'but he must explain himself to Wilmer.'

'Sempal doesn't feel he needs to answer to someone from outside the village,' Marna said.

'He must speak with Jona, then.'

'Jona's behaviour has been odd too.'

'You are making excuses. Why is Sempal hiding if he has nothing to conceal? You are his friend. You must persuade him to return.'

Thork's tone told Marna it was an order, not a request. 'I'll do my best.'

She knew she wouldn't be able to influence Sempal, but agreeing to try kept Thork happy. It gave her an excuse to seek him out. She was worried about how he would survive. Sempal was a storyteller, not a hunter. He spent his time thinking complicated thoughts, not learning which plants were edible and which gave stomach cramps. The weather had been kind so far, but even in the fruitful months storms could blow in from the sea with little warning. Anything above ground and not tied down with strong nettle rope, could be swept to the furthest side of the island and left battered on the shore. Sempal had only his tattered cloak to protect him.

Marna stopped to gather berries on her way to the shore. The birds had snaffled the juicy ones, leaving the over-ripe or not quite ready berries. Marna knew where to look, though, and found a bush left untouched. She gobbled a handful, but knew not to stuff herself with too many or her stomach would pay.

She gathered berries for Sempal and her family then continued. A few tumbled from her pocket as she reached the cliff path and began climbing. At the top she paused for breath before putting her fingers to her mouth to blow a long note. It was the call Sempal taught her. To the unknowing ear it sounded like the mawing of the gulls. She waited as terns flew over, diving close, as if they wanted her hair to line their nests. Marna knew they were protecting their young and steered a path away from them. There was no sign of Sempal.

'I have brought ripe berries.' She turned with her arm outstretched to show the food. It was early for haws or rowan berries, but as well as the cluster of bilberries she had found tiny, early strawberries. There was no-one about. She could see down to the caves at the bottom of the cliff. They were invisible when the tide was high and difficult to reach even at low tide. Instinct told her that was where Sempal would be.

Bother.

It was light enough to reach the caves, but Marna didn't relish the descent. She cursed her friend as she stomped along the path and clambered across the pebbled beach towards the rocks. If she were as nimble as Jona's sheep, she would have no trouble scampering to the caves. Since she wasn't, it took both hands and feet to crawl over the slippery boulders to the inlet, with the waves rustling in her ears, inviting her into the water.

Come away with us, Marna. Come away. We can show you such wonders...

A small stream crossed her way as it ran to join the sea. Someone had placed flat stones on the bed to act as a bridge. They were shiny with green slime and Marna wobbled as she stepped on the first one. She flapped her arms. The water wasn't deep, but it rushed and eddied and the rocks were sharp. If she toppled in there was a danger of serious injury. The next stone was underwater and she stretched over it towards the larger stone, lying in mid stream. As she tipped her weight forwards, the foot balancing on the first stone slipped from under her. The berries fell from her pocket and she struggled to keep her balance. One leg was in the air, the other hopping on the stone while her arms flailed like a swan taking flight. It must have seemed comical to an onlooker, but not to Marna as she tried in vain to stop herself falling sideways into the chilly water.

Her head grazed the bottom and her vision turned black. When she regained her senses her mouth was full of water. She tried to breathe through her nose, but water spurted up her nostrils. In a panic she beat her arms and kicked out. There was a noise above her. She stopped moving. It was laughter.

Marna managed to scramble to her knees and sit up in the water. Her hair was dripping down her face and she pushed a lock from her eyes. Sempal was standing at the side of the stream with his hands on his hips.

'Seen something funny?' Marna said. She tried to make her voice sound annoyed, but she guessed she looked ridiculous. 'Give me a hand up.'

Sempal reached out a hand to help her. Marna took hold of it and for a second was tempted to drag him in the water, but she stopped herself. She was shivering as she stepped out of the stream.

'Here, take this.' Sempal removed his cloak and placed it round Marna's shoulders. It was the woollen cloak Marna had dyed for him the previous summer.

'Thank you,' Marna drew it close. 'I brought you strawberries and bilberries, but they were lost in the stream.' She looked wistfully at the flowing water.

'They won't be wasted. The gulls will pick them out and enjoy them.'

'The gulls are fat enough, but you have lost weight.'

'I get by,' Sempal brushed aside her concerns. 'I'd rather be here than in the village where my neighbours think I am a murderer. Even my sister believes I killed

Roben – no doubt Joel too.'

'Henjar would never think that,' Marna said.

'Henjar thinks what others tell her,' Sempal answered. There was bitterness in his voice, but then he smiled. 'We need to get you warmed up. I've made a home in that cave.' He pointed. 'I've a fire burning.'

'How…?' Marna demanded.

'A trader showed me how to twist a wooden rod over a board and catch the sparks on dried heather.'

'A wooden rod?' Marna doubted her friend.

'Aha,' Sempal liked to tease her.

'Why didn't you tell anyone?' Marna accused. 'The village has been struggling to make fire since Roben's disappearance.'

Sempal shrugged. 'They think I'm stupid and useless.'

'Not everyone. Besides, that would have been your chance to prove them wrong.'

'And given them a reason why I killed Roben.'

Marna looked blank.

'To take over his position,' Sempal explained.

'Nobody would think…' Marna was about to deny it, but she guessed Sempal had a point.

'You're shivering, come on.' He took hold of Marna's hand and led her to an opening in the side of the cliff, no wider than a slit.

'In there?'

'Breathe in.'

The gap was wide enough for Marna to squeeze through if she sucked in her stomach. There was no way Jona or the village elders could pass.

'You go first. I'll be right behind.'

Marna turned sideways and edged herself through. The passage smelled of seaweed and fish. Marna felt pressure on her back and jumped.

'It's only me. Go on in,' Sempal said.

There was a thin line of light on the floor from the entrance slit and as her eyes adapted Marna became aware of an orange glow. It grew larger as she shuffled nearer, keeping a hand on the wall of the cave. The passage opened into a chamber. Sempal's fire was almost out. Marna huddled close to capture its warmth.

'Watch out.'

The fire crackled and spat out new flames as Sempal added driftwood from a pile in the corner.

'The wood is damp,' Marna said, jumping back. Once it settled she hunkered down to heat her body and dry her clothes. Sempal sat next to her and they watched the shadows change in the light. She couldn't see his face, but she sensed he was watching her. She removed his cloak and handed it to him.

'Keep it,' Sempal said.

'Don't be silly. This fire won't keep you warm through

the night.'

Sempal grunted at her disparagement of his fire, but held out a hand to accept the cloak.

'Oh, it has a tear.' Marna stuck her thumb through a diamond shaped rip in the material to demonstrate.

'You're making it worse.' Sempal snatched the cloak. 'I caught it on a rock when I was snaring birds.'

Marna laughed. 'Limpets more like. Would you like me to mend it?'

'It's an old cloak. What is one more tear?'

'I can mend them all. I'd like to.'

'Everybody knows this is my cloak. If you took it to the village to mend, the others would know you'd seen me. They would ask where I was.'

'I hadn't thought of that, but what does it matter? Thork asked me to look for you. Why won't you come back? You have nothing to be ashamed of.'

Sempal bent over the fire and Marna felt his breath on her neck. She looked up. He was gazing into the fire as if the glowing ashes would give him answers to his problems. 'I'll go back when I am ready,' he said.

'When?'

'If I can find Joel's boat it will give a clue to what happened. Perhaps it was hit by a whale or seals.'

'Joel's accident was so long ago. Surely after months in the water, the waves will have beaten the boat into bits?

This driftwood you are burning could be it.'

Sempal was about to toss a piece of wood onto the fire, but hesitated. 'Joel's body came ashore. Why not his boat?'

'Boats aren't like dogs. They don't return home when they are hungry.'

Sempal made a face.

'I should be getting back.' She shook as she tried to stand. Sempal put a hand on her shoulder.

'You could stay here.'

'Don't be silly. Mother would worry and send Thork to search for me.'

'And Thork would waste no time in telling Jona.'

'Finding Jona won't be easy. He doesn't spend time in the village. Wilmer is in charge.'

'We don't need someone from Barnhouse to run our affairs.'

'There's no need to be like that. Wilmer is doing his best.' Marna stepped away from the fire.

'You're going the wrong way,' Sempal said. 'The exit is behind you. That water must have got into your brain as well as your chest.'

Marna wanted to say something cutting, but she couldn't help laughing.

'Will you come again?' he asked.

'It seems I will have to.'

'Oh?'

'The coastline reaches from Hoy and the Flow round Birsay and out to Eynhallow and Rousay. It will take more than two eyes to spot an empty boat.'

'Thanks. You are a good friend.'

'I'm not your only friend, remember that.'

'Mmm,' Sempal was unconvinced. He took her hand and helped her along the passage. 'Will you manage the stream?' There was a glint of mischief in his eyes. Marna flapped him off.

The sun was sinking and a feeble moon rose. She had stayed out longer than she planned, but she took her time negotiating the stream before scampering towards the village. It was wiser to get home before her mother asked questions. No matter how convincing an excuse she thought up, her mother knew when she was lying.

'There you are.' Her mother was whisking the top of the milk to make butter. 'I could do with a hand before my wrist stiffens attached to this spoon.

Marna sat down and took the wooden spoon from her. She began stirring the cream.

'Not like that. How many times must I show you?'

'Sorry.'

'Where have you been? Caran has arrived from Orphir. She is asking for you.'

'Caran is here?' Marna looked round the hut. It was one of the smaller houses in the settlement. Three cots, shielded by stone slabs lain on their sides surrounded the fire. There was a dresser for storing pots and ornaments, against the front wall, but nowhere a person could stand without being seen. 'I guess she's with Thork.'

'He is showing her his new bow.'

'Being in love must be fascinating.'

'You would know, if you made an effort. Here give me that.' Marna was unable to master the task of whisking and her mother took the spoon back. Marna stood up and prodded the fire with a stick. The dying flames leapt up.

'Careful,' her mother warned. 'We don't want it to go out. Wilmer has already lit it twice. If I ask a third time he will think I am putting it out deliberately.'

Marna tried to think of her mother and Wilmer together. She liked the jeweller, he was kind and funny, but the thought of him as a step-father...no, she couldn't picture it. She thought of Sempal and his bow drill. 'Soon we won't need Wilmer,' she said.

'What have you heard? Is there a new fire maker?'

'Maybe,' Marna teased. She was saved from explaining by the arrival of Thork and Caran. Thork had his arm around Caran's waist and she laughed as she stopped him sliding his fingers down her tunic. Marna's mother lifted her bowl out the way. When Caran saw Marna she broke from Thork and rushed to embrace her.

'Marna, it is so good to see you again.'

'That is because you want her help,' Thork said.

'Don't listen to him,' Caran released Marna from a bear hug.

'I rarely do,' Marna answered.

'The tunic you dyed red for me two summers' ago is too small now,' Caran put on a wheedling voice.

'You've been eating too many geese,' Thork said, giving his girlfriend a poke in the stomach.

'Only because you catch them,' Caran brushed him away. 'Say you'll dye me a new one, Marna.'

'I will need bog-iron for the colouring.'

'I have some with me. We have plenty in Orphir.' Caran reached into a willow bag slung over her shoulder and brought out clothes. 'This is a new tunic and matching shawl. Can I leave them with you?'

'Of course,' Marna accepted them.

'Thank you.' Caran gave Marna a peck on the cheek. 'When will they be ready? We have a village celebration in ten days. My cousin is getting married.'

'They should be ready by then,' Marna agreed, 'as long as the sun shines to dry the dye.'

'You are amazing, Marna.' Caran gave her another hug. 'I have to return before the wedding to help prepare the food. In seven days.'

'I'll see what I can do.'

'I shall make sure there is no slacking until you have

finished,' Thork joked. 'Is dinner ready, mother?'

'Do you need help?' Caran offered.

'Everything is ready,' Marna's mother glared at Marna, reminding her of the little help she had given. Marna blushed.

'Sit down and we will serve,' Caran said, nudging Marna.

They ate supper of stuffed duck eggs and bannocks before retiring to sleep. Caran was staying with them and Marna allowed her to sleep in her heather lined cot while she made a bed for herself by the fire. It was a warm night, but the cold from the stream was in her bones and she shivered. It was hard to sleep. Thoughts bounced through her head like hares; the tear in Sempal's blue cloak, fire making, dyes. She worried there wasn't enough meadowsweet and dock leaves to dye Caran's tunic and shawl. Perhaps there was some left over from when she dyed Jona's leggings. Perhaps not - Jona had long legs. Two of them. She pictured Jona with three legs, then four. At five, she opened her eyes.

The room was dark, with only a glowing ember smouldering in the hearth. Marna rubbed her head and got up. She shuffled to the fire and prodded life into it then made her way to the dresser, careful not to disturb the others. Thork was snoring like a wild boar and Marna hoped Caran was able to sleep through the whistling snorts.

She reached for the stone pot that kept her plants dry. It was empty. No meadowsweet. What had she done with it? She looked at the sleeping figures. The sun rose early during summer. She could make her way to the loch, gather what she needed and be back to cook breakfast before the others woke. They wouldn't know she was gone.

Her cloak and bag were kept at the bottom of her cot. She tiptoed across and teased the cloak from beneath Caran's feet. Caran rolled over, but didn't wake. The bag was harder to recover, but she needed it for carrying home the plants without damaging them. Henjar had woven it for her from strong nettle fibres.

She gathered her cloak around her and slipped the bag over her head before making her way out. She heard Boda crying as she past Henjar's house and was about to go in to comfort him when she heard Henjar's soothing voice. If she stopped to speak to Henjar she wouldn't get away until midday. She sidled past the door and along the passage. There was a breeze blowing up from the sea. She loved the smell of the seaweed and the tang of salt on her lips. The rhythmic lapping of the water soothed her, but her journey was inland, towards the freshwater loch.

The dock leaves were easy to find. Their tough stems hurt her fingers as she gathered them. One of her nails was torn and it bled. She gave up and looked for meadowsweet. There was a clump a little way off and she found enough to fill her storage box. The search took less time than Marna imagined and she decided to look for watercress. The taste was tangy, but her mother enjoyed it on her meat. She was wading through a patch of reeds in the shallow waters at the side of the loch when a loud quack made her startle.

Stupid, it was only a duck. The quacking got louder and Marna sensed the bird was in distress. The wild ducks knew to fly off when people were around. Perhaps she was too close to its nest.

'Don't worry Mrs. Duck, I haven't come for your eggs,' she said.

The quacks merged into one long drone. Marna followed the sound until she found the problem. The mother duck was paddling in the water with two ducklings at her side, but the third duckling was trapped in the reeds. It had got its tiny leg stuck and the more it pulled, the tighter the stem entangling it became. A crow was watching the scene with beady red eyes. Marna imagined it was licking its lips.

'Not today,' Marna waved a fist at it. The bird didn't fly away. She picked a pebble and threw it towards the crow. Her aim wasn't good. The bird cawed and flew a few feet to wait.

The duckling had given up its struggle and was lying limp. It didn't resist as she unwound the fibres of the plant. It felt cold and its fluffy body was still. The mother duck chaperoned her remaining infants away from Marna, but was watching. Finally the duckling's leg was free. The bird didn't move and Marna feared she was too late. She lifted the duckling in her hand and cuddled it close to her chest. The mother duck flapped its wings and quacked. Marna felt a tickle in her hand and opened her palms. The duckling stirred. It shook water droplets from its coat and gave a yap.

'Time to go back to your mother,' Marna said. She waded into the water to find a clear patch then gently lowered it into the water. The duckling bobbed up and down before its feet began paddling and it returned to the mother duck. Marna smiled.

She grabbed hold of a branch to drag herself to the bank, but something caught her eye - something blue. She reached out to tease it from the wood. It was a triangular scrap of material, identical to the piece missing from Sempal's cloak. She was standing on the spot where the figure she saw on the day Jona had his vision would have been. Her eyes hadn't deceived her.

She was convinced the person she saw had something to do with Jona's vision. She rubbed the material between her fingers. It had a familiar feel and for the first time in her life, she had doubts about Sempal.

Chapter 7

Henjar's mother was amusing Boda at home while Marna and Henjar sat outside, gossiping and weaving willow baskets.

'Here comes Thork to annoy us,' Marna laughed.

'And Albar,' Henjar added. 'He follows your brother like a little dog.'

'Albar has his own reason for being here,' Marna said. Henjar blushed and brushed back her hair.

'Have you heard the news?' Thork said.

'What news?' Marna said.

'It will cost you a willow basket,' Thork teased.

'What use do you have for baskets?'

'I can give it to Caran.'

'You'll need more than a willow basket to impress Caran once she sees the handsome and wealthy travellers from the south,' Albar said. Thork scowled.

'Visitors are coming?' Henjar squeaked. 'How many? When? I must be ready.' She stood up and wiped the willow twigs from her tunic.

'These traders are causing a stir,' Marna said.

'And Caran is a pretty girl,' Albar teased.

'Caran is loyal, not like the girls you know,' Thork defended his girlfriend.

'The girls I know are the same ones you know,' Albar laughed. He winked at Henjar.

'Why should any of our girls want to be with an uncouth sailor smelling of fish and piss, when there are strong lads here?' Thork argued.

'Strong lads in the village, like Henjar's brother?' Albar countered.

'He was strong enough to kill Roben,' Thork said.

'That isn't true,' Marna threw down her basket and jumped up to face her brother.

'I wasn't complaining. Roben was no friend to us.'

'He was my friend,' Henjar said.

Thork pushed his tongue round his cheek and shuffled his foot in the earth. 'I meant...'

'But now he is dead, I would go with a travelling sailor,' Henjar finished.

'Me too,' Marna agreed, hoping to lighten the situation. 'It is time we had some adventure.'

'Ho, listen to her,' Albar said. 'If Marna was my sister, I would keep her confined to the house until I found her a husband.'

'Don't think I haven't tried. No-one in the village is brave enough to take her,' Thork answered with a smile at Marna. 'Perhaps a foreigner who doesn't know how strong minded she is will be fooled.'

'Be careful what you say, brother,' Marna answered. 'I know about poisonous plants. I know which ones have no taste when added to mutton stew.'

'You wouldn't poison Thork?' Henjar gasped.

'Marna was joking,' Thork reassured her. 'She knows I wouldn't dare interfere with her affairs.'

'If you can't find a husband, I'm available,' Albar said with a grin.

'You are more like a brother than a husband,' Marna scoffed. He wasn't any good at hunting, but Thork made sure he brought a hare or wild goose home for his younger brothers and sisters. In his favour, he did have a fine singing voice. That might sustain him if he toured the villages entertaining gatherings, but it wouldn't feed a family in winter.

'You say these traders are wealthy?' Henjar said. 'Where are they from?'

'From a land where they have coloured gemstones and fine threads in their cloaks and tunics,' Albar said. 'A land where men ride on snow white steeds and shoot arrows at fierce water creatures that eat children whole.'

'Not little Boda,' Henjar said, clenching her fists. 'I wouldn't let them.'

'He is only teasing you,' Thork gave his friend a punch on the shoulder. 'You had better watch out; you are starting to sound like Sempal.'

'The gods forbid.'

'I should like to meet these men,' Henjar said.

'Me too,' Marna agreed.

'Then I suggest you start preparing food. The traders have brought fine whale bone and coloured gems. Wilmer is keen to do business and has invited them to the village. He hopes our hospitality will secure good deals. I'm no matchmaker, but I think a plate of stew and dumplings washed down with sweet ale will encourage them to stay and get to know the folks here,' Albar said.

'Especially the womenfolk,' Thork added.

'I shall tell my mother to grind grain,' Henjar rushed to leave, forgetting her baskets. Marna gathered them and the willow strands.

'I'll bring the berries I collected this morning,' Marna said. 'Have you any meat you can spare?'

'What will you give me?' Thork asked.

Marna reached over and planted a kiss on his cheek.

'I might have meat to spare too,' Albar said, turning his face for Marna to kiss. She duly obliged.

'There, now we had better get on,' she said.

Thork and Albar followed Marna into the village and laughed as she and Henjar ran from one hut to another, collecting stone pots and cooking implements and spreading the news.

'You'd better hurry,' Albar tormented them. 'I can hear them coming.'

'Then you must have enormous ears like an ass,' Marna scolded. 'Why don't you and Thork practise drumming and get out of our way?'

'What's the fuss?' Marna's mother appeared from Jona's hut.

'Shh, it's a secret,' Henjar giggled.

'You'll have a job keeping a secret in this village.'

Marna wanted to ask her mother what business she had in Jona's house, but Henjar grabbed her arm and pulled her away. 'Joannet is coming,' she explained.

Her words echoed along the passageway and Marna hoped Joannet hadn't heard the distaste in her voice. Joannet did not appear, but they were joined by four other girls, wanting to know how they could help.

'How many men will there be?' one girl asked.

'Enough to go round,' Thork quipped.

'Will they enjoy these limpets I collected?'

'We can't have a feast without limpets,' Thork joked.

'They bring you out in spots,' Marna reminded him.

'And it's no feast,' Henjar sighed. 'Just left-overs.'

'Poppycock girl, it's what you do with the food that counts. There will be a banquet by the time we are finished.' Joannet had joined the gathering without anyone noticing, but it didn't take her long to assume command. The girls were given their tasks and Joannet hovered over them to make sure everything was in order. 'Greena, stop beating the flour or the dough will stiffen.'

'I like it stiff,' Henjar said and was surprised when the

others laughed.

Marna loved the banter and giggling when the girls got together. Joannet was skilled at preparing wonderful meals from basic ingredients and although the others moaned, they were happy to follow her instructions.

'Instead of ruining the broth, go and find out when the men will arrive,' she ordered Henjar and Marna.

Marna was happy to escape the heat of the cooking room. Henjar was glad too.

'I look a mess. I need to sort my hair,' she wailed.

'Why? They are just men,' Marna answered.

'Healthy, wealthy men,' Henjar reminded her. 'With Joel and Roben gone, I need a father for Boda.'

'Seth and Walf will help and there is Sempal.'

'Uncles aren't the same as a father.'

'Wouldn't Boda be better with a father from our own people?'

'Where is all your talk of adventure?' Henjar scoffed. 'You are like my mother. Lin worries about travelling a few miles from our village. Or are you jealous that the men will prefer me to you?'

'You had better watch Boda doesn't toddle towards a river in this new country with his new father, and be eaten by one of the terrible creatures Albar spoke of.'

Henjar gasped and Marna felt bad. She took Henjar's hand and rubbed it. 'Perhaps we shall both find a husband

and sail over the seas together.'

'It would be nice if we could stay together,' Henjar said. 'I must go now. Don't tell Joannet.'

Henjar scurried towards her house. Marna heard her making baby noises at Boda when she passed. The travellers had arrived by boat, but she hadn't seen their vessels. It made sense, though, to moor their boats in the sheltered bay round the coast. The hill to the back protected it from winds and the islands broke the waves.

From the bay, they would have made their way to Barnhouse. Wilmer had been home attending to business and would have met the travellers there. Inviting them to Skara Brae was clever. Barnhouse was near the Ness. Wilmer would not want interference from the priests.

She spotted Wilmer coming towards her, struggling to pull a small sledge against the wind. She joined him and took a handle.

'Where is your ox today?' she asked.

'I lent him to friends gathering logs from the birch wood,' Wilmer answered. 'I thought I could manage this myself, but if you hadn't come I fear the wind would have blown the sledge and its contents into the sea and perhaps me with it. I have a fear of drowning.'

'What have you got?' There was an animal skin covering stone bowls and clay pots – no doubt containing the jewellery Wilmer wanted to trade. Marna was keen to see it.

'Bits and bobs,' Wilmer re-arranged the cover. 'I hope to persuade the men from Ireland to take bone charms and good luck brooches for their womenfolk. They are a superstitious race. I left them in Barnhouse to enjoy the ale, but they will be here soon.'

'Ireland?' Marna was disappointed. 'Albar said they were from the south…'

'… where it never rains, the sun shines all year and rich food can be picked from trees,' Wilmer added. 'Albar was pulling your leg.'

'It doesn't bother me, but Henjar will be upset,' Marna said. 'She was hoping to win an exotic husband.'

'I expect there will be a man to suit her among the visitors, if that is what she wants,' Wilmer said. He tugged on his handle and one of the wooden runners caught on a rock. The nearest pot wobbled and toppled to the ground. Wilmer tried to grab it, but the clay shattered and the brooches spilt out. Marna put her handle down and bent to pick up the goods.

'Thank you. That was careless of me, but it looks like we have found everything,' Wilmer placed the jewellery on the sledge.

'No, there's something beneath the runner. It looks like a comb.'

'You have sharp eyes,' Wilmer bent to pick up the

object. 'It's a knife. It may be small, but I can get a good price for it.' He slipped it in the pocket of his coat.

With Marna's help they steered the sledge towards the village. She stood back to allow Wilmer to manoeuvre it through the doorway then followed behind.

'You don't approve of Henjar marrying one of the foreign traders?' Marna said.

'It's not for me to approve or otherwise,' Wilmer answered. 'I am not her father or brother and even if I were, she has a mind of her own. My advice would be unwelcome and go unheeded.'

He dragged the sledge along the passage towards the workshop. Marna walked at the back to make sure nothing fell out. Passing the house where the women were baking, they heard squeals of excitement dampened by Joannet's rough commands.

'Something smells good,' Wilmer said.

'Joannet wants to know when the men will arrive,' Marna remembered her task. 'We are preparing a feast.'

As she spoke, Marna eased a hand towards the sledge. Wilmer tugged it forwards. 'A feast?' he said. 'These men are not gods that require sating.'

'Gods have no need of feasts,' Marna answered, 'Whereas men seem always to be filling their bellies.'

'Indeed,' Wilmer laughed.

They reached the workshop and Wilmer positioned the

sledge against a wall, but seemed reluctant to pull back the skin while Marna was there. 'The men should be here any time. I should light a fire in the guest chambers.' He spoke with urgency, but didn't move, keeping a hand on the sledge.

'I can light the fire,' Marna offered.

Wilmer made a noise that sounded like a chortle. 'Who taught you? Surely not Roben?'

It was on the tip of Marna's tongue to blurt out Sempal's name, but she held back. 'I have watched men make fire by twisting a wooden rod until it gives sparks.'

'Where was that?' Wilmer's voice was severe.

'Well...I don't remember...' Marna took a step back.

'I'm sorry, I didn't mean to frighten you,' Wilmer smiled again. 'Watching is one thing, but it takes a great deal of practise, and failures, to get it right.'

'Let me try,' Marna said. She had found a twig and wound a dried grass stalk round it the way Sempal had. She practised when no-one was watching and at the last attempt had created a spark that could be nursed into a flame. She was eager to show off her new skill.

'Very well,' Wilmer agreed. 'I shall be through shortly when I have finished here.'

'Thank you,' Marna rushed at him and gave him a hug. She had hidden her fire rod outside the village, piling stones into a cairn round it. She didn't want Thork mocking or her mother asking questions until she was confident she could demonstrate without failure.

She hurried to retrieve it and twirled it between her fingers as she headed back.

'Where have you been?' Joannet's voice was louder than a lowing ox.

Marna jumped. She thrust her hand with the fire drill behind her back. 'I was helping Wilmer.'

'About time he returned. Where is he?'

'He's unloading his sledge in the workshop. I don't think he wants to be disturbed,' Marna answered.

'We'll see about that,' Joannet took a step then stopped. 'What are you hiding?'

'Nothing.' Marna felt her face burn. Joannet side-stepped to see what was in her hand, but Marna swapped hands and hid the drill beneath her cloak. She held out both palms for Joannet to inspect.

'Humph,' Joannet folded her arms, blocking Marna's way. 'Where is Henjar?'

'Boda was crying. She had to attend to him.'

'A likely story! I'm surprised she even remembers she has a son. I've no doubt she'll abandon him to her mother the minute she finds a new man.'

'That is a horrible thing to say.' Marna took a step towards Joannet, but felt the drill slipping from beneath her cloak and grabbed at her chest.

'What's wrong with you now?' Joannet said.

'Stomach cramp. I've eaten too many berries.'

'Then it serves you right.'

They stood watching each other for a few seconds until the impasse was broken by the arrival of Wilmer.

'No fire?' he said, looking pleased.

'We'll leave that in your capable hands,' Joannet said. 'The food is ready. I'll instruct the girls to lay it out.' She gathered her shawl and swished past Marna with a beam on her face.

'Joannet interrupted me. I didn't have time,' Marna said, but Wilmer wasn't interested in excuses. 'Would you like me to fetch Thork and the others?' she asked.

'Yes, if you can prise them from their games. I saw your brother throwing stone balls at a stick. He has a good aim, unlike his friend. Albar has other talents. He may sing for us tonight and you could ask Thork to bring his drum. The visitors would appreciate entertainment.'

'Oh...but...'

'Yes?'

'Jona doesn't like drums being used for merriment. They should be kept for important parades and burials.'

'That seems like a waste, but Jona is set in his ways,' Wilmer winked. 'Jona isn't here now, is he?'

'Isn't he?' Marna recalled seeing her mother come out of Jona's hut and assumed she was speaking with him. 'Has he gone to visit Fara on Eynhallow? I heard she is expecting her first child.'

Before Wilmer could answer, barking from the dogs outside the village announced the arrival of the strangers.

'Our guests are here and the fire isn't lit,' Wilmer worried.

'We'll keep them occupied until it is,' Marna promised. She left Wilmer and scrambled outside. A group of villagers, led by Joannet, were waiting to greet the newcomers. Marna squeezed to the front. The strangers were a little distance off, striding towards the village from the path by the loch. She counted five men and one boy – or perhaps a shrunken man. She had heard Sempal speak of dwarves, but not in Ireland.

As they approached, Marna saw that it wasn't a dwarf, or a boy. It was a woman. Her red hair was cropped and she wore breeches like the others, but her slight build and developed chest made her gender clear. She wore a leather cord round her neck with a set of pipes dangling onto her shirt. The wood was painted with figures of winged children with pointed ears.

Normally Jona would have selected three elders and they would greet the guests and exchange gifts of stone tools or sweetmeats before inviting them into their homes, but the village was lacking in elders. Jona was absent, Roben and Joel were dead and Wilmer was indoors trying to light the fire. Seth and Walf had gone hunting. Thork would have relished the role, but he was fetching his drum and the others were too shy to speak. They stood gazing at the Irish contingent.

'What, have we come upon a village of mutes?' one of the strangers said. He was a tall man with flaming hair. Marna supposed he was the leader.

'There is no need to speak when you are around, Finn. You talk enough to wake the dead,' his friend said. The other three men laughed, but the woman was silent.

There was a glazed look in her eyes, like the blind calf Marna saw last year. She seemed sad, like the calf before it died.

Although she was at the front, Joannet didn't answer. Marna was about to step forwards when Henjar pushed through, dressed in her best tunic and hardly recognisable with the amount of colour plastered on her face and arms. She carried a stone basin with water which she offered to the red-haired leader.

'Welcome to Skara Brae,' she said. 'Wash the journey from you then come inside and rest. We have prepared food and entertainment.'

This was a big speech for Henjar and she stepped back and lowered her head.

'Thank you,' the leader showed his approval by dipping his hands in the water. The others did likewise, including the woman. Henjar had forgotten to provide a towel. The leader shook his hands dry, covering Henjar with water like a wet dog. The others wiped their hands on their clothes. 'What is your name, my pretty one?' The leader put out a hand to raise Henjar's chin.

'Henjar.'

'A bonny name for a bonny lass. They call me Finn. These are my men, Mickel, Brann, Conel and Pog.'

'Pog?' Henjar sniggered.

Finn didn't introduce the woman, but nobody said anything. With the welcome complete, the male guests were ushered into the village with a clamour. The strange woman hung back. Marna lingered too.

'Are you no going wi' the rest?' the woman asked.

'It wouldn't be proper to leave you alone,' Marna answered. Although the woman wasn't much older than her, she felt like a young child in front of her and gave a curtsey. The woman laughed and fingered her pipes.

'Are they children?' Marna was intrigued.

'Them be the faerie folk,' the woman said, 'As mischievous as bairns, aye – but no half as magical.'

Marna smiled. 'I don't have children, but my friend has a little boy. I know what you mean. I'm Marna. I live here.' It was a stupid thing to say, but she felt awkward and the questions she wanted to ask wouldn't come. There was something about the sparkle in the stranger's brown eyes that Marna liked, but at the same time she felt afraid. Not of the woman herself, but of the dangers she might find herself in if she were drawn into the woman's sphere.

'Marna, you say?' The woman lifted the pipes to her lips and fluttered her fingers over the small holes along the tubes. Her eyes smiled and she blew into them. The first note was a shrill whistle, but the tune mellowed into a lilting lullaby. Marna could hear the songs of familiar birds and the call of the sea.

'Are you homesick?' Marna asked.

The woman finished her tune before removing her pipes. 'How can I be homesick when I have no home?'

'Everyone has a home,' Marna argued. 'It is where we belong. Perhaps you have not found yours yet.'

'You are wise for your age, Marna,' the woman answered. 'My home is with the faerie folk. They know my true name, but the others call me Erin.'

Marna wanted to know Erin's true name, but instead she asked, 'Are you hungry?'

'You're one for the questions,' the woman said softly, staring through Marna at a spot in the distance. Marna turned, but there was nothing there.

'I meant, if we don't go in the food will be eaten.' A stomach gurgle betrayed her motive.

'There are more important things than eating,' Erin answered, 'but sharing food is a sign of friendship and trust.

I can tell you enjoy your food.'

Marna sucked in her stomach. Erin laughed and put an arm on Marna's shoulder. 'Let us go in.'

Marna got the feeling things were being turned upside down and that Erin was the one welcoming her. The strange woman's arm was light on her shoulder, but she was being steered towards the entrance.

Once inside Marna led Erin to the gathering. The men were making themselves comfortable, accepting the best places and sampling the food on offer with approval. Marna nudged her way through, but when she looked round Erin hadn't followed her. She was standing at the back of the room, her clothes merging with the stone of the wall, so that she was almost invisible.

'Where have you been?' Henjar poked Marna in the back with her elbow. She was holding two goblets of ale and the sticky liquid trickled down Marna's tunic.

Marna was about to invent an excuse, but the leader of the Irish traders looked towards them and Henjar fluttered her eyelids. 'I must go.'

Henjar collapsed at the feet of the Irishman. He leaned over to whisper something as he took his goblet and she blushed.

'Marna.'

She looked across to see who had called. Wilmer gave a wave and she joined him. Thork was beside him.

'Marna, can't you persuade your brother to play for us?' Wilmer said.

'Please no. I've heard enough drumming for a life time,' Marna answered, holding her hands over her ears.

'Indeed?' Thork said. 'Wait until I fetch my sticks. Jona had us practising a new rhythm. Brum, pum, pum, tiddly, idly um, pum.' Thork marched out of the room, humming. Wilmer nodded his appreciation to Marna.

'It doesn't take much to get Thork to do what you want. The trick is in knowing how to phrase it.'

'You speak of your brother as if he is a dog you can train,' Wilmer said, but Marna could tell he was joking. 'Music and singing should soften our guests. Once they trust us, we will be able to bargain with them. They have brought flint, whalebone and linen. We have only pots and jewellery to trade in return.'

'Our pots are strong and pretty,' Marna said. 'The merchants who came last year wanted more than we had. We also have bone needles and nettle rope.'

'You make it sound like the Irishmen will be getting the better deal. You should join us for the negotiations.'

'Wilmer,' Marna's mother appeared. 'I wondered if you could light my fire. It has gone out again.' She linked arms and led him away as Thork returned.

'Albar, will you sing for us?' Thork encouraged.

Albar claimed his throat was dry. He was handed a

118

flagon of ale by Henjar. Marna didn't miss the grin on his face as he accepted. He began with a ballad, but as the ale took effect he sang the cheerier ditties the men knew from working with the cattle. The Irishman called Conel had a good voice. He joined in with a sailor's chant and the others were ready for dancing.

A space was cleared in the centre of the room. The men and women danced apart at first, but it wasn't long before partners were chosen. Marna crept to the back of the room to watch, while Henjar made sure she found herself in the arms of one of the Irish guests.

Marna tapped her feet to the music, hoping Erin would join in and play her pipes.

Where was Erin?

She searched among the crowd, but the strange woman had disappeared. Marna supposed the stuffy room, with the smell of cooked fat mingling with the smoke, was too much for her. She was about to go outside to look when she spotted Erin enter the hall from the passageway leading to Jona's house. She moved through the crowd like a shadow. The dancers hardly knew she was there. Erin stopped beside Finn and ushered him away from the girl he was kissing. It was one of Horen's daughters, who gave Erin a filthy look before stamping off.

Marna moved closer, but couldn't hear the conversation between Finn and Erin. From the grim look on

119

Finn's face she suspected something was wrong. She picked up a goblet of ale from a table. Offering it to the leader would serve as the excuse she needed for eavesdropping. The visitors were speaking in a strange language. Marna had heard Irish spoken before, but this was different. The good humour Finn showed when chatting with the village girls was gone.

The music and dancing stopped. Everyone was staring at Finn and Erin. Nadea, the girl Marna had seen with Finn, was standing with her twin sister.

'Dance with him now you've got him,' Nadea called.

'Who would want to dance with her?' Eada added.

Erin made a hissing sound like an angry owl. Finn banged his fist against the wall. 'There will be no more dancing. It is time for us to leave.'

'What is the hurry? We've just arrived,' Pog grumbled. He had his arms around Henjar.

'You wish to leave?' Wilmer stepped into the room, straightening his cloak.

'It will be dark soon. We must return to our boats.'

'They are moored several miles away. The wind is rising and the sea will grow rough. There will be no comfort for you on board. I hoped...' Wilmer looked round at the villagers, '...we all hoped, you would honour us by spending the night here.'

'Aye, we have no wish to journey out,' Mickel

answered. He spoke to Finn, but he stared at Erin.

'There are bad omens here,' Finn warned. 'No good will come if we tarry.'

The villagers muttered and the Irish men moved to form a group.

'Bad omens?' Wilmer gave a shallow laugh. 'What do you mean?'

'My sister has the gift of knowing. Some call it a sixth sense.'

'It would be better if she used the other five. Your sister talks nonsense,' Mickel answered. Finn reached for a stone knife at his belt, but didn't draw it.

'Erin can tell when something is ill with a place. She can tell when there have been unexplained deaths.' Finn emphasised the last word. 'There have been unexplained deaths in this village. Do you deny it?'

Henjar gave a cry and dropped the goblet she was holding. It fell to the ground and the ale spilt and ran across the floor like blood from a severed vein. She stood dumbstruck, allowing one of the women to stoop and pick up the cup. Marna was too far from her friend to comfort her, but she saw Albar move towards her and put an arm round her waist.

'The woman's reaction proves I am right,' Finn continued. 'There are men who are not here that should be - a lame boy and a red-haired man.'

'Impossible, how do you know...?' Wilmer began.

'I can see their shadows,' Erin answered. 'Dark shadows. Those of men who walk in the realms of...'

Marna thought she was going to say 'the faerie folk' and was disappointed when she ended with 'secrecy.' Erin spoke softly, but the room was hushed to listen. Marna shivered, thinking she could feel the shadows cross the floor. But no, that was silly. Jona had gone to visit his daughter and son-in-law, taking gifts for the new child, and Sempal was in his cave boiling limpets. His shadow was attached to him, sitting by his fire.

'Why, if there are shadows here, I'll beat them out with my drum,' Thork said. He had swallowed more than his share of ale to impress the Irishmen and he reeled as he stood up. His drumming was loud and erratic. Marna held her ears, but Wilmer forced a laugh.

Others joined the laughter to tease Thork, who was proud of his playing. The situation was defused with merriment. Finn looked at his sister then sat down.

'Don't you want to dance?' Mickel asked.

'Later,' Finn answered. He cast an eye towards Henjar and smiled.

'Then drink more ale,' Wilmer offered. 'It is known to keep the shadows at bay.'

Marna was standing near Finn. She had forgotten about the cup in her hand, but he reached out to take it, bending his face close to hers. She could smell his foul breath and wondered what Henjar found attractive.

'Have you fresh water?' Erin asked Marna.

'I can fetch a mug from the loch,' Marna answered.

'That is too far to go in the dark.'

Erin leaned over to speak to her brother. He nodded and she left the gathering. Marna was anxious to speak with her, but sensed she wouldn't welcome company. Henjar had escaped from Pog and pulled Marna aside.

'Hasn't he got the most wonderful blue eyes?'

'Who, Pog?' Marna feigned ignorance.

'Finn. He has such strong muscles.'

'And a wife at home waiting for him,' Marna said.

'His wife died last year,' Henjar said.

'Is that what he told you?'

'Why do you always drown any dreams I have?' Henjar said then put her hand to her mouth. 'I didn't mean drown, I meant...'

'Kill?' Marna suggested.

'What has got into you, Marna?'

'You've barely met him. You don't know what he's like.'

'He is brave, wealthy and generous. He has more cattle at home than he can count.'

'So, he can't count.'

'Pog says he is good with children.'

'Which means he has a brood of his own.'

'He is an uncle.'

'If he truly wishes to take you home as his wife and adopt Boda as his son, then I am happy for you,' Marna said. 'But I can't believe you are the only girl he has fallen for on his travels. Perhaps you should ask your brother's opinion before losing your heart.'

'My brother? Don't make me choke. He is the one who got me into this mess.'

'What do you mean?'

Henjar made a gesture with her arms to suggest rocking a boat.

'You don't think Sempal caused Joel's accident?'

'Roben's death too. You heard Finn speak of a deadly shadow.' She had been drinking and her temper was rising. So was her voice. People were looking over.

'You don't know what you are saying,' Marna wanted to slap her friend. Words raged in her head, but she knew it was the ale and the giddiness of having men interested in her that turned Henjar's head. 'If Finn is to be your next husband, you had better rescue him from Sylva,' she said, before pushing past Henjar and marching to the door.

She paused to watch Henjar stride over and pull Sylva off Finn's knee by the hair. The Irishman gave a roar and leaned over to spank Sylva on the behind as she was dragged away. Marna had seen enough.

It was a warm evening with light for Marna to see her way past the bere strips and across the scrub towards the shore. The sun cast an orange glow on the rippling water, but she wasn't afraid of shadows. The warm colours lifted Marna's mood. The gods were showing approval, whatever Erin thought. As she neared the water, the sun's reflection darkened and the tide ebbed and flowed a deep blood red.

A gust blew from the west, knocking Marna back. She stumbled and fell, landing on the pebbles. Her palm was bleeding and she sat on the shingle to rub the blood down her tunic. She was about to get up when she spotted a figure creep out from the long grass on the bank and walk across the shore. She couldn't tell who it was, but she imagined it was Erin. Another figure appeared, walking towards the first. Only Sempal hobbled with such a slouch. The meeting was planned, but what had Sempal to do with the Irish woman?

Marna got to her feet and hurried towards them. Ten feet away she stopped and struggled to breathe. Erin and Sempal weren't talking. Sempal had his arms around Erin's shoulder. She had her limbs all over him, legs wound round his, arms grabbing his waist and fingers clambering down his thighs. She pressed her body and lips towards him, drawing him to her.

Chapter 8

'Sempal,' Marna cried, galloping towards them.

The figures broke apart as she tumbled into Sempal. He teetered and grabbed at her arms. Erin stood for a moment then dashed to the bank and disappeared. Marna hit out at Sempal. 'How could you?'

'How could I do what?'

He shielded his face and chest from Marna's flailing arms until her anger died. She stepped back. There were tears dribbling down her cheeks.

'How could you?' she said again, but with less spite. 'After what she said.'

'What did she say?' Sempal's voice was calm. Marna pulled at her hair, hoping the pain would wake her. She stamped her foot and turned to run. When she reached the sandy ground at the water's edge she was sweating. The waves rippled at her feet. She stood listening to the beat of the waves. The incoming water rose round her ankles and lapped at her shins. She felt a hand on her shoulder.

'Come on, tell me what's wrong,' Marna looked round. She was blinded by the sun on the water and for a moment her vision was blurred. She hadn't seen her friend for several days and as she focussed she was surprised to see hairs grown on his chin. Soft, downy hairs – not like the thick, brushwood growth Thork had, but definitely the start of a beard. When he held her, she could feel strength in his grip. It frightened her and she drew away.

'What's up Marna? You look scared.'

'What were you doing with Erin? How long have you known her? What has she told you?'

'Hold on, one question at a time, please.' Sempal had his familiar smile and Marna relaxed.

'What are you doing here?' Marna said.

'It's a beautiful evening,' Sempal said. 'I was admiring the twinkle in the water's eye.'

'If you said that to Thork he would think you had lost your mind,' Marna answered, moving closer to him.

'Thork gets his wisdom from the earth. I get mine from the sea and sky.'

'I wouldn't try explaining that either.'

'There's more to life than eating, sleeping and making love.'

'So what was Erin doing here?'

'She came to see the water.'

Marna gave him a push. 'I bet that wasn't all.'

'You are no better than the others.' Sempal looked at her in a strange manner, gauging whether to trust her. 'I thought you would understand.'

'Understand what? You may share a love of the sea, but Erin is no friend to our village.'

'Why do you say that?' There was a shadow in his eyes, the look of someone smitten with love or lust. Marna

127

wanted to take his hand, but he stepped away. 'You've made up your mind. You don't want to listen.'

'You weren't there. You didn't hear what she said.'

'Tell me then, what did she say?'

'She said there were bad omens. She could smell the reek of death. She tried to turn her friends against us.'

Sempal puckered his lips. 'She's right. There is fear and doubt in the village.'

'You can trust me.'

Sempal bent down and picked up a pebble. He turned it between his fingers then thrust it out to sea. It bounced three times on the surface before plopping under. He watched the ripples fade before walking away.

'Sempal, please don't go,' Marna called.

He paused then moved to sit on a nearby rock. It was big enough for two. He sidled along the stone so she could squeeze beside him.

'You're shivering,' he put an arm round Marna's shoulder and they watched the sun go down.

'It's beautiful,' Marna said, leaning closer to Sempal. 'I suppose Erin could describe it in more poetic language.'

'Don't be silly,' he gave her a hug. 'I met Erin a few days ago. We talked about the sea and her homeland. Her brothers and their families...'

'What about their family?'

'She has three brothers. Two are in Ireland, but Finn is

here. If you came from the village you must have met him.'

'Yes,' Marna agreed. 'He's the leader.'

'Not someone to argue with. He refuses to speak to his eldest daughter because she married a foreigner.'

'He has a daughter?'

'Two daughters and three sons, according to Erin. He did have four sons, but he killed one in a fight.'

'That's awful. Was this after his wife died?'

'His wife is in Ireland expecting his seventh child. Who told you she was dead?'

'No-one, perhaps Pog, but I must have mis-heard.'

'What is this about? Don't tell me you've fallen for him.'

'Of course not,' Marna answered. 'Is Erin married?'

Sempal laughed. 'Do I detect a glint of jealousy?'

'I was just curious.' Marna got up from the stone and moved to stand behind Sempal. She rolled up her sleeves and began massaging his shoulders, kneading the muscles with her fingers. They felt knotted. Sempal squirmed and rolled his shoulders, but let her work away the tension. 'What were you talking to Erin about?'

'I asked her to find out a few things for me.'

'You could have asked me.'

'They were questions you couldn't have asked.'

'Like what?'

'Finding out what questions Wilmer is asking about

me. I need to know who suspects me of murder.'

'I could have told you,' Marna protested. 'Wilmer has finished his investigation and talks of returning home. No-one suspects you of murder. We need you back.'

Sempal made a face. 'Do you know where Jona is?'

'Who told you he has left the village?'

Sempal rubbed the side of his nose with his finger and Marna tweaked his muscle.

'Ouch,' Sempal dodged to the side. Marna stepped in front of him.

'You told Erin about Roben's death. That's how she knew, not some sixth sense or talking to faerie folk.'

'Faerie folk? What has Erin been saying?'

'Why should I tell you when you don't trust me?'

'You are being petty,' Sempal answered. 'Just like a little girl.' Marna stubbed her foot into the sand and kicked it up at him. 'I can't tell you what I know without putting you in danger.'

Marna sat down. 'What danger?'

'I didn't kill Roben, but somebody did. Somebody he knew.'

'Somebody from our village?'

Sempal nodded.

'That is ridiculous. We know everybody here.'

'The others don't seem to think it ridiculous. They were quick to blame me.'

Marna knew it was useless arguing with him when he was in a mood. She was cold sitting on the stone and her arms were popping out in goosebumps. She rolled her sleeves and as she did, she remembered the blue material she found by the loch.

If she had brought it with her she could have shown it to Sempal and asked him what it meant. He wasn't wearing a cloak that evening.

'Who do you think killed Roben?' she asked.

'Jona of course,' Sempal didn't hesitate. 'That's why he's left the village, before Wilmer gets on to him.'

'I don't think Wilmer suspects Jona of murder,' Marna said. 'Why would he kill Roben?'

'They were always arguing, with Roben under-mining Jona's authority. He didn't think Jona was fit to be priest. I imagine he wanted the job himself.'

'The village would not have accepted Roben as priest and he knew that. Besides, if that were true, surely it would be more likely for Roben to kill Jona.'

'Perhaps Roben attacked Jona and he defended himself. What happened isn't important.'

'No?'

'The question we need answered is why Jona would kill Joel.'

'He wouldn't,' Marna said. 'They were friends.'

'But Roben may have wanted to kill Joel,' Sempal

said. He was mumbling to himself.

'What was that?' Marna asked.

'An idea.' He stood up and rubbed the hairs on his chin. 'I have to find Erin. We have things to discuss.'

Marna took this as a rebuke for interrupting their tryst. 'I can help. Erin will return to the village to find her brother. I can speak with her.'

'Best if you stay away from Erin. You've upset her.' Marna was about to object, but Sempal stopped her. 'If you want to make yourself useful, you can keep an eye on my sister. Erin said she was throwing herself on any man, whether he would have her or not.'

'That isn't fair. Everyone was keen to make our guests welcome. Henjar was more enthusiastic than the others.'

'You don't have to make excuses. I know my sister. Flirting with the village men is one thing, but I don't trust these Irish lover boys, especially not Finn. His temper matches the colour of his beard.'

'I have red hair,' Marna objected.

'But not a beard.'

Sempal didn't wait to hear Marna's response to her lack of manliness. She watched him stride across the sand, kicking at seaweed and trying not to drag his leg. Marna gave a yawn. It was time to get back.

She strolled through the bere stalks, digesting what Sempal said and wishing things could be like before.

Before what? Erin's arrival? Roben's death? Joel's accident?

As she reached the stone walls she caught sight of Erin, on her knees searching in the shrubs.

'Have you lost something?' Marna called. The strange woman was startled by the voice and tumbled forwards. She got up and rubbed the mud from her hands on her breeches.

'Marna, isn't it? Are you spying on me?'

'I was talking to my friend, Sempal and now I'm going to bed.'

'You won't have seen my pipes flying around, will you lass?'

Marna cringed. She was a grown woman, not a child. She wanted to say something caustic, but she was intrigued by the notion of the pipes flying around.

'There,' Marna pointed.

'What?' Erin seemed distracted.

'Your pipes. They're round your neck.'

'Why, so they be. She fingered the wood. 'My darlings.'

'Will you play them for me again?' Marna asked.

'Again?' Erin looked confused.

'You played when we met. They told you things.'

'Did they, indeed? Things about you, Marna?'

'I...I don't know,' Marna stuttered.

'I'll have to be asking the faerie folk if you want me to play. I can't perform without their guidance.' Erin lifted the pipes to her lips and blew gently before raising them to her ears. She swayed her head then jerked to a halt and stared into Marna's eyes. 'The faerie folk know you,' she said. 'Marna the Wise, they call you, but maybe that's just their little joke.'

She blew on the pipes again and listened.

'What is it?' Marna asked. She didn't believe in faerie folk, but she was worried by Erin's behaviour. She had seen old Bruan act in a similar manner last year, before he slavered at the mouth, grabbed hold of his neck and dropped down dead. Her mother put it down to eating foxgloves and Marna wondered if Erin had been chewing any seeds that she shouldn't have.

'The Sidhe,' Erin's voice was hoarse. It seemed to take on a deeper tone. 'They tell me you know things that no human should know.'

'Things like what?' Marna didn't know whether to laugh or feel afraid. 'Who are the Shee?'

'Do not speak ill of the wee folk.' Erin put her arm across her face to shield her eyes from Marna. 'Beware of the colour blue.'

'What has Sempal been telling you?' Marna pulled Erin's hand away from her face. Her skin was as pale as a scallop shell and her hair clung to her head like strands of seaweed on a rock.

'Do not touch me.' Erin pushed her away. 'I must speak with my brother.'

Marna felt a chill from the woman's body as she brushed past. She watched Erin move towards the village as if she was floating on a heather bed of air. It took a moment before she came to her senses and followed her.

She heard raised voices as she bent to pass through the entrance tunnel. The Irish men were unhappy. The voices came from the workshop. She quickened her pace and when she reached the workshop, peeked in. Finn was standing over his sister.

'Damn your faerie folk. I knew I shouldn't have brought you, witch.'

The music and dancing was over. Erin was lying on the floor, rubbing her cheek. Marna could see a red bruise spreading from beneath her fingers. The few villagers who remained watched, but didn't interfere.

'You tell her, Finn,' one of the other Irishmen slurred. Marna didn't see his face. 'We're lucky our boats didn't capsize on the voyage over. We could all be sleeping with the fishes.'

The men laughed. Brann moved towards Erin. She lashed out with her fists.

'That's enough,' Wilmer spoke from the corner of the room. 'We are tired and have drunk too much. It is time to sleep. Things will be brighter in the morning.'

'Pity the family who sleep with her in their house,' Finn spat.

'Erin can stay with us,' Marna said, stepping into the room.

'What?' She recognised Thork's voice.

'Thank you, but I know when I'm not welcome,' Erin said. Wilmer offered her a hand. She reached for it, but drew back before deciding to accept his help. She whispered something in his ear once she was on her feet and Wilmer smiled. Glaring around the room, she spat at her brother. 'Take care, Finn of Fingal's Cairn. It doesn't do to speak ill of the Sidhe.'

'And what can the wee folk do to me?' Finn broadened his shoulders to show off his muscles.

'Physical strength will not help you,' Erin scoffed. 'You cannot fight what you do not wish to see.'

The room was silent. People moved aside to let Erin pass. She stopped in front of Marna.

'Only by using what is inside your head can you stand a chance of surviving the wrath of the Sidhe.'

Marna nodded, but didn't answer.

'Heed my words, for they are those of the faerie folk. Beware of what you do not wish to believe.'

'What was that about?' Thork whispered to Marna over-loudly as Erin departed. Marna shrugged. 'She is some woman. I wouldn't mind her as a sister.'

'You wouldn't stand a chance,' Marna grinned. 'Better to stick with the one you know.'

Thork grunted and gave his drum a thump.

'I think we've had enough entertainment for the evening,' Wilmer said, holding his head. Marna imagined a drum roll would not be appreciated.

The visitors gathered their travelling bags and followed the villagers to their houses. Henjar appeared at the doorway carrying a bundle of seal skins. She advanced on Finn and took hold of his arm. 'You can have my brother's empty bed,' she said.

'Steady on, girl,' he laughed, but he seemed happy to go with her. By the time they reached the door he had his arm on her backside, helping her out.

'Sempal's bed will be too small,' Thork observed.

'I don't think he will need Sempal's bed,' Marna said. 'I hope Boda keeps them awake all night.'

'Tut, tut, don't be jealous.'

'Me?'

Thork gave her a pinch. 'Come on, you heard what Wilmer said, things will look brighter in the morning.'

Thork took hold of Marna's hand and they returned to their house. The fire had died, despite Wilmer's attention and their mother was asleep.

'Have a good night,' Marna said to Thork.

'Looks like mother has,' he grumbled.

Marna snuggled under the sealskins in her cot. She heard her brother groan as he turned over and hoped he wasn't going to be sick. Luckily he nodded off. Marna closed her eyes, but instead of Thork's snoring she heard voices. Little voices, like those of children. They were gone when she opened her eyes and sat up. There was a coldness in the air that couldn't be muffled by ale or animal skins.

She got up to light the fire. She hadn't time to hide her drill that afternoon and had stuffed it on the top shelf of the dresser. She fetched it down, but there was no fuel in the box. Marna shivered. Erin was right; there was something dark hanging over the village. Something evil.

Chapter 9

Marna tossed on a sea of dreams she couldn't make sense of. When the first rays of sunlight shone into the village, she got up. Thork was never an early riser and her mother wasn't used to the ale. She left them to search for berries and leaves. There were yellow irises growing by the side of the loch, which she'd spotted a few days ago. When the spear-like leaves were dried, but not shrivelled, they could be woven into mats. Laying them on the floors of the huts took away the coldness of the stone and if she dyed them in bright colours it would add cheer to the house in winter.

She walked on tip-toe along the passageway, hoping not to disturb anyone. If they were waking up with heavy heads, they might assume she was breaking into the village to do mischief. The Irish visitors might strike before they asked questions. As she passed Henjar's house she heard Boda crying and expected to hear Henjar comfort him. The baby's cry turned to a scream. Marna bent her head to enter the house.

'Is everything all right?' she called. There was no reply, apart from loud snoring from the bed in the corner.

Henjar's mother was deep in sleep with Boda in the cot beside her. Marna saw his clothing was wet.

'You need cleaned up,' she said to the child. 'Where is your mother?'

Both Henjar's cot and Sempal's bed were empty

although Marna noticed the Irish leader's satchel placed against the dresser. She gave Henjar's mother a nudge. It took a good shake to get her to wake.

'Boda is crying, Lin,' she said. Half the village could hear him, but Lin seemed oblivious to his wailing. 'He has wet himself. Where is Henjar?'

'Isn't she here?' Lin looked round in a sleepy daze.

'No and neither is Finn.'

'Finn?'

'The Irish trader,' Marna answered.

'There has been no man in this house since Joel drowned and Sempal left,' Lin said.

'His satchel is...' Marna was about to explain, but thought it easier not to confuse Lin. 'Will you take care of Boda while I look for Henjar?'

Henjar's mother rubbed her eyes and rose to attend to Boda. Marna made her way out of the walled village. It was a pleasant summer morning with a light breeze, although the ground was wet. An arch of coloured light joined the sea to the land. The air was fresh and Marna gulped it in, glad to be free of the village odour. If Henjar and Finn had gone somewhere secret, it would have been towards the shore, where they could snuggle up in the banks of sand and watch the stars, or shelter in the caves when it rained. She hummed as she neared the sea, loud enough to give anyone a chance to hear her coming.

'Henjar,' she called. 'Are you here?'

Marna hurried along the shore towards the cliffs. The tide was on its way out and the sand was sticky. Her feet sank into the soft mud leaving prints. There was no sign of Henjar. Her head told her she should continue to the loch for plants, but her feet took her nearer the caves where Sempal might be found.

As she thought about Henjar and Finn, or tried not to think about them together, it came to her that Sempal might not be alone. Erin would have needed somewhere to sleep. Sempal's cave was warm and secret.

She didn't want to risk disturbing them and gave a snort then a chuckle. Erin's decision would have depended on what the faerie folk advised. The faerie folk had a way of advising Erin what she wanted to hear.

She turned back and headed up the bank and inland towards the loch. She was near the bere strips when she spotted Henjar coming towards her. Her tunic was rumpled and her hair uncombed.

'Marna, have you seen Finn?'

'I thought he was with you.'

'He went looking for his sister. But that was some time ago, before the sun came up.'

'I'm sure he will turn up. He left his bag in your house. Meanwhile, Boda needs you.'

'Isn't my mother taking care of him?'

141

'Your mother is old. She doesn't have the energy to look after a young boy.'

Henjar took hold of Marna's arm. 'Guess what? Finn and I are to be married. I am sailing back with him to Ireland. Boda shall come too. Finn will be his father.'

The excitement beamed from Henjar's face. Marna felt a lump in her stomach. 'Oh, but he is already married with children of his own,' she said.

Henjar let go of her friend's arm. 'Why do you say that? Who told you such nonsense?'

'Perhaps in Ireland men have more than one wife,' she answered. 'And women more than one husband.'

'Don't be silly, Marna.'

'I have heard of such customs.'

'But not in Ireland. Finn's wife is dead,' Henjar insisted. 'Tell me who told you these lies.'

Marna hesitated, but Henjar needed an answer. 'Erin.'

Henjar grunted. 'Then it isn't true, because Finn says she is a liar. Her mother dropped her soon after birth and she hasn't been right since. Finn told me that her head wasn't put on properly. She tells tales and pretends she has seen visions. You heard her at the gathering talking rubbish and frightening everyone. She does it to gain attention. And that's not all.' Henjar moved closer to Marna and grabbed the sleeve of her tunic. 'Finn says she almost killed a man in Ireland. She took a stone axe to him as he lay in bed.'

Marna's mouth fell open.

'She claimed it was in self defence, but the man was sleeping like a mouse in winter and she thrust the axe through him seven times.'

'That would take strength.' Marna considered the accusation and didn't believe it

'It's the reason she came on the voyage - to get away. She has the temper of a starving dog, the talons of an eagle and the brawn of an ox when she is roused.'

'Maybe you shouldn't believe everything Finn tells you,' Marna said. 'Erin is different from the women we know, but she is no monster.'

'She is weird. Weird and dangerous,' Henjar said.

'If she did attack this man, no doubt she had good reason for doing so. Perhaps she was protecting a child.'

'Finn says she hates children.'

'Eats them for supper, does she?' Marna couldn't believe she was defending the woman. 'Enough about Erin.' She pictured the Irish woman with an axe in her hand and a smile on her face, standing over Sempal. 'I'm concerned about you. Are you sure you want to go to Ireland with a man you know next to nothing about?'

'You said that before, but Finn and I got to know each other last night,' Henjar answered. 'Finn has promised to get me a new comb to replace the one I lost. He says it will be a betrothal gift to prove he is true.'

Marna knew it was hopeless arguing with Henjar. In that sense she was like her brother. 'I will miss you and Boda. When will you leave?'

'When the men have traded and the tide is high.'

'Oh Henjar.' Marna threw herself on her friend and gave her a hug. Henjar was crying when she let go.

'Ireland is only across the ocean. On a clear day, you might see me wave.'

'I would need good eyesight.' Marna wiped a tear.

'I'd better go to Boda,' Henjar said. She gave Marna another hug and headed towards the village.

Marna watched her go. Hopefully Sempal would advise his sister against doing anything rash. Henjar might listen to him. She looked towards the loch. The irises would have to wait. She had to find Sempal, whether Erin was there or not.

As she neared Sempal's cave, Marna heard a whistling sound like the wind through the slits in the rock. Her ears grew attuned and she recognised notes. The music settled in her head and she pictured leafy woods with birds singing. Whoever was playing was a skilled musician and Marna guessed it was Erin working her magic on her pipes. She stopped to listen, keeping still lest Erin hear her and flee. She was lulled by the melody. Although the tune was light she could hear darker notes in the background. The song was one of sadness, of lost love, of death. The music ended abruptly and Marna heard a wail. It jerked her into motion and she clambered across the rocks to the cave.

'Sempal, are you all right?' she called. There was no reply and she prepared to squeeze through the gap, but stopped when she heard footsteps. Erin's head appeared, then the rest of her body. She stood upright, but her eyes were glazed as if she were walking in her sleep. A purple bruise was developing on her cheek.

'Where is Sempal?' Marna demanded. 'What have you done with him?'

Erin didn't answer. Marna pushed past and slid into the cave. She felt her way along the damp wall to the chamber. Sempal was sitting cross-legged, with his eyes closed, beside a small fire. His chest was bare, and the flames illuminated strange designs painted on his skin with red dye. Erin had followed her in and stood beside her.

'Did you do this?' Marna accused Erin.

'These marks show the faerie folk that he is a friend. They will know to protect him,' Erin replied.

'Tush,' Marna clicked her teeth. 'Why should Sempal need protection?' She was going to add "except from you", but caught her tongue.

'There is evil in your village. Evil breeds fear and fear gives birth to further evil.'

'Not helped by your omens.'

Sempal was beginning to stir. Marna knelt beside him.

'What plants has she given you to chew? Salvia?'

'It is Seer's sage,' Erin replied. 'You would do well to try it.' She offered Marna a handful of leaves. Marna took them and tossed them into the fire. The flames lit up a deep sea blue.

'It is foolish to test the spirit world,' Erin warned.

'I am not afraid of invisible folk. Where is your brother?' Marna asked.

'I haven't seen Finn since the feast.'

'What were you arguing about?'

Erin laughed. 'That is none of your business.'

'Yes it is. Your brother was rough with you. He has promised to marry my friend Henjar - Sempal's sister. I need to know if he will take care of her.'

'Henjar? What about her?' Sempal heard the name.

'She means to sail to Ireland with Finn.'

'You said your brother was married,' Sempal turned to Erin.

'That he is, unless Gudrun has passed on since we set out.'

'Then Finn is a brute. When I get my hands on him...'

'He is twice your size and has three times your strength,' Erin reminded him with a laugh.

'So?' Sempal puffed out his chest, but he was fooling no-one. 'We must warn Henjar.'

'I have, but she won't listen,' Marna answered.

146

'Perhaps I should speak with her,' Erin offered.

'She won't listen to you. Your brother says you are a liar. He told Henjar that you almost killed a man.'

Marna was eager for Erin to explain, but the Irish woman scratched the back of her head and picked at a nit.

'Did he now?'

'Is it true?'

'Tell me, how can you almost kill someone? You either do or you don't.'

Sempal was pacing round the fire as they talked. 'What about Boda?' he said. 'I won't have him brought up as a stranger. How can we stop Henjar?'

'I'll need time to think of a plan.'

'We don't have time. Erin says her brother will return home on the next favourable tide,' Sempal said.

'That is true,' Erin said, 'Whether you think me a liar or not.'

'I didn't say I thought that,' Marna answered, but her voice belied her words.

'You may wish to hear our plan,' Erin said. She looked to Sempal. He nodded. 'It is a plan to save Sempal.'

'Save Sempal from what? Nobody believes he has done anything wrong, except Sempal himself.'

'What do you mean?' Sempal said.

'You think people accuse you because you feel guilty. You weren't with Joel to save him and you spoke ill of

Roben before he died. You don't have to prove anything.'

'Then we must save Sempal from Sempal,' Erin said.

'How?' Marna asked.

'By proving to the villagers it was Jona who killed Roben.' Sempal said.

Marna gave a sigh. 'You have been chewing too much salvia. There is no way you can prove Jona is guilty unless you plan to use false evidence against him.'

'Whose side are you on, Marna?'

'I'm on your side, but I won't do anything stupid.'

'If Jona is innocent, why is he hiding? I saw him yesterday, talking to his gods. He was drunk and in a trance, so he didn't spot me.'

'It would be good to know what Jona is up to,' Marna agreed. 'I thought he was in Eynhallow visiting Fara.'

'You see, he has fooled everyone in the village.'

'Nobody actually said he'd gone there,' Marna replied. 'I assumed…'

'It doesn't matter now. Erin will go to him...'

.'..with one of my special love potions...'

.'..and seduce him. With gentle questioning, Jona will tell her everything.'

'Even if Jona has something to hide and he falls for Erin's charm and confesses, no-one will believe you,' Marna said.

'That is where you come in, Marna,' Erin said.

'Nobody will believe me, a stranger and a liar, but you are respected. You must bring a group of elders to an agreed spot, where they can hear my conversation with Jona.'

'Eavesdropping?'

'Don't sound so shocked. You are pretty good at it,' Sempal said. Marna huffed, but Sempal took her hand. 'I need you to help me.'

'How can I persuade anyone to come? Nobody will want to listen in on lovers' chatter.'

'I bet you a painted pot they would,' Sempal said, 'but that isn't what you tell them.'

'What do I tell them?'

'You'll think of something.'

'What's in it for her?' Marna glared at Erin.

'This Jona is your head priest?' Erin said.

'Was our head priest,' Sempal corrected.

'Our only priest,' Marna added.

'And he knows about inducing trances?'

'He's good at trances,' Marna said.

'About the only thing he is good at,' Sempal agreed.

'Jona spends a lot of time talking to gods,' Marna said.

'Talking to himself,' Sempal muttered.

'I want to know how he does it,' Erin said.

'Talking to the faerie folk isn't enough. You want to talk with gods. You would get on well with my brother Thork.

'Really?' Erin's eyes lit up.

'When do you intend carrying this out?' Marna changed the subject.

'As soon as we can,' Sempal answered.

'Then we'd better work out the details.'

Marna resigned herself to the plan and they spent the rest of the morning discussing it.

'What if I am delayed?' Marna considered the possibilities for failure. 'How will Erin know?'

'You could give a call when you arrive,' Sempal suggested. 'What bird sounds can you do?'

'I might manage a kittiwake.'

'There are too many of those flying round the cliffs,' Sempal said. 'Erin won't know which one is your voice. Try an owl.'

Marna wasn't convinced, but she hooted to please him.

'I won't confuse that with the real thing,' Erin said.

'Then we'll have to think of something else,' Marna said. 'Jona isn't stupid.'

'You are looking for faults in the plan,' Sempal showed his impatience.

'Jona is a powerful man and if he murdered Roben he is a dangerous one. We can't put Erin's life at risk.'

'Don't worry about me. I've handled worse men than this Jona,' Erin answered.

'We are wasting time,' Sempal said. 'Who will you

bring?'

'Thork will come, if he thinks I need protection,' Marna said. 'Albar too, if he's free. Who else?'

'What about Wilmer?' Sempal suggested.

'The plump old man at the feast, who was falling over himself to please Finn and stop any trouble?' Erin asked.

'Wilmer is in charge of investigating Roben's death,' Sempal explained.

'He is no fool,' Marna said.

'Then he acts like one to deceive,' Erin said. 'That is not such a bad thing, but I fear his aura is broken. It didn't belong with him.'

'He isn't from our village,' Marna said. 'He has taken over as fire-maker.'

'And general village organiser,' Sempal added. 'He'll know what to do once Jona confesses.'

'If he confesses,' Marna said. Sempal was about to argue, but Erin choked a mouthful of phlegm into the fire.

'I do not see this fool surrounded by fire.' Erin rolled her eyes until the whites showed then jerked her arms in front of her. 'He carries a water mark. The sign is strong. I fear for him.' She shivered and Marna felt like shivering too. 'His aura is weak. It will not stay long in this world.'

'Best not to tell him that,' Marna said. She was tempted to ask about her own aura, but before she built up courage, Erin had regained her senses.

151

'What happened?' She looked around.

'Nothing,' Sempal answered. 'If we've finished making plans, I'll show Marna my boat.'

Erin and Marna followed Sempal outside. His boat was secured under a pile of seaweed.

'That's it?' Marna didn't hide her disappointment. Sempal had bound driftwood logs together to build a raft. 'It looks too flimsy to put to sea.'

'It lacks finesse, but I have tried it out. If I paddle near the shore it will take me to the bay where Jona is fasting and taking advice from the gods.'

'It might hold you, but not Erin as well.'

'I shall be in the water, holding to the raft for support,' Erin answered.

'You will freeze before you leave the bay.'

'It is the same water I swim in back home.'

'When Erin rises from the water, Jona will be awestruck,' Sempal said.

'He will believe I am a sea goddess. He'll do anything I say. Tell me everything.'

'Take care when he finds out you are human,' Marna warned.

'I shall have your brother Thork to protect me.'

Marna wished she hadn't mentioned him.

'We'll go late this afternoon,' Sempal answered. 'It will be easier to paddle the raft when the tide is low.'

'There is a wind coming, I can sense it in the air,' Marna said. 'You should wait.'

'The sooner we expose Jona, the sooner I can return to the village and take my place with the elders,' Sempal said.

That was it. Sempal wanted to be an elder.

'Fine,' Marna agreed. 'I'll speak with Thork.'

'You do that,' Erin said. 'Sempal and I shall go over our part of the plan.'

Marna didn't stay to find out what that involved. At the base of the cliff she looked back to see Erin draped across Sempal. Their lips were locked and one of Erin's hands was tight around Sempal's buttocks. Maybe she was rehearsing how to seduce Jona, but it didn't seem like she needed any practise.

Chapter 10

Marna expected Thork to be hanging around the village, sharpening an axe or lifting rocks to impress the girls, but when she didn't find him she asked her mother.

'He has gone hunting wild boar with Albar. We can have pork roasted with sorrel and wild mushrooms tonight,' her mother said.

There weren't many wild boars nearby and although her mouth watered at the thought of the dish, Marna hoped Thork wouldn't decide to trek miles across the island after them. She needed him back.

'Did he say when they would be home?' she asked.

'They didn't take supplies, so they won't be long unless he intends visiting Orphir on the way.'

Marna decided to look for Wilmer. He wasn't in Jona's hut and she ventured outside. A group of the younger men were working to repair the stone wall round the village. It was heavy work, cutting and lifting stones, and their bare chests were smeared with sweat and dust. Marna guessed Thork's hunting trip was an excuse to get out of the work party. She stopped to joke and asked if they'd seen Wilmer.

'You're not asking him for permission to sail away with the Irish lads too?' one of the boys asked. Marna assured him she had no thoughts of travel.

'Henjar said you might go with her, to mind Boda.'

'Did she? I shall need to speak with her.'

She left the men and found Wilmer sitting on a rock near the loch, carving a charm from a piece of antler. Remembering what Erin said, Marna took a good look at his face. It couldn't be rosier if it was a wild hip. Everything about Wilmer beamed good health. Having a broken aura didn't seem to hinder him.

'Can I help you?' Wilmer looked up and Marna flicked her glance to the ground. A young dog was sleeping at his feet. Marna leaned down to stroke its shaggy head. The pup stirred and gave a contented yelp.

'Who is your new friend? He's gorgeous.'

'This is Pip,' Wilmer put aside his carving to stroke the dog's ear. 'Walf's bitch had seven good pups before she threw out this one. It should have been knocked on the head, but I took him. I'm soft when it comes to dogs.'

'What is wrong with it?' Marna asked.

'Up boy,' Wilmer raised his hand to instruct the dog. Pip rolled over to show his tummy. 'He isn't very obedient. Up,' Wilmer repeated. The dog kicked his legs in the air. Marna noticed that one back leg was shorter than the other and the foot was skewed at an angle.

'Oh,' she gasped. 'Can he walk?'

'He gets around, but he won't make a hunting dog.'

The dog gave a whine and nuzzled its nose towards Marna. 'There is more to life than hunting,' Marna said.

'I couldn't agree more,' Wilmer answered. 'So what

brings you here? Shouldn't you be stirring dyes, or stirring up the young men? The boys working on the wall will need refreshments.' He gave her a wink.

'I saw them,' Marna said, 'but I have no interest in finding a husband.'

'Not like your friend Henjar.'

'She has a fatherless child to think about.'

'Of course, that was insensitive of me.' Wilmer picked up his carving and began to whittle the antler, but he couldn't keep silent for long. 'Albar is a good lad or what about Sempal? I know you're close to him. Don't deny it.'

'We're just friends,' Marna answered, but her face burned. Sempal hadn't objected to the attention Erin spooned on him, but she couldn't imagine kissing him the way Erin had. 'I came to see you, to give you this.' She reached in her pocket for Roben's black fire stone.

'Where did you get that?' Wilmer put down his carving and took it from her, rolling it between his fingers.

'It was Roben's,' Marna admitted. 'I found it in the meeting room, after Roben and Jona argued.'

'When was that?'

'The night before Roben left the village.'

Marna expected Wilmer to be angry, but his voice was calm. Perhaps it was the soothing effect of the stone. Marna enjoyed rubbing it too.

'I didn't know what to do. I kept it to annoy Roben,

but after he disappeared I was afraid,' Marna said.

'Afraid of Roben? Jona?'

Marna didn't answer. She looked at Pip, who was sitting up, balancing on his one good hind leg.

'Afraid of me?' Wilmer asked.

She looked up at Wilmer and he stuck out his tongue and rolled his eyes, the way he made faces to please the young children. She laughed. 'No, I'm not afraid of you.'

'Good.'

'Can I have the stone back?' Marna asked.

Wilmer held it between his thumb and first finger. Marna thought he would make up an excuse to keep it, but he handed it to her. 'It's not much good on its own.'

'I know, but I like touching it. Is that odd?'

'Not at all,' Wilmer chortled. He took up his carving and began working on it.

Marna stood fiddling with the stone, hoping to find the words to introduce Sempal's plan. 'People say Jona killed Roben,' she blurted out.

'Do they?' Wilmer didn't look up. 'Why?'

'I heard them argue.'

'So you said, but people argue every day. It doesn't mean they kill one another. You argue with Thork.'

'All the time,' Marna agreed. 'But why should Jona leave the village, unless he has something to hide?'

'Jona is in tune with a more spiritual reality than most

men.'

'He scares me.' Marna tried to sound afraid.

'He won't return to the village until he has answers to the questions that bother him,' Wilmer said.

'But he isn't far away, is he? He's watching us.'

'Have you seen him? ...Damn.' Wilmer let his blade slip and the antler he was carving snapped.

'That was my fault,' Marna apologised.

'Not at all. The antler is poor quality. It is too weak for jewellery. You were telling me about Jona.'

Marna hated deceiving Wilmer. She wanted to tell him the truth, but she had promised Sempal. 'Erin told me where Jona is hiding. She has seen him. She said there was a dark aura round him. Perhaps Jona is ill.'

'The Irish woman speaks in riddles that can be interpreted whatever way you like, but I would not be surprised if Jona was ill,' Wilmer agreed. 'He takes little care when picking berries and mushrooms.'

'My mother is skilled with medicines and potions. She may be able to help, but I doubt she would want to go to him if there was danger involved.'

'Your mother has sense. The gods alone know what mischief is dancing in his head.'

'What should we do?' Marna asked.

Wilmer ran his tongue round his mouth while he thought. 'Someone should go to him.'

'He is living in a cave. There's a path over the cliffs.'

Wilmer put his knife and the broken antler in a pouch and stood up. 'There's no time like the present for getting things done.'

'You can't go alone,' Marna added a touch of concern to her voice. 'What if something happened? There is a wind blowing up. The cliffs are not safe. If you should slip...'

'I have walked on these cliffs since I was a child,' Wilmer answered. 'Granted I am not so light on my feet these days, but I have no fear of falling.'

'What of Jona? He is a strong man.'

'I will give him no reason to mistrust me.'

'If he is ill he may not think straight. He may feel everyone is against him.'

Wilmer frowned. 'You have thought this out.'

Marna didn't reply, but she pretended to shiver.

'If there is trouble, I would be no match for Jona,' Wilmer agreed.

'Thork will be home soon. He could go with you.'

Wilmer blew out a chestful of air. 'I had better wait, then.'

'We can meet when the sun starts to go down.'

'We? You intend coming too? I thought you were afraid of Jona.'

'If Thork and you were with me...' Marna made patterns with her toes in the dirt. 'Please.'

'I doubt I could stop you.'

'Thank you.' Marna gave Wilmer a hug and the dog gave a whine. 'I haven't forgotten you.' She buried her head in the dog's coat.

'Best not to tell anyone of our plan, apart from Thork,' Wilmer said. 'We don't want the entire village following us over the cliff.'

'My mother could make a potion to calm Jona,' Marna almost believed her own story.

'We should see how Jona is first. Meanwhile, it is a pleasant afternoon. Why don't you spend it gathering plants?'

Marna took Wilmer's advice and headed to the loch to gather meadowsweet, nettles and bog myrtle. Oddly, she kept thinking about the boys at work on the wall. They thought their bare chests and muscles made them attractive to the girls. Sempal didn't have bulging biceps, but Erin found him worth kissing.

She can have any man, why pick on Sempal?

It was just a kiss, Sempal would know better than to let her seduce him.

What did it matter? Sempal was a friend, not a lover, besides Erin would return to Ireland soon.

The sooner the better.

'Ouch.' She was usually careful, but that was her third nettle sting on the same finger. It was red and blistered and she sucked away the pain. Her legs were scraped by the gorse she clambered through to find the bog myrtle and with her head in the clouds she'd mistakenly gathered poisonous toadstools instead of mushrooms. When she realised she had thrown away the heads of the plants and kept the useless stems, she knew it was time to give up. She would return home and make pads for the stone chairs until Thork returned.

Her brother was late home. Marna bit her nails as she imagined Sempal and Erin setting off in their small raft. Wilmer would be ready to leave. If they went without Thork and Jona attacked Wilmer, she wouldn't be able to stop him. That was stupid, why would Jona attack Wilmer? She was starting to believe Sempal's crazy ideas, but decided to give Thork until she finished sewing the cushion.

Marna was about to slice the end of the thread and tie it off when she heard Thork's voice. Half the village would have heard him shouting at Albar. They had failed to catch a boar and Thork blamed his hunting partner. Albar was having none of it and they were exchanging insults.

'My father is losing his eyesight, just like you. It is a problem with age,' Albar said.

'Your father spends too much time looking at the sun,' Thork objected.

'Stop it, you don't have time for arguing,' Marna

grabbed her brother's arm.

'Why? What's wrong?'

'We have to find Jona.'

'Now? Why? I haven't had anything to eat since midday and I could do with a nap.'

'Wilmer is waiting for us.' Marna pulled him along.

'Albar, help me. My sister has gone mad.'

'I need you too, Albar,' Marna said.

'No you don't. I have to get back to my family. I promised to sing for them.'

'Songs can wait,' Marna objected.

'Not in my household.'

'What is this about Jona? Where is he? Where are you dragging me?' Thork asked when Albar departed.

'I don't have time to explain,' Marna said. 'Wait here. Don't move.' She kept an eye on her brother as she ran to the house to fetch a handful of stale bannocks.

'I need more than that,' Thork complained.

'We're late. Wilmer may not have waited.'

Wilmer was on the shore, looking out to sea. He turned and waved when he heard them.

'You will need to be stealthier than that when we find Jona,' Wilmer warned.

'I didn't realise it was a hunt. Just as well you didn't bring that half-legged mutt with you,' Thork greeted him. 'Walf did a good deal trading him for three arrowheads and

162

a stone ball.'

'Pip is a worthy companion. He isn't a hunter, but he has more sense than half the young men here.'

'That's you told,' Marna gave her brother a friendly nudge. 'Come on.'

Thork tried to work out which young men Wilmer meant as Marna led the way up the path. The track ran close to the cliff face and they could hear the water battering the rocks. Wilmer stayed as far from the edge as possible, but Thork played the dare-devil, pretending he would climb down and fetch eggs.

'What is that on the waves?' He pointed.

Marna held her breath, hoping it wasn't Sempal on his raft. He should have reached the bay, unless he was in trouble. She looked down, but could see nothing.

'Albar is right, your sight is worse than a blind mole's.'

'It was a whale,' Thork said. 'It has gone under the water. Pity I don't have a spear.'

'You would need a barn full of spears before you hit a whale from this distance.'

Wilmer didn't join in the banter. He turned his back against the wind and continued at a steady pace. Marna followed him, but Thork waited. Eventually he gave up trying to spot his imaginary whale and caught up.

'That's the bay Erin mentioned,' Marna said as the

path dipped. 'The one with two large stones on the shore.'

'We should keep our voices down,' Wilmer advised.

They crept down the path. Thork managed to stifle a cry when he slipped on the wet scrub, but he couldn't stop laughing when Marna did the same. Wilmer took his time descending, holding onto the thick scrub. Thork helped him with the final step. As they approached the long grass backing onto the bay Marna heard the chirrup of a meadow pipit, joined by the sounds of chaffinches and blue tits.

'It sounds like we're in a wood,' Wilmer said. 'But there are no trees.'

'It's Erin. She's playing her pipes,' Marna said.

'What is she doing here?' Thork and Wilmer spoke together.

'She comes here often,' Marna invented.

'The Irish traders have only been here a few days.'

'We should hide,' Marna said, ignoring Wilmer's remark.

'Why?' Thork was puzzled. Marna gave him a look, but it was Wilmer who explained.

'Erin and Jona won't wish to be disturbed.' Thork didn't comprehend and he was forced to speak plainly. 'This is a romantic liaison.'

'Jona is old enough to be Erin's father.'

'Nevertheless…' Wilmer took hold of Thork's sleeve.

'I suppose you would know about these things,' Thork

said pointedly.

'There's a bush over there,' Marna ignored their banter.

'It's a gorse bush,' Wilmer moaned.

'I can see Jona,' Thork said. 'He has an axe. That's not romantic.'

The priest was a little way off, coming from the far side of the bay. Wilmer reckoned thorns were safer than axes and scurried after Marna. Thork joined them.

'Move up, or we'll be spotted,' Thork gave Wilmer a push and he fell into the bush. The branches swayed.

'The wind is getting up,' they heard Jona say. Marna watched through gaps in the branches. Erin was with him. She stopped playing to linked arms with Jona. He said something Marna couldn't hear and Erin let go. She sat in the sand, spread her legs then reached for Jona to join her.

'It's cosy in the long grass,' she said, loud enough for eavesdroppers to hear. Marna wondered if that was her cue to hoot, but kept quiet.

'It's wet,' Jona said, kneeling beside Erin.

'Lie here,' Erin encouraged, stroking her breasts.

Jona lay on the sand with his head in Erin's lap. She stroked his hair then leaned over to kiss him. Marna heard Thork mutter something about it being disgusting. Wilmer was removing thorns from his cloak.

Erin looked at the bush. Her eyes caught Marna's and

she nodded before returning her attention to Jona.

'Tell me about your village,' Erin said, raising her voice. 'Why did you leave?'

'I wasn't wanted,' Jona answered.

'But you are the head priest. You know everything about the village. You know all the secrets.'

'You talk too much. You can't talk and kiss at the same time.' He leaned to kiss her again, but she slid away. 'Why do you want to know our secrets?'

'They interest me, but if you don't know any...'

'What I don't know about the village isn't worth a cow's spit,' Jona answered. 'I know the things people would rather were buried with the dead.'

'What does he mean by that?' Thork whispered.

'Hush,' Wilmer was starting to pay attention.

'The dead have no secrets,' Erin said, 'Only the living. The faerie folk rely on me to tell them things. What do you know about the young man with the limp?'

'Sempal?'

'That is the name I heard. I see a watery shadow round him. He is not welcome in the village, I think.'

'You know what I think? I think you are a spy.

Erin put her pipes to her lips and played another tune. Marna recognised it. The bird songs were gone. This was a cheeky tune the Irishmen sang words to at the feast. It was about women and love.

'Is that the music people play in Ireland?' Jona asked when Erin finished playing. 'I prefer it to the awful drumming we hear here.'

'Thank you,' Thork took a step out of the bush, but was dragged back by Marna.

'Tell me your secrets,' Erin said. 'I promise I will tell them to no-one. Not even the Sidhe.'

'It isn't wise to keep knowledge from them,' Jona sat up. Marna couldn't tell if he was serious or not. He reached in his cloak for leaves and offered one to Erin. She accepted. He shoved one in his mouth, positioning it below his tongue. Erin copied him, but made a face.

'You want to learn secrets like who is to blame when objects go missing?' Jona asked.

Erin removed the leaf from her mouth. 'I am not interested in magpies.'

'What about fathers seducing their daughters or brothers and sisters kissing on the lips at night?'

'Not guilty,' Thork said, a little too loud for Marna's liking.

'I know who pays to have young boys in his bed,' Jona was warming to his subject.

'Not guilty,' Wilmer said in a whisper.

Jona looked to the bush. 'Did you hear a noise?'

'The mussels I ate don't agree with my stomach.'

'From over there.'

'It's a hare, look.'

Thork turned as if trying to spot Erin's hare. Marna gave him a nudge. Erin managed to calm Jona and soon he was recounting more tales of village life. Marna didn't believe the stories. Jona avoided naming names, but when he spoke of a young girl who didn't like boys touching her, she felt her cheeks redden. She avoided Thork's eyes, but he was unaware she was the subject of Jona's invention otherwise he would not have remained hidden in the bush.

'Is that enough or do you want names?' Jona said.

'Why would I need names?' Erin answered. 'I do not know your people.'

'You know the lass Sylva?'

'I have heard the name.'

'She went missing from the village two years back. Ran off with a traveller and had a child. She came back when he had enough of her, but where is the child, I ask you? In a ditch in Deerness, no doubt.'

Beside her, Marna could feel Thork gripping onto his stone knife. He had a soft spot for Sylva.

'Jona has been chewing too many of the mushrooms that grow by the loch,' Wilmer said. 'He imagines weird happenings and believes they are true.'

'I'll cut his tongue out if he says anything more against the people I know,' Thork swore.

'Shh,' Marna quietened him. 'Erin is speaking.'

'I have heard the villagers speak of Roben, the fire-maker. They say he was a bad man.' Erin rubbed her pipes, hoping the faeries would protect her.

'He was a good man, until he lost his eye.'

'Was it an accident with fire?' Erin said.

'He lost his eye to a woman. He couldn't think straight after that.'

'Love does terrible things,' Erin stroked Jona's hair.

'This wasn't love, it was lust. He couldn't have the girl while her husband was alive, so he plotted to have a good man killed to get entry to her bed.'

Erin gave an unconvincing gasp. Wilmer gave a real one. His face was white and Marna thought he was about to faint. She gripped his hand. 'It's the mushrooms talking.'

'Who does he mean?' Thork asked.

'He thinks Roben plotted to have Joel killed. Perhaps Roben asked Jona to help him. We need to hear more,' Marna whispered back.

'Roben is dead,' Erin said. 'He deserved to die.'

'Aye,' Jona agreed.

There was silence and Marna wished Erin would hurry up. Her knees were stiff from kneeling and she was trying to stop herself sneezing with the flower pollen.

Ask him if he was involved - Marna willed her thoughts towards Erin.

'Do you know who killed Roben?' Erin asked.

'Aye.'

'Did you kill him?' Erin spoke rapidly. 'As the village priest, you had the right to deliver justice.'

'Aye, that I had...'

Marna looked at Thork and Wilmer. This was the confession Sempal wanted.

'...but I didn't kill Roben,' Jona continued.

Marna exhaled. Jona sat up and looked round. 'I can hear that noise again. There's someone watching us.'

'Don't be silly.' Erin moved to sit between Jona and his view of the gorse bush.

'I can hear breathing. Ugly breathing.'

'There is no such thing as ugly breathing. All life is beautiful,' Erin lifted her pipes and blew a note. She moved them from her lips. 'It is a wicked thing to say otherwise.'

'You said Roben deserved to die.'

Erin didn't answer him. She leaned over and picked flowers to make a chain. When it was long enough she wound it round Jona's neck. 'Who did kill Roben?'

'Why are you so keen to know?' Jona pulled the chain from his neck and threw it towards the gorse bush.

'Have some salvia.' Erin offered him a handful of dried leaves. He stuffed them in his mouth then lay down.

There was a danger Jona would fall asleep and Marna's nose was itchy. She wiped it on her sleeve. Erin was signalling to them, but it wasn't clear what she wanted.

'Did the gods tell you who killed Roben?' Erin asked, giving Jona a nudge. He sat up and hugged his knees before beginning to rock.

'Aye, the gods spoke to me. They revealed the evil and burdened me with the task of retribution,' Jona declared. 'While Wilmer was asking his questions in the village, I fasted for three days and nights and made a blood offering. The gods rewarded me with a vision. I saw a beam of light and I followed it.'

'It led you to the killer?'

'It led me to the evidence I needed. It wasn't clear, but with help from the gods I pieced the clues together.'

'You must go to the village elders,' Erin said. 'You must tell Wilmer what you know.'

'I will in good time,' Jona laughed. He got to his feet. Erin held out an arm to be helped up, but he brushed her aside and stepped towards the gorse bush. He raised his voice, as if making sure Marna could hear. 'Before I do, Roben's killer will be on their knees begging for mercy.'

Chapter 11

'Blackmail.' Thork didn't muffle his word.

'There it is again,' Jona said. He reached for his axe as he strode towards the bush.

'It is the wind in the branches,' Erin said.

'I have been alive thirty five summers and have never heard wind like that.'

'He knows we are here,' Marna whispered. She could see from Wilmer's frown that he was debating whether to step out and challenge Jona or wait. She decided he would have stepped out if could disentangle himself from the gorse without looking a fool. Thork had no such problems. He raised his knife and leapt out, charging towards Jona.

Jona was taken by surprise, but he braced himself and took Thork's weight on his chest. Thork's knife and Jona's axe were knocked from their hands. Thork locked arms with Jona and the pair wrestled to the ground.

'We're here to discuss matters rationally. What has got into your brother?' Wilmer said.

'You'll have to stop them.'

'Yes. How?' Wilmer didn't move from the bush. Marna crawled out, sneezed then approached the fighting men. She stopped two feet away. They were rolling on the sand. Thork had his hands around Jona's throat, squeezing his breath from him. Jona was tugging handfuls of Thork's hair and beard.

'Thork stop it,' Marna shouted.

'He can't hear you,' Erin said.

'Can't you do anything?'

'Like what?'

'I don't know. Play your pipes or something.'

Erin laughed. 'Even the faerie folk would struggle to stop these two. They'll tire soon enough.'

Marna felt helpless. Jona freed himself from Thork's grip and beat his fists into Thork's face. His hand slipped and the younger man swung round to win the advantage. Thork bounced on Jona's chest until, with a heave, Jona sat up, knocking Thork off. His head hit against a rock with a crack that made Marna wince. Before he could recover, Jona was on top of him, banging his head on the ground as if opening a shellfish. Marna gasped as she saw blood.

'Leave him alone, you great bully.' Marna swung her leg and kicked Jona's backside. She got most of her weight behind the kick and as Jona turned towards her voice, she hit him in a delicate spot. Jona groaned and tumbled forwards, landing across Thork's face. Both men were stunned and lay still.

'Give me a hand to pull them apart,' Erin said as Marna stood with her mouth open.

Wilmer took the opportunity to emerge from the bush. He saw blood on the ground and turned away.

'What sort of man are you?' Erin chided.

'A sensitive one,' Wilmer answered. He helped Erin and Marna roll the men apart. Thork rubbed his dazed head and got to his feet, but Jona lay motionless.

'Is he dead?' Wilmer asked.

'If he's not, I'll finish the task.' Thork staggered towards Jona, banging into Marna.

'No you don't,' Marna held him back.

'Are you all right?' Sempal was hobbling towards them from the shore. He was speaking to Erin, not Marna. 'What happened? Has Jona confessed?'

'Jona said Roben plotted to kill Joel,' Marna said.

'Did he confess to killing Roben?' Sempal repeated.

'No, but he knows who did.' Erin made a show of putting an arm around Sempal's waist.

'Jona spouted a load of vile rubbish,' Wilmer said.

'I've put him straight on that,' Thork added.

'What did he say about Roben?' Sempal asked.

Thork pouted, but didn't reply.

'Jona made false accusations about everyone in the village,' Wilmer said. 'I doubt there is a seed head of truth in anything he said.'

'Roben could have sabotaged Joel's boat,' Marna suggested.

'Roben didn't know about boats, besides, I was in it that morning and it was fine. There was no opportunity for anyone to tamper with it,' Sempal explained. 'Joel would have checked the boards and the oars before setting out in the afternoon.' He removed Erin's arm from his waist. 'Why didn't you get him to confess? That was the plan.'

'He couldn't confess if he didn't do it.'

'Jona was about to say who the killer was when Thork jumped out,' Marna said, glaring at her brother.

'He knew we were there,' Thork said.

'Thork has a point,' Wilmer agreed. 'Jona suspected we were listening. He would have invented a story to send us on the wrong track.'

'He only knew we were there because Thork couldn't keep his big mouth shut,' Marna said.

'He made me mad, with his talk,' Thork said. 'He is our priest. He is supposed to help and support us.'

'So you made the decision to sabotage the plan?' Sempal pointed a finger at Thork.

'Don't get uppity with me,' Thork raised his fists.

'Stop fighting, boys,' Marna stepped between them. Erin looked disappointed.

'There are five of us, we can make Jona talk,' Thork said.

'I'm afraid we can't,' Wilmer said. 'He seems to have vanished. So has his axe.'

Marna spotted a trail of flattened sand and vegetation leading from where Jona had fallen towards the bank. There was no sign of the priest.

'I'll find him,' Thork said. 'He won't get far.'

'He won't tell you anything. We need to be clever,' Marna said.

'My plan was clever,' Sempal sulked. 'It would have worked if you hadn't spoiled things.'

'Don't blame me, you little runt.'

'Stop it. Marna is right,' Wilmer raised his voice. 'We need time to think. I'm not sure what Jona told us or what it meant. His words were garbled and spoken to deceive, not helped by the plants he's been chewing.'

'I gave him dried dandelion,' Erin said. 'I told him we used it in Ireland to ease the pain of child birth.'

'Fools will believe anything,' Thork scoffed.

'He isn't the only fool,' Sempal was still fuming.

'Your plan was a good one,' Marna said, putting a hand on his arm.

'We should return to the village,' Wilmer said. 'You too, Sempal.'

'I need to find Finn,' Erin said. 'He means to return home tomorrow and there are things that must be said before we leave.'

'I'll go with you,' Sempal said. 'I'm not going back to the village. Not yet.'

'You can't come with me,' Erin answered. 'The words are between a brother and a sister.'

'I have words to say to Finn too,' Sempal said. 'Words

between a man and his intended brother-in-law, but I'll wait until after you have spoken with him. I won't return to the village until Roben's murderer has been named and outcast.' He glared at the others in turn, daring anyone to stop him. Wilmer opened his mouth, but closed it again.

Sempal turned and hobbled towards his boat. Wilmer gave Thork a nudge. 'Go with him. The tide is turning and the waves are angry. He will need help.'

'Aye,' Thork agreed.

'The boat won't hold you both,' Marna said.

'Well, it won't be me getting my feet wet,' Thork said. Sempal was almost at the water's edge and Thork jogged after him.

'I shall see you again, Marna,' Erin said.

'You may not, if you leave early in the morning.'

Erin raised her right hand with the palm facing outwards and circled Marna's face, drawing energy from it. Marna felt a draught, as if greeting the wind. 'I shall see you again,' Erin repeated. She walked a few steps then stopped and turned to Wilmer. Marna thought she was trembling, but she smiled and said, 'I will not see you again, Wilmer. Not unless I swim with the Naiads.'

Marna and Wilmer watched her walk off with a swagger. She raised her pipes and blew a farewell note.

'She is quite some lady,' Wilmer said. 'Songs will be sung about her antics. It is sad she is leaving.'

'But she will see me again,' Marna tried to make a joke, but Erin unnerved her.

'Perhaps. Now, since the others have gone, will you accompany me to the village?' Wilmer said. 'It is getting late and it is not safe to be on the cliffs alone.'

Marna took hold of his hand. It felt cold. 'I shall ask mother to make you mittens before the winter arrives.'

'That would be welcome.'

They made their way along the cliff path. There were rays of shadowy light from the dipping summer sun, but a breeze was rising. Wilmer regained his spirits and chattered about the weather, birds and something about baking pies. Marna was only half listening. Her mind was on Jona. She had thought he was dead. Thork hit him hard. He wouldn't be able to fend for himself. Someone should look for him.

'Careful.'

Marna heard Wilmer's warning too late. She jerked aside to avoid a stone and her toes jabbed into a dip in the ground. She lost her footing and stumbled towards the cliff face, swinging her hands to keep her balance. The ground was damp and her feet slid as if they were on an icy pond. The earth was crumbling beneath her and she was falling. Around her was the rumble of rocks clattering against the cliff and she pictured her father. He was holding out a hand to welcome her.

'Dad.' She reached for the hand.

Fingers grabbed hold of her arm. The grip was strong, tugging her to safety. Her legs scrambled to reach the rocks and find footholds. Her heart was piercing holes in her chest and her shoulder socket ached from the strain, but she was on firm ground. She bent over and took a long breath of salty air then rubbed her shoulder. Wilmer was beside her, breathing hard.

'I thought you were gone,' Wilmer's voice caught. He reached to push a lock of hair from her eyes. 'Are you all right?'

'Yes, thank you.' Her throat was dry and her voice trembled. Her whole body was shaking.

'Come here,' Wilmer put his arms around her and drew her in to a warm hug, the way her father did when she was small. He patted her back to soothe her.

'I'll be fine now,' Marna said as he released her. She wiped a tear from her eye. 'Let's get back.'

They continued their journey, with Wilmer walking on the cliff side, shielding Marna from further harm. It was brave of him, she knew, considering his fear of drowning. He didn't speak as he concentrated on his footing. Marna imagined her father, falling to his death in a rushing sea while searching for eggs. He had been alive when he hit the water, or so people said. He drowned because he couldn't swim. Her mother made sure Marna and Thork could survive in the water, but Marna doubted she would stand a chance if she fell from such a height.

Wilmer increased his pace as they neared the bottom of the cliff, but paused when they arrived at the track heading inland to the village.

'I will ask mother to make us hot honey ale,' Marna said. 'That will warm us.'

'Honey ale is tempting, but I have work to do.'

'This evening?'

'There are things I wished to speak with you about,' Wilmer said. 'But now isn't the time.'

'Things like what?' Marna asked.

Wilmer took hold of her hand before answering. 'Don't take this the wrong way, but I can't help feeling there was more to it than ...madness... when your brother attacked Jona.'

'What do you mean?'

'I have only been here a short while, but I can see that Thork is keen to take over as village priest.'

'I don't think...' Marna began.

'It is common knowledge. I feel he may have been looking for a reason to discredit Jona.'

'Thork admires Jona, or he did,' Marna said. 'He was upset when Jona insulted his drumming. I don't see what that has to do with Roben or Joel.'

'Thork argued with Roben before his death.'

'So did everyone in the village, including me,' Marna

answered. 'You don't mean...? You can't think Thork had anything to do with murder.'

'No, no, of course not. It was an evil thought. These are evil times. I shall banish it from my mind.' Wilmer rubbed his forehead with a smile. 'There, it is gone.'

They circled the bere strips. The crops were not doing well that year, whether due to the gods' disfavour or the weather.

'You said there were things you wanted to talk about,' Marna said. 'What else is on your mind?'

'I am an old man and I can't help worrying, but I should mind my own business.'

'Tell me what you are worrying about,' Marna said. 'Has it to do with me?'

'I am concerned about your friend Henjar. I thought it was a joke, but now I believe she intends leaving the village with the Irishman. Has she spoken to you?'

'Yes.'

'She has made up her mind?'

'I think so.'

'You don't sound happy.'

'How can I be? Erin says her brother has a wife in Ireland who is expecting a child. No doubt he has other wives and children in trading villages.'

'That is not good, but if Finn has asked Henjar to go with him, that must mean something.'

'He promised her a comb as a betrothal present.'

Wilmer was about to say something, but his pup was lolloping towards them.

'Pip wants to make sure we arrive home safely,' Wilmer said with a laugh. He lifted the dog in the air, giving it a kiss on its long nose. Pip returned the greeting by slobbering on Wilmer's cheek.

'It will never be a hunting dog if you spoil it,' Marna said, repeating Thork's words in a mock-scolding voice.

'And I will never be a hunter,' Wilmer replied. He put the dog on the ground and it sniffed around the bottom of Marna's tunic. She bent to stroke it.

'He likes you,' Wilmer said. 'But you had better return home and let your mother tend to your grazed leg.'

Marna hadn't realised her leg was scratched, but she felt blood trickle down below her knee. She rubbed the skin and the wound hurt.

'I shall have to leave you. My business cannot wait. Good night and take care.'

Wilmer headed along the shore and Marna made her way to her house. Her mother was stirring broth over the fire.

'That smells good,' Marna removed her cloak and picked up a bowl.

Her mother steeped dock leaves in heated water while Marna ate. When she finished her mother bathed her leg with the dock and applied some self heal leaves. She didn't ask what happened.

'Is Thork back?' Marna asked.

'I thought he was with you.'

'We split up. I'll go and look for him.'

'No you don't, my girl. You need to rest.'

'I won't be long.' Marna side-stepped her mother and recovered her cloak.

Her leg was stinging and she limped towards the shore. Before she reached the beach she spotted Thork marching from the cliff path carrying a stick. He obviously hadn't trusted Sempal's boat, Marna thought. She increased her pace to meet him, but a spasm of pain stopped her. Thork saw her and waved the stick.

'Look what I have found,' he called as he strode up.

Marna looked. The willow stick was etched with intricate carvings, painted red and blue. She recognised the figure of the large bird, wings outstretched, carved from a sheep horn, attached to the top.

'That's Jona's staff.' She reached to touch the stick, but Thork drew it away.

'It's mine now. I found it lying in a cave, with this.' He shook a dyed blue skin at her

'Jona's cloak? He'll need it when it turns cold. You shouldn't have taken it,' Marna rebuked. 'It's stealing.'

'Stop moaning, sis. If he was so concerned he

shouldn't have left them lying unguarded. Here, you can have the cloak. It's no use to me. Give it back to Jona if you want. I have the staff and that makes me head priest.'

'Does it? I'm not sure Wilmer would agree.'

'Wilmer is not head of this village. He doesn't belong here, though he wriggles his way in. Tomorrow I'll call the village and announce my claim.'

'Sounds grand,' Marna mocked.

'If you want to be useful, tell your friends to prepare for an inauguration ceremony at the stones. It will mark a new era in our lives.'

'In *your* life,' Marna mumbled.

'What did you say?'

Marna thought about asking what Caran would say, being married to the village priest. She would have to settle in a strange village and the role would bring added pressure, with Thork being in demand to settle disputes.

'Where is Sempal?' she asked instead.

'Sulking in his cave like a wounded animal, if that branch of wood he calls a boat hasn't sunk. I expect he's waiting on Erin to comfort him.'

Marna didn't rise to his taunting. She snatched Jona's cloak. 'Mother has made soup with mutton bones and mint. I imagine village priests have to eat, or do you need to ask the gods' permission?'

Marna avoided her brother's swipe and stomped home.

Chapter 12

Marna tried to sleep, but she couldn't settle. The house was quiet which allowed her mind to be active. She thought of Sempal and Erin, Henjar and Finn and Thork becoming head priest. There was something else, a thought she couldn't tie down. Then she was falling, tumbling over the cliff, her arms flailing. Purples, greens and browns blurred on her way down towards the blue ocean. Blue...

Her mother woke her with a beaker of warm ale. 'Is your leg bothering you?'

'Jona's cloak isn't blue, it's red,' Marna said. 'I dyed it for him last year.'

'Of course you did. Now drink this.' Her mother pushed the cup into her hand and lifted it to her mouth. The drink tasted bitter. Marna spat out the first mouthful, but her mother insisted she drank it.

She swallowed the last of the liquid with the segments of leaves and seeds that settled at the bottom then rolled her tongue. Her throat was burning.

'Where is Thork?' Marna croaked.

'There's a problem with the Irish guests. He's gone to sort things out.'

'Can't Wilmer do that?'

'Thork fears it might get physical.'

'What sort of problem is it?' Marna struggled to her feet and handed her mother the empty beaker. She hurried to the door.

'Put some clothes on before you go out.'

Marna was wearing only a thin vest. Her mother must have removed her tunic during the night.

'You were sweating, dear,' her mother said. 'I thought you were too warm.'

Marna found her tunic and pulled it over her head, but her mother wouldn't allow her to leave until she tied her belt and sorted her hair. A crowd had gathered outside, mainly men, but a few women stood with arms folded. They formed a circle, with Thork and four of the Irishmen in the centre. Marna didn't see Finn among them.

Thork was wearing a headband with a hawk feather sticking out above his ears. A sheepskin cloak was draped over his back and right arm. He raised Jona's staff to gain silence. Marna thought he looked foolish, but the crowd waited for his instructions. Marna squeezed between Joannet and Albar. Thork cleared his throat.

'Where is Horen?' he demanded. 'Let him step forth.'

Horen was standing behind Thork. He tapped him on the back and Thork jumped, knocking his head-dress over his eyes.

'I am here,' Horen answered. 'Nadea and Eada too.'

The group parted to allow Horen's daughters to enter the ring. They made the most of the attention, swinging their hips and pushing up their breasts.

'What is your complaint?' Thork asked. He repositioned his headband, but it wouldn't stay in place.

'My accusation is against the man they call Finn,' Horen said.

'Where is Finn?' Thork asked.

The scene was becoming ridiculous, Marna thought. Why did Thork have to make a show of everything? He could make shooing mice into a village hunt.

'I wish we knew,' Mickel answered. 'The gods have set fair tides for our journey homewards, but we haven't seen Finn for near on a day.'

'Have you searched for him?' Thork asked.

'What do you think?' Pog didn't hide his irritation. Marna saw Conel make signs to Brann. They were ready for a fight.

'Where have you looked?'

'He'll be in the sand dunes, wooing a lass,' Horen said. 'He has lain with both my daughters.'

'He promised to marry me,' Eada said.

'And me,' her sister Nadea asserted.

'He loves me.' Eada stamped on her sister's toe. Nadea grabbed her hair.

Thork stepped in to separate them.

'The girls are mistaken,' Mickel said. 'Finn has a wife in Ireland. She is my sister Gudrun. I'd strike him on the head with my hammer if he thought of leaving her.'

Marna heard a cry from across the circle. She hadn't spotted Henjar, but it was her friend's voice. The twins stopped squabbling. Thork twisted round. Henjar was standing with her hand over her mouth. When she realised all eyes were on her she pushed past the men next to her and rushed away.

Marna felt she should go to her friend, but she wanted to hear the outcome. Everyone looked to Thork for a solution. He lifted his head to the sky and knocked his staff on the ground three times. Marna knew he had no idea what to do and was playing for time.

'Where is Wilmer?' someone called 'He will know what to do.'

'We are wasting time,' Conel said.

'Aye. Finding Finn is our priority,' Brann agreed.

'When we do, he will be called to account,' Thork declared. There was a murmur of approval from the villagers. 'We will send a party to search for him.'

'We'll find him,' Marna's neighbour Jedd shouted, but before Thork could pick volunteers and organise groups, the majority of the villagers shuffled away.

'Sorry, I have my animals to attend to,' Jedd said.

'And I have a meal to prepare,' Joannet added.

'Finn may be dangerous,' Horen voiced his fear. 'He is a large man and he could be armed.'

Thork watched the people leave until he was left with

Albar, the Irishmen and Marna. His headband had won the
battle and slipped round his neck. The tip of the feather
tickled his nose. As he swiped it away the sheepskin cloak
fell from his shoulder into a puddle.

'Marna, you look down by the loch,' he instructed,
trying to regain dignity.

'I can't. I have to go after Henjar.'

'Albar, you take the woods to the south,' Thork turned
to his friend.

'I promised to help mend my cousin's boat.'

'We'll find Finn ourselves,' Mickel said, signalling to
his companions.

'Erin might know where her brother is,' Marna said.

'You've spoken with her?' Pog asked. 'When ?'

'She was looking for Finn yesterday evening.'

'We'll find them both and be gone from this place,'
Mickel said. He turned to Thork. 'We would not wish to be
a burden on your people any longer.'

'Aye, we won't miss your hospitality,' Brann added.

Mickel spat on the ground at Thork's feet and pushed
past him. The other three copied him.

'And we won't miss you,' Thork shouted back. Albar
put a hand on his shoulder to stop him going after the men.
Wilmer was coming towards them from the shore. Thork
saw him and gave a grunt. He shook off Albar, picked up
his cloak and marched off.

'He'll be fine,' Albar said, 'Once everything is back to normal'

'I'm not sure what normal is any more,' Marna said. She didn't wait on Wilmer. Albar could explain. She needed to find Henjar. Lin was washing tunics at the loch.

'Have you seen Henjar?' Marna called.

'She has taken Boda to play in the sun.'

Boda was heavy to carry and Marna guessed Henjar wouldn't have gone far. She took the path towards the meadow, knowing Henjar liked to sit there and make flower chains with Boda. The young boy was picking daisies, with his mother sitting at his side. She had been crying, but wiped her eyes when she saw her friend approach. Marna sat beside her without speaking.

'What a fool I've been,' Henjar said. 'He kissed so sweetly that I believed he loved me. He promised to give me a comb. He asked Wilmer to make me one.'

'Wilmer said nothing of this when we spoke.'

'Finn arranged to meet me here yesterday evening, but he didn't turn up. I bet he gave the comb to one of the twins.' Henjar began crying again.

'Don't cry,' Marna handed her friend a strip of cloth to wipe her eyes. 'I know many men who would give more than a bone comb to be your husband.'

'Oh, who?'

'Albar, for one. I've seen the way he looks at you.'

'Albar is fond of me? But he is always teasing, making silly boasts and acting the fool.'

'That is because he is shy.'

'He does have nice eyes,' Henjar said.

'Eyes?' Marna laughed. 'Since when have you been interested in a man's eyes?'

'Did I say eyes? No, you heard me wrong, I said thighs,' Henjar gave a smile.

'He is fond of Boda,' Marna added. 'He would make a good father.'

Henjar handed Marna her handkerchief and stood up. 'I can feel a chill in the wind. It isn't good for Boda.' She took Boda in her arms. He was holding a buttercup, which he offered to Marna.

'Thank you, Boda,' Marna accepted.

'I'll see you later,' Henjar said and started walking towards the village.

'He is helping his cousin mend a boat on the shore,' Marna called. Henjar turned and gave a smile.

'That's funny, I was going there myself after leaving Boda with my mother.'

It was a bright morning and Marna couldn't decide what to do. She could go to the loch and look for Finn as Thork suggested, but the mewing of the gulls invited her towards the cliffs. Her mother would be grateful for eggs. It was late in the season and most of the sea birds had forsaken their nests to fly out to sea, but there might be leftover eggs that were unlikely to hatch.

Not everyone in the village could gather eggs. There was a skill to edging along cliff face, feeling the clefts in the rock to secure foot and hand holds. Marna had been doing it since she was a child, learning from her father who was a master. He had supplied eggs for most of the village. After he died, her mother tried to discourage Marna from taking over his role, but she had no fear of the cliffs.

When he was younger, Thork had confided to Marna that he was afraid of heights. He denied it now, but he was always too busy to accompany her on gathering trips.

There was a sea mist rising to hinder the view as she walked along the top of the cliff, eyes straining to make out abandoned nests cradled in the cracks. It took a while, but the mist cleared and Marna spotted a single egg in an empty nest a third of the way down the cliff. The cliff face was overhanging and she couldn't climb down from where she stood. Keeping one eye on the nest, she looked for a suitable place to begin her descent. From the top, she worked out a path to the ledge. Once she was level with the nest she could sidestep her way along.

She took her sandals off, laced them together with the cord bindings and fastened them to her belt. When she was satisfied they were secure, she lay with her belly on the ground and used her arms to crawl backwards, dangling her legs over the edge, searching for a foothold. Her left leg touched a boulder jutting from the side. Her fingers grasped at the thick plants on the top while she transferred her weight to her leg, testing to make sure the rock would hold.

Taking the first step took the most courage. She found finger holds and eased herself down to balance with both feet on the boulder then paused for breath. She was facing the side of the cliff and didn't look below her feet. Sliding her right foot beneath her, she felt a cleft in the stone, big enough to take her toes. A loose stone fell away as she lowered herself down. For a second Marna was reminded of her accident the previous day. There was no-one with her now to save her. She took another breath and cleared her mind.

I know what I'm doing.

She repeated the thought. Working her way along was a slow process, but a steady one. She was closing in on the nest and stopped when she reached the ledge to look along. The nest was half hidden and Marna struggled to make out the egg she spotted.

The object gleamed white in the sunlight, but it was flattened and oblong – not egg-shaped. Marna hit her tongue against her teeth, making a sound of disapproval. Her effort was wasted. She raised her hand to find a hold above her, but curiosity made her look again at the object. *What was it? A shell? She may as well find out.*

Retrieving it wasn't as simple as Marna hoped. It involved a tricky manoeuvre, bending her knees and folding her back, maintaining her balance while holding tight to the cliff face. When she was in position, Marna waited for a gust to pass. She shuffled closer, darting her hand out so her fingers snatched at the nest. Her first attempt was useless. Her knuckle scraped the edge of the nest, pushing it further away. She flung out her left hand and the nest rocked, threatening to cascade down to the bay, taking the object with it.

After two more tries, Marna accepted that she was too far away. The ledge was narrow, with barely room for her to stand on tiptoe. As she tried to inch along, the rocks cracked. She jerked back in time to prevent clattering down to the sea with the loose stones. Taking a deep breath, she stretched a toe across to touch the ledge with the nest, but kept her weight on the larger rock. There was a root burrowed in the rock above her. She grabbed it, which allowed her to free her back leg from the ledge.

For a second she hung from the root, with one toe resting against the nest. She feared the root would give, but she managed to lodge her free leg against the rock face. Her position was stable, but she was stuck. She remained there for a minute, searching for holds. The gods were kind. She spotted a notch in the rocks at the level of her waist and reached for it with her right hand. Feeling more secure, she was able to lower herself onto a protruding rock the shape of a sheep's nose.

Exhausted, she rested on the ledge. The nest was now above her. She reached up and felt along the stone. Her fingers touched the bundle of twigs and seaweed. She stood on her toes and stretched her arm. The object was cold. The edges were smooth, like weathered bone. Her shoulder and arm ached as she willed the object into her hand. It slipped between her fingers and she teased it from the nest.

'Aargh.'

It felt like she was being bitten by a fish with tiny, needle-sharp teeth. She drew her hand back. The tips of two of her fingers were bleeding. She sucked away the blood. The wounds were no more than scratches and she reached up again. Nudging the object to the edge of the ledge, she grabbed it before it toppled to the water. Opening her fist, she looked at her prize.

It was a comb. Marna guessed it hadn't been in the nest for long. One of the teeth was broken, but it was in good condition. The quality was first class. She turned it in her hand. There were symbols etched into the bone. It was Wilmer's handiwork. She recognised the intricate carvings that made his pieces so wonderful.

'Henjar's comb,' Marna thought.

It was made from whale bone, like Henjar's, but Wilmer could have made several combs from the bones of the whale washed up the previous winter. He may have brought them to Skara Brae to trade with the Irish.

Marna wiped the dirt from the comb and secured it in the pocket of her tunic. She was nearer the top, but she spotted ledges and chips in the rock below her that she could use to work her way down. She pondered over her find as she scuffled across the rocks and decided to take it to Wilmer. He recognised all his pieces. He would remember who he made it for.

What if it was Henjar's? Could a bird have stolen it? The nest looked like that of a guillemot. They weren't known for pilfering and the comb would be awkward for an auk to carry. Besides, the comb had disappeared from her house. No seabird would be there. Not alive at any rate.

Marna stopped concentrating and the rock she was reaching for broke free and bounced down the cliff to land on the stones on the shore. Her foot dangled in mid-air and Marna made the mistake of looking down. She was about thirty feet up and the ground swirled beneath her. The water beat against the rocks. If a fall didn't kill her, it would break enough bones to guarantee a slow death.

It took a few minutes to realise there was a shape floating in the shallow water. It could be driftwood, but it looked like a seal in trouble. Marna regained her balance. She wanted to rush down, but had the sense to watch her footing. It was likely the animal was dead. If so, it would provide welcome meat, oil and skin for the village.

The closer she got, the less the shape looked like a seal. More like a porpoise. Marna loved watching them jump from the water in rainbow arches. They swam so well, but it was hard to tell if they were fish or not. They came up to the surface for air, but unlike the seals, they couldn't live on land for long. She was watching the mass bob on the water and misjudged her final step. She landed with a thud on the shingle, stumbling and catching her ankle. It twisted round and she gave a yelp. Her foot hurt when she tried to walk and she sat on a rock to examine her leg. The bones didn't grate, but the skin was beginning to turn deep red and starting to swell.

She unfastened her sandals from her belt, slipped one onto her good foot and laced it up. It was harder fitting the other sandal on her bruised foot, but she managed to squeeze her toes between the straps. She stood up and hobbled towards the water. The object was larger than she imagined. She would need Sempal and his boat to get it round the bay.

The tide was going out, taking the thing with it. Marna cursed herself for putting her sandals on. She hated walking on pebbles with her bare feet, but the sea water would ruin the leather. There wasn't time to ease them off. If she waited, the object would be pulled too far out. Marna stepped in to the cold water, shivered and waded towards it.

When the water was above her knees she knew she should turn back, but she was so close. She could almost reach out and touch it. A few more steps and the water lapped at her waist. The current dragged her tunic, drawing her further from the shore. It would be easier to swim rather than wade, but the current was strong. She had no trouble keeping up with Thork when they swam in the loch, but a wild sea was different.

Her goal was within her grasp and she lunged forwards, hoping to grab the end. Her hand touched the cold surface and she screamed. Her fingers were rubbing against a human leg.

Chapter 13

Screaming resulted in a mouthful of salt water. Marna
spluttered, but only succeeded in swallowing more. She
feared letting go of the body to wipe her mouth. Buoyed by
the swollen flesh, she was able to look back towards the
land.

It was so far away.

The tide had washed her level with the outcropping of
the cliff. Her feet didn't touch the seabed.

The body was too heavy for Marna to drag. It was a
grown man, arms and legs spread-eagled, floating face
down. Fronds of seaweed were wrapped around the limbs
and a foul smell rose from it. There was nothing Marna
could do except hold on to the corpse as it drifted out.

It was mid afternoon and she hoped someone would be
at sea and spot her. If Albar and his cousin finished
repairing their boat, they would want to test it - hopefully.
The water was colder than cold. Marna had heard tales of
ice mountains in the seas further north and imagined they
had come travelling down to Orkney. She couldn't feel her
toes although she assumed they were there, unless a fish
had snaffled them. Her teeth chattered. Her bedraggled hair
covered her face. It was an effort to push it behind her ears.
It didn't stay there long, but she couldn't see with it over
her eyes.

On three occasions she was convinced she saw a boat and gathered her energy to wave. The boat would disappear beneath the waves, never to rise, and she realised it was the sea playing tricks. Her eyes stung with the salt water and her sight was blurred. A dark shape was coming towards her- another wave to weather, unless it was a shark. Her imagination was working although her fingers were numb. She was losing her grip on the body. Once she lost it she would be dragged under. She had been too young to understand the grizzly details of her father's death, but she pictured Joel and how they had dragged his puffed up body from the water.

Her head was light. She closed her eyes and felt herself drifting below the water. There was an intense pressure on her ears like the rumble of thunder when the gods were drunk. She tried to kick out, but didn't have the strength.

Then her whole body felt light. She was being lifted from the water. Her heart was beating. She could hear it echoing against her ribcage, like the sound of Thork's drum inside the funeral cairn. It felt like Erin's faerie folk were using her chest to spring on instead of heather. Her eyes were glued shut by the salty water, but she felt something touch her. There was a rush of air to her lungs and she sat up and spewed out a mouthful of water.

'Is that the thanks I get for saving you?'

She rubbed her eyes open. They stung and her vision

was glazed, but someone was beside her, pushing on her chest.

Marna screamed, but no noise came out.

It was the dead man.

She remembered the body, the reason she was in the water. They were both dead.

'Don't touch me,' she squeaked. Her voice was hiding deep in her throat.

'It's me,' the man said. 'I thought you were dead.'

'Dead,' Marna echoed.

'Not yet, but you will be if you don't let me dry you.'

Marna screwed her eyes. 'Sempal?'

He held out his cloak. She tried to rise and toppled forwards. The ground rocked. Sempal swayed. Water rose to sweep over Marna's knees and Sempal grabbed her arm.

'Careful.'

She was on Sempal's boat. He had lengthened and stabilised it, but there was little room to move. He wrapped the cloak around her and she hugged the material to her skin. It smelt of Sempal.

'The body, where is it?' Marna asked, twisting to look at the water.

'What body? What happened?'

'Don't fluster me,' Marna tried to remember. 'I was on the cliffs looking for eggs.'

'Eggs? At this time of year.'

'I saw something, but it wasn't an egg. Then I spotted the shape in the water. I thought it was a seal.'

'You swam out for a dead seal?'

'It was stupid, I know, but ...it was horrible…all bloated and slimy. It can't have gone far.'

'Steady on,' Sempal stopped Marna toppling over as she leant to look over the side.

'There,' she pointed.

Sempal had stopped paddling his raft to attend to Marna, allowing the boat to drift on the waves. He picked up the wooden oars and lowered the ends in the water. It took an effort to steer towards the object.

'You're right, it is a dead man,' Sempal's voice was shaky. He reached towards it, but it was weighed down with water.

'What can we do?' Marna asked.

'We'll have to secure it to the back of the boat and drag it to the shore,' Sempal said. 'There should be rope behind you.'

Marna handed him the twine. She didn't have the strength to help with the body, but she held onto the oars and had the sense to sit still while Sempal worked. She was surprised how well he managed to manoeuvre the body, pull it round and tie it into position.

'Who is it?' she asked.

'I don't know. I didn't see his face. I don't think he's

from our village. From his clothes, I would say he is a stranger to the island.'

Marna turned to look over the side at the body. The sea water had swollen the man's flesh, making it bulge against his sodden tunic. The hair was matted and covered with seaweed, but she could see a red tint to it.

'Finn the Irishman has gone missing. His friends haven't seen him since yesterday evening when Erin was looking for him. You don't think it is him?' she asked.

'Erin's brother?' The side of the boat sank as Sempal peered over at the body. 'If it is him, then I am not sorry he has come to such an end,' Sempal answered, pulling harshly on the oars. The raft didn't move.

'You have spent your energy. You can't do it alone,' Marna said. 'Let me take an oar.'

'You are barely back from the dead.'

'Rowing might heat my chilled bones.'

'Break them, more like.'

'You sound like my mother.'

The boat was going nowhere. Sempal relinquished an oar and showed her how to avoid blisters. It was hard, but the thought of a fire and her mother's warm broth kept her going. Helped by the wind, they steered the boat round the cliff towards the bay in silence, neither having the breath to speak. As they neared the shore Sempal stopped rowing.

'What's wrong?' Marna asked.

'I've been thinking.'

'Oh no, not again.'

'If it is Finn, I may be suspected of killing him.'

'Finding the body doesn't mean you killed him.'

'No, but I have a reason. He bullied Erin and betrayed Henjar.'

'But you haven't met the man. I can testify that you found us both in the water.'

'The villagers know you, they'll listen, but the Irishmen won't. They will look for someone to blame.'

Marna stopped rowing as she realised Sempal might be right. It wasn't only Finn who was hot-headed. His countrymen were quick to act before they thought things through. 'We need a plan.' She looked towards the shore. 'There is no-one watching us. We could release the body and hope it is close enough to the beach to be carried with the waves onto the sand.'

'The tide won't turn until the sun goes down,' Sempal said. 'Finn may be in Ireland before his countrymen.'

'Then no-one could blame us.' She sighed and looked again at the body. 'I suppose it may not be Finn.'

'Who else can it be?

Marna blew out some air then pulled on her oar.

'What are you doing?'

'We can't sit here. We could leave the body in the bay where we found Jona. Someone will find it soon enough.'

Sempal raised his eyebrows.

'I'll give hints, if they don't,' she added.

The sun had dipped by the time they reached the bay and rowed to the shore.

'Do you think Jona is here?' Marna asked.

'Spying on us, you mean?' Sempal took a stone knife from his tunic and stretched past Marna to cut the ropes holding the body. It drifted beside the boat until Sempal gave it a shove. They watched as it dipped in the water.

'It doesn't want to float to shore,' Marna worried.

They were within a hefty stone's throw from the land. Sempal lowered himself into the sea to guide the body to the beach. He left it face down on the sand and waded back to the boat. Marna gave him a hand up.

'Let's go,' Sempal said.

They took an oar each and pulled hard. The boat circled, but they managed to direct it round the cliff.

'What now?' Sempal asked. Marna had stopped rowing to rub her reddened palms.

'Drop me off in the bay here and I'll head to the village. You'd better get dried then find Erin and tell her the news.'

'That won't be easy,' Sempal muttered.

'I'll find her companions and direct them towards the bay.

'You'll do no such thing. You need to get warm, fed

and put to bed.'

    'And miss the excitement?'

    'Haven't you had enough of that for one day?'

Chapter 14

Marna was cold, hungry and exhausted, but her mind was active. She agreed to get rest, but as she staggered up the track and wove through the flower meadow towards the village, she was making plans. She would find Thork and tell him she spotted a body while gathering seaweed. If she pretended to look shocked, her brother wouldn't ask questions or wonder why she didn't have any kelp or bladderwrack to show. Considering what had happened, she wouldn't need to pretend much.

She hoped to speak with Thork alone, but she saw him talking to a group of people outside the village. Wilmer was there, and Horen. Joannet was trying to prevent the giggling children playing with Thork's staff. Wilmer was the first to spot her.

'Marna, what has happened? You are pale and shivering.' He removed his cloak and wrapped it round her shoulders. The wool was fresh and warm and she snuggled against it.

'I saw a body, in the sand,' she gasped.

'A body? Thork took hold of her arm. 'Where?'

'Give your sister space,' Wilmer chided. 'She is stricken by the sight and needs hot, honey ale.'

'She is soaking wet. What have you been up to, sis?'

'Gathering seaweed. I saw a man lying on the shore. I think it is Finn.' Marna stuck to her story although the words were lame. Wilmer furrowed his eyebrows and she could tell he wasn't convinced.

'Leave it to us,' Thork said. 'You go with Joannet.'

'But I can show you where the body is.'

'I'm sure we'll spot it ourselves,' Wilmer said. Marna made a face as she tried to think of a reason to go with them. Wilmer shook his head and relented. 'Put on dry clothes, first. We'll wait for you.'

Marna handed Wilmer his cloak and scurried to her house to change. Her mother was out, so there was no need for a lengthy explanation. When she returned, Wilmer handed her a beaker of ale. It was sweet and clawing, but she drank deeply, glad to clear her throat of the salt from the sea.

'Thork is organising a work party to shift the body,' Wilmer told her. 'He won't be long.'

A few of the womenfolk were keen to follow, but Thork didn't want hangers-on. 'It isn't something to goggle at,' he told Joannet. Marna thought Joannet would hit him behind the ear, but Wilmer pacified her by suggesting she prepare food for the men on their return. Albar brought a rough-haired pony for Marna to ride on and she directed them up the cliff path to the bay.

The body was lying where Sempal left it. The tide had turned and the water had retreated a few feet, allowing a gull to perch on the corpse's back and peck the clothes.

Albar rushed to scare it off. He, Thork and Horen managed to lift the body and stagger with it to the bank. They rolled it so the face was uppermost. The flesh was swollen and white as bone. The eye sockets were empty, but it was Finn's body. Marna turned away, to see a green-faced Wilmer, holding his sleeve over his nose.

'He's been murdered,' Horen said. 'See the wound on his forehead. It is through to his skull.'

'We can't say it was deliberate,' Wilmer argued. 'The body has been in the sea. That causes changes to the natural state of things.'

'Was he drowned, or was he dead when he reached the water?' Thork asked.

'A good question,' Wilmer said. 'He may have been on the cliff top and slipped. His head would have knocked against the rocks during the fall.'

'Why would he be so near the edge?' Horen asked.

'Checking the tide, perhaps. Looking for favourable weather to return to Ireland.'

'Perhaps he didn't slip, perhaps he was pushed,' Horen said.

While they were talking, Marna spotted the Irishmen marching towards them. She gave Thork a poke.

'Just what we need,' Thork groaned. 'How did they know we were here?'

'You should have let Joannet come with us,' Wilmer

replied.

Mickel had taken over as leader. He walked past Marna and Wilmer to stand in front of Thork. 'What is going on?' he demanded. 'They say in the village that a body has been found.'

'Marna spotted it on the shore,' Thork answered.

'It was in the shallow water,' Marna said. 'The tide has retreated now.'

Mickel looked around the group. His gaze rested on Horen. 'Aye, and we can guess who put it in the water.'

'What do you mean by that?' Horen advanced towards Mickel, but Wilmer stood between them.

'He wanted to off-load his daughters on Finn because he couldn't find husbands for them here,' Brann said.

'Finn laughed and he got angry,' Conel accused.

'Don't be ridiculous,' Wilmer said. 'No-one in the village has a motive for murder. The summer has been wet and the greenery on the cliff tops is slippery. It is likely your friend slipped. Marna fell near the edge last night.'

Everyone stared at Marna. 'That's right,' she agreed.

'Marna can hop across the rocks like an auk,' Wilmer continued. 'If she can slip, I'll wager Finn did too.'

'This place is evil,' Pog spat, 'As Erin warned us. He moved to examine the body. 'What are those strange marks on Finn's ankle? The bite of a sea goblin?'

Wilmer gave a small laugh. The others stared at him,

not finding the remark amusing. 'Sea goblins, you can't think...?' Wilmer let his words tail off, but he shook his head in disbelief.

Marna forced herself to look at the body. There were strange puncture wounds on Finn's right ankle and it was easy to imagine they were made by an angry goblin. The skin was torn and the area around the marks had darkened.

'The sooner we leave this place the better,' Conel said. The others agreed.

'No-one is stopping you,' Thork answered.

'We'll give Finn a decent burial in Ireland,' Mickel said. 'His spirit will not rest until the truth is out and whoever is responsible is brought to justice.' He placed his cloak over Finn's head. 'Gudrun will be heart-broken.'

The Irishmen lifted Finn's body. They took a limb each and carried it towards the cliff path. No-one from the village offered to help, but they followed in silence.

Joannet and her friends had gathered outside to greet the party. They rushed forwards to crowd the Irishmen.

'Clear the way. There is nothing to see,' Wilmer tried to part them. 'Go back to your homes.'

'No, wait,' Thork contradicted him. 'Let the Irishmen pass, but do not go to your homes. While everyone is gathered, I have an announcement.'

Everyone stared at Thork. Wilmer gave a look of irritation, but he said nothing. The visitors moved through the crowd to carry Finn inside. Marna dismounted from the pony and Albar led it away. Wilmer looked undecided whether to follow the Irishmen and offer his assistance, or stay and hear what Thork had to say. He hovered at the entrance to the village.

'Finn is dead,' Thork began. The villagers murmured, but Thork raised his right arm to quieten them. 'Our visitors fear there is evil at work in the village and I agree. The gods are angered by our lack of respect.'

Marna saw Wilmer roll his eyes. She knew he had no time for talk of gods or faerie folk. Joannet was nodding and encouraged the people around her to do the same.

'Jona has failed us,' Thork said. 'The gods have chosen me to be their new mouthpiece.'

'How do we know?' Walf called.

'I have the staff of the high priest,' Thork answered. Since finding it in Jona's cave, he carried it everywhere.

Marna heard a cheer and looked round to see Albar. He was carrying his drum and gave a heavy beat on the stretched skin. 'Tho-ork, Tho-ork,' he chanted.

Wilmer gave him a dismissive look, but Albar continued drumming and chanting until others joined in. Horen clapped and the children copied.

'Tho-ork, Tho-ork.'

The name was repeated with feeling, the sound growing louder until Marna could no longer hear "Thork", but a hypnotic call to arms. She was surprised to see Walf clap, although he didn't repeat the name. Wilmer had slipped away. Thork raised his hands for silence.

'We must hold a feast for the gods,' he declared.

'Fee- east, fee-east,' Albar drummed. Thork frowned.

'It will be held at the Stones of Stenness. Everyone must bring an offering; whatever you hold most dear - jewellery, pottery, goats, cattle. We must purge our village and stop these unnatural deaths.'

The crowd had worked itself into a frenzy. A group of young men jostled to the front and lifted Thork on their shoulders. They carried him round the walls, with the others following, chanting his name. Marna waited until they had gone then scrambled indoors. Her legs felt heavy and her head was pounding, but before she reached her house she spotted Wilmer at the entrance to the workshop. She guessed the Irishmen were there, preparing Finn's body. Wilmer gave a wave and came to join her.

'I don't know what has come over Thork,' Marna apologised. 'He's been like it since he found Jona's staff.'

'Longer than that,' Wilmer answered. 'The staff has given him confidence to speak out.'

'He is planning an inaugural celebration at the old stone circle. Everyone must sacrifice a precious gift.'

'A celebration at the Stones is not a bad idea. We need something to take our minds off death. Thork may make a good priest and a feast is always welcome.'

'What will you bring to sacrifice?' Marna asked.

'Some bracelets or neck chains. I've polished pretty stones that should please Thork's gods.'

'I don't know what to give,' Marna said. 'I have nothing of value.'

'You have a sharp mind and a generous heart.'

'But I can't offer those to the gods unless…' Marna stopped, remembering how close she came to being sacrificed in the sea.

'Then I shall carve you a bone figure to offer instead.'

'Would you? That would be kind.'

The mention of bone carvings reminded Marna of the comb she found. 'There's something I want to show you,' she said, reaching in her pocket. 'I found this on the cliff.'

Her hand patted the edges of her pocket, but she couldn't feel the comb. She stuck her hand in and turned it outside in. The pocket was empty, apart from a puddle of water. 'It was here. I must have lost it in the water.'

'In the water? What were you doing?' Wilmer asked.

'I found a comb,' Marna said, skipping over his question. 'A whale bone comb, like the one Roben gave to Henjar. The one she lost. I thought I'd found it, unless you made others like it.'

'All my combs are unique,' Wilmer said. 'The carvings are etched to suit the personality of the user.'

'That's what I thought,' Marna answered. 'I didn't get a good look, but the one I found had circles.'

'The comb I made for Henjar had waves on the side. It is unlikely Henjar would have dropped her comb on the cliff. Did you show it to her?'

'I didn't have time. She said Finn asked you to make a similar comb for her. Perhaps that is the comb I found.'

Wilmer shook his head. 'I'm afraid Finn did not ask me for a comb.'

He didn't face Marna as he spoke. His attention was on a small speck, trundling lop-sidedly towards them. Marna smiled as Pip was unable to stop and crashed into Wilmer's legs.

'You know you are not allowed indoors,' Wilmer pretended to scold the dog as he bent to rub its nose.

'The gods will not be pleased with you,' Marna said.

'Oh?'

'You do not intend offering them the most precious thing you have.'

'Ah, let's keep that between ourselves,' Wilmer said. 'Although now Thork is priest and you are able to make fire, I can return home to Barnhouse before the feast.'

'Must you go? We'll miss you.'

'I have neglected my business there for too long. I shall still visit and Barnhouse is not so far that you can't go there. Pip will be glad of someone to throw sticks for him.'

Marna gave Wilmer a hug.

'I'd better see if our Irish guests need help,' Wilmer said. 'Would you mind taking Pip outside to his kennel?'

Marna took hold of Pip and led him away. She was so used to seeing Wilmer and Pip she would miss having them around. With the fervour Thork was stirring, the village needed Wilmer's down-to-earth approach and a lick from Pip always made things better.

'Where have you been?' Her mother was busy soaking nettles when Marna arrived in the house, having seen to Pip. 'I saw the Irishmen arrive.' She mashed the plants in the stone cauldron.

'They have laid Finn in the workshop,' Marna said.

'They can't keep him there for long, not with the smell.'

'They are sailing soon and will take Finn home.'

'They will need fresh cloth to wrap the body in. Skins will make the body reek like middens. Be a good girl and gather me sweet smelling herbs from the meadow.'

'Yes mother.'

Marna was exhausted after the day's activity, but she didn't want to explain. She collected a woven basket and helped herself to a bere bannock before heading out.

Chapter 15

Over the next two days, dried, carded nettles were spun into threads then woven into cloth to cover Finn's body. The villagers worked together to help the Irishmen prepare their leader for his final journey home. A stone chamber was built outside the village, set against a small mound to give protection from the wind. It was used to shelter the body while the work of washing, laying out and binding was carried out. Marna carried sheets of cloth to the men and lingered to watch them work.

'Those are the sea goblin marks.' She pointed to the strange, circular lesions on Finn's leg. 'What do you think caused them?'

'I don't know. Maybe Wilmer is right and Finn fell from the cliff. He could have grazed his leg on the way down, struggling to grasp the rocks. Or maybe it was a hungry fish once he was in the water.'

'Aye, and maybe it was the black dog from the depth of the earth that seeks to drag men down,' Pog said.

'Don't scare the girl,' Mickel chided.

'I'm not afraid of sea goblins or pixie dogs.'

'Pog is worse than Erin with his stories.'

'Where is Erin?' Marna asked. 'I haven't seen her since... How did she take the news?'

'Not well,' Mickel admitted. 'She's a strange one. The two were always arguing when Finn was alive, but when she heard he was dead she screamed like a trapped wolf. Those scars on Brann's face were made by her nails. She took off to the hills when we tried to restrain her.'

'She'll be back before we sail,' Conel said. He was sharpening Finn's axe to place in his leader's hand.

'She had better be,' Brann said gruffly. Marna saw the scars on his cheeks and winced.

'When are you leaving?' she asked.

'When the sun rises, at the first tide,' Mickel replied.

'I'll tell my mother. She will prepare honey bannocks and dried meat for your journey.'

'That would be well received,' Mickel said. 'The journey will take several days.'

'I'm sorry things didn't turn out well for you here,' Marna felt ashamed of her village although she wasn't sure why. 'Will you be back?'

Mickel looked towards his friends. Brann grunted.

'We were able to trade our flint for good pottery and brooches,' Pog said, 'but there are other places we can trade that don't hold such memories.'

The men looked at Finn and bent their heads. Marna knew not to ask further questions about their visit. 'Do you need any more cloth?'

'We have plenty,' Mickel said.

Marna returned to the house. Henjar was with her mother, stirring a pot of something green and foul-smelling over a fire. When she heard Marna's news she burst into tears and ran out.

'Watch the pot,' her mother said as Marna turned to go after her friend.

'But...'

'She will be better on her own.'

News spread and when the sun rose the next morning, the villagers had prepared enough food to load the Irish boats twice over. The two boats were moored to the south east, where there was a sheltered harbour cut in the rocks. Some of the villagers travelled with the Irishmen to see them off, pulling sledges loaded with supplies. Marna didn't go with them. If she climbed the hill she could watch the ships round the coast and head west.

It was a pleasant morning. The sky was clear and she spotted the boats bobbing in the water. She kept her eyes on them until they faded into specks. With the strangers gone, Henjar would forget about Finn. She rarely mentioned Joel and never Roben.

She had spoken with Henjar when they gathered nettles for Finn's shroud. Henjar was in denial and talked about life in Ireland. The man's death was a shock, but Marna couldn't go along with it when Henjar sang Finn's praises. After ten minutes she invented a reason to leave.

With the boats gone from sight, Marna realised she could talk to Sempal, without fear of Erin being draped over him. Her prophecy had been false; they hadn't met again and never would. Cheered by the thought that the faerie folk didn't know everything, Marna went to find Sempal. There were things to discuss, not least the problem she was having with Thork. His new, self-appointed position was going to his head and he was unbearable. Even the devoted Caran wished he hadn't found the staff. She called it a 'stupid lump of wood,' although not to Thork's face.

Marna was smiling as she neared Sempal's cave. The sun was shining and her feet skipped over the rocks, taking care when she crossed the stream.

'It's me,' she called. It was unlikely he would be inside on such a brilliant day, but she could wait. She heard footsteps and raised her arms to embrace Sempal.

'To what do I owe this honour?' the voice was mocking. It wasn't Sempal's. 'Surprised?' Erin laughed.

'What are you doing here? I saw the boats leave.'

'Without me, unless I have a double which is possible.'

Sempal appeared behind Erin and put his arms round her waist. Erin's voice changed to a whine. 'How could I go back without knowing how my brother died?'

'It was an accident,' Marna said.

'I do not believe that. A mischief has entered my brother's body. Everyone witnessed the mark of the beast on his leg. As I speak, it is worming its evil way through his muscles and sinews, ready to open his dead eyes and raise his rotting body. The boats are cursed. They will never make it to Ireland, not with their crews alive on board.'

'What will happen?' Erin's voice was mesmerising and Marna almost believed the boat would sink.

'I see a storm,' Erin covered her forehead with her left arm.

'But the weather is fair,' Marna said.

'That is what Mickel said when I tried to warn him. He mocked me.' Erin made a sign in the air with her right hand. Marna assumed it was protection against evil.

'How long are you going to stay in this cursed place?' she asked. Erin looked at Sempal.

'Don't be like that, Marna,' Sempal said. 'Erin is welcome to stay with me as long as she wishes. I can protect her.'

'She has the faerie folk on her side. Shouldn't you be looking after your sister and nephew, or are sweet kisses more important to you?'

'I'll take a walk on the shore while you talk about me, shall I?' Erin interrupted.

'Now look what you've done,' Sempal turned on Marna as Erin swaggered off.

'Are you blind to her game?' Marna said. 'She might be the one who pushed Finn over the cliff.'

'Don't be ridiculous.'

'They fought often, according to Mickel. She has attacked a man before. If she killed Finn, it would explain why she doesn't want to be on the boat with the body.'

'You think Finn will rise up and accuse her? You are talking nonsense. Jona killed Finn,' Sempal argued.

It was Marna's time to feign a laugh. 'Why would Jona want Finn dead? He never met the man.'

'As far as we know. You said Finn was absent from the village most of the time.'

'He was busy with half the women of the island.'

'Erin told Jona about her brother's temper. He could have challenged Finn. Jona has a temper of his own.'

'Jona was in no state to pick a fight with anyone when we left him,' Marna reminded him.

'Perhaps Finn sought Jona out. He may not have been happy about Jona's attentions on his sister.'

'If that is the case, you are lucky Finn didn't know what you were up to with Erin.'

'What do you mean?'

'You know what. Your feelings towards her are blinding you to her failings. Give me a good reason why Erin wouldn't kill her brother.'

'He had twice her size and strength.'

'But a quarter of her intellect,' Marna countered. 'Erin knows how to manipulate people. If you're set on Jona being the killer, perhaps he was encouraged to do it by Erin.

It would be like her, to get someone else to do the dirty work.' She mimicked Erin's accent. 'My brother is a terrible man He beats me with his fists.'

'Stop it,' Sempal said.

'Stop what? Telling the truth?'

'You are the one blind to the truth,' Sempal moved past Marna to look out to sea. 'Finn's death was an accident, like you said. His kinsmen have gone home. The matter is over.'

'Not to Erin it isn't,' Marna said.

'We're wasting time arguing when we should be finding who killed Roben. You can't blame Erin for that.'

Marna reached for Sempal's hand and gave it a squeeze. 'I thought you would be alone. I wanted us to be alone together.'

'How can we be alone together? That is a very Marna-like thing to say. I'm glad you've recovered from your drowning.' He kissed her on the forehead. 'We're still friends, aren't we?'

'Of course.'

'What have you been thinking since then,' Sempal said. 'Don't say "nothing" because friends don't lie.'

'I don't know if I've been thinking or just dreaming,' Marna answered. 'There are too many things that don't make sense. The man on the cliff; the blue cloth at the loch; the wound on Finn's leg; the lost comb; the found comb;

Jona's accusations. I can't weave them together and I don't see where Finn fits in to any of it.'

'Let's take one thing at a time. The man on the cliff, do you mean the person you thought was me on the day Joel drowned?'

'Yes.'

'Are you sure it was a man?'

Marna was about to say 'yes,' but thinking about it, she wasn't certain. 'What woman would be on the cliff?'

'You were, but what about this comb?'

'I told you. I found a bone comb in the empty nest.'

'When you were looking for eggs in autumn. You think it was the comb Roben gave to Henjar?'

'Or the comb Finn promised her. She said he had asked Wilmer to make a new one, but he hadn't.'

'Henjar would recognise her old comb.'

'I know, but I lost it. It fell into the sea when you rescued me.'

'Blame me, as usual.'

'Don't be silly, I wasn't...stop teasing. This is serious.' She gave Sempal a light push and he pretended to stumble across the pebbles. Marna laughed until he did catch his foot and tumbled to the ground.

'Are you hurt?' Marna knelt beside him.

'No, I'm dying,' he croaked, drawing Marna towards him and kissing her. His lips were warm and she felt his breath on her face. She pulled away.

'Before we can do any more investigating, we have Thork's feast to think about,' she said.

Sempal sat up. 'I wouldn't mind going to a feast. I'm tired of shellfish and half-cooked crabs. You should see the muck Erin cooks. Insects and worms wrapped in seaweed. I would kill for one of my mother's bannocks.'

'Kill who?'

'You know what I mean.'

They sat in silence for a moment with the sun shining on them. 'You could go to the feast,' Marna said. 'There will be people there from Barnhouse, Stenness and Harray. Even from Smerquoy. Their heads will be covered and their faces painted for the ceremony. Nobody would recognise you.'

'Not if they had drunk enough ale or honey mead, but what about my leg?'

'I didn't think of that.' Marna couldn't come up with a solution. 'I'd better be going,' she said as she spotted Erin dragging a driftwood branch. 'I have to help Thork with the preparations. He's kept too busy sorting out quarrels to arrange anything.'

'Is that a coded message to mean Caran is visiting?'

'I meant now that Wilmer has left, he is called upon to resolve everybody's problems. Caran is not happy. She hoped he would move to Orphir with her and she is jealous of the time he spends on this feast when he could be arranging their wedding celebrations. They argued yesterday and she has returned to her family in a huff.'

'Thork should be grateful. Erin says weddings are pointless. It isn't natural to tie one man and one woman together for life. The animals don't.'

'The swans do,' Marna said. 'I have seen them on the lochs. The same pairs nest every season.'

'I suppose Caran is like a swan,' Sempal mused, 'With her long slender neck and pale skin.'

'Not like Erin,' Marna said coldly. 'She has the weather-beaten appearance and fiery feathers of a skua.'

'That is harsh, Marna.'

'It's as well your sister can't hear your views on marriage.'

'No doubt you will tell her. Anyway, I won't keep you,' Sempal answered, waving at Erin.

Marna knew he was acting upset so she would kiss him for Erin to see, but she wasn't playing his game.

'Going so soon?' Erin said as Marna strode past her.

'Don't worry, I'll be back.'

Her temper was hot as she went in search of Thork. He was outside, arranging axe heads on a flat stone.

'Are these new?' Marna asked. All axe heads looked the same to her, but these were polished and the blades lacked the usual chips. She had to admit they were quite pretty.

'Flint heads from Ireland. I traded dried hog meat for them. Bonny, aren't they? Which do you think is best?'

Marna lifted the nearest one and felt its edge. 'Ouch.'

'Careful. Trust a girl to pick up the sharp end.'

'You could have said something before I touched it.'

'I mean to offer the finest axe to the gods at the feast, but I can't decide which is best.'

'That one,' Marna decided. 'It has the nicest shading.'

'But this one is sharper and that one fits the handle I've carved from hazel.'

'Then I cannot help you. You will have to offer the gods all three.'

Thork screwed his nose.

'Do you want help with the preparations for the feast?'

'It is not a feast. It is an inauguration ceremony to prove to the gods that we are serious about our devotions.'

'That's what I meant.'

'Joannet is in charge of the bread, bannocks and honey cakes,' Thork said. 'Perhaps she needs help.'

'Wouldn't it be easier to do the baking in Barnhouse?' Marna said. 'It's only a short walk from the circle. If the food were prepared there, it would be warm for the fea...ceremony.' She could taste the fresh bread as she spoke and licked her lips. Thork scowled, but his expression changed as he considered her idea.

'You have a point. Tell Joannet your suggestion.'

'Ah.'

'Good,' Thork took her hesitation to be a "yes". He returned his attention to the axe heads.

'Eeny, meeny, miney, mo,' Marna muttered. Thork looked up. 'Will you be finished here in time for dinner? Mother will want to know.'

Thork grunted and Marna left him. She knew Joannet wouldn't listen to her, but her mother was respected. Joannet would pay heed to her words. She skipped to the village and into her house. Henjar and Boda were there. Boda was playing with small stones, throwing them in the air and giggling if they hit anything. One of the stones bounced off the dresser.

'Be careful he doesn't hurt himself,' Marna said. She was worried one of the stones would knock the delicate whalebone figure of a person sitting on the dresser. Wilmer gave it to her before he left. The base was flattened to sit perfectly on a rock, or on her palm. The mouth was carved large enough to satisfy the biggest appetite and the eyes were as mischievous as Wilmer's own. It was a gift to offer to the gods.

Henjar lifted her son into her arms. 'You are getting too heavy, my lad,' she said with a smile. Boda pulled the end of her hair with his chubby fingers and sucked it in his mouth. 'He's getting fine teeth,' Henjar said. 'But it means he is chewing everything. That's what I came to see your mother about.'

'Here,' Marna's mother offered Henjar a woven wreath of herbs and plants, the right size for Boda to bite on without choking.

'What's in it?' Henjar asked.

'Mint and garlic.'

Marna made a face. 'I used to hate the taste of the garlic, but it stopped me getting toothache.'

'I've sweetened it with honey,' Marna's mother said.

Boda didn't mind the taste and chewed on the dummy while Henjar helped Marna's mother grind cereals.

'That should be your job, Marna,' her mother chided. 'What have you been up to while we have been working?'

'Talking to Thork. He wants you to speak with Joannet.'

'Does he now?'

'He thinks the baking for the feast would be best done in Barnhouse. The bannocks would be warm and soft.'

'It would save carrying to and fro. Thork may have had a sensible idea for once.' Her mother winked at Marna. 'You help Henjar and I'll speak with Joannet. I'll make it sound like it is her idea.'

Her mother left and Marna played with Boda.

'I wish Wilmer had made me a figure to give to the gods,' Henjar said. 'It is beautiful.'

'You wouldn't want to give it to the gods.'

'No,' Henjar paused. 'Have you seen Sempal?' Marna hesitated. 'You have seen him, I can tell.'

'Yes, but...'

'But what? Is he ill?'

'He's with Erin.'

'The mad Irish woman? I thought she left with her husband.'

'Her husband?' Marna was swinging Boda in her arms and held him suspended in mid-air.

'Finn said she was married to Brann, the short, tubby one with the grey beard.'

Marna recalled the greasy, little man who spoke aggressively. 'No wonder she didn't go home.'

'But if she's got her cat claws into Sempal...'

'Sempal is a grown man,' Marna said. Henjar made a face. 'No, you're right. He needs rescuing.'

Marna had no idea what to do about Sempal's infatuation for Erin. After what he said about marriage, it would be pointless telling him about Brann.

'Watch this, Henjar said. She put Boda down and stepped back. The infant took a tentative toddle towards his mother before wobbling. Henjar put her arms out to steady him. He was interested in the flour she pounded and reached out his chubby fingers to grab a handful.

'He eats everything, just like his father did,' Henjar

said. The thought of Joel brought a tear. Marna put an arm around her friend.

'I'll never find another man like him,' Henjar wept.

'There are good men about if you look. Have you spoken with Albar?'

'Not yet.'

'Sylva has intentions towards him.'

'Sylva, but she is fat and stupid...'

Marna screwed her eyes.

'Well, thin and clever, but she has no sense of humour.'

Marna spent the day with Henjar. After the meal was ground they went out to pick flowers, berries and early nuts. For a few hours Marna put aside the troubles of the previous months and pretended everything was fine. She slept well that night.

Chapter 16

Marna woke to serious banging. Joannet and a group of women, accompanied by their husbands, were preparing to set out with a sledge load of pots and cooking utensils. Her mother was rushing in and out with bowls of grain and herbs. Marna listened from her cot. After the clattering and babbling, the village was quiet. Marna rose and washed her face from an urn of loch water. Her mother returned from seeing the catering party off.

'Where is Thork?' Marna asked.

'He and Albar have gone to set up an altar. They've taken the young men and boys to gather wood for a fire they'll build in the centre of the stone circle. He won't be back until after the feast. We have to make our own way to the stones. Me with my legs, too. Some son, he is.'

'I'll help you,' Marna offered.

'You can start by mixing the pigments for the decorations.

Her mother was in and out of the house that morning more times than a hare from its burrow. Having finished the pigments, Marna felt she was in the way. It was a warm day that should be enjoyed and she made her way to the meadow to smell the intoxicating aroma of the summer flowers. Her mother had left a beaker of honey ale on the dresser. She assumed it was for her and she took it with her, drinking the ale before lying on the grass. It tasted sweet and she licked her lips, enjoying every drop her tongue could capture. She closed her eyes and tried to empty her mind, but that was like telling Thork he could no longer hunt. Her brain took the chance to arrange everything that had happened since Joel's death.

Was that the beginning?

Jona said that Roben planned Joel's accident so he could marry Henjar, but Jona was not in his right mind.

Had there been signs of Roben's lust for Henjar before Joel's death? Roben couldn't have been in the boat with Joel. He was seen in the village arguing with Jona while Joel was fishing. Everyone remembered that.

Roben couldn't have sabotaged the boat. Joel checked the boards, skin and rudder before setting out. He carried spare oars and hides to patch up leaks.

Perhaps Joel had taken ill at sea, but he was a healthy man. He hadn't complained of ailments.

If Joel's death wasn't an accident, the only answer Marna could think of was that there was someone else in the boat with him. Was this person acting for Roben? If so, why? What did anyone have to gain by it?

Why would Joel's killer attack Roben? Were the two incidents connected? The killer may have fallen out with Roben. There would have to be trust between them and Roben wasn't a man who could be trusted.

No matter how many times she thought about it,

backwards, forwards and topsy turvy, it didn't make sense. The sticking point was Finn? A number of people may have wished to get rid of the Irishman, but none of them were connected to Joel or Roben.

Was Finn's death a tragic accident, muddying the water? Or did he find out something? He was only in the village a few days. What could he have found that she hadn't in weeks of searching?

That thought annoyed Marna and she concluded that Finn slipped to his death as Wilmer said. He may have inflicted the strange marks himself as some Irish rite. If it was to do with pleasing the gods, Jona might know about it. She had to find him, preferably alone and before he got high on plant substances. She opened her eyes.

'Come on sleepy head, the parade has started. I've been sent to find you.'

Marna rubbed her head. A shadow above her pulled her arms. The sun was flashing lights in her eyes. It took a moment to recognise Albar. 'What parade?'

Albar gave an exaggerated sigh.

Marna sat up. 'I thought the feast was at night, by torchlight.'

'Look about you. The sun is setting. You have been away all day, according to your mother.'

Albar was dressed for his duties as a ritual drummer. The deerskin apron she'd dyed for him covered his best tunic and his drum was slung round his shoulders. His face and arms were painted with blue dye.

'Beware of the colour blue,' Marna muttered.

'What has got into you? Have you been drinking Jona's poppy juice? That stuff can make you blind if you're not used to it.'

'I wouldn't drink anything like that. It was something Erin said.' Marna ran her tongue across her lips and tasted a bitterness hidden beneath the sugary reminder of the honey mead. 'I'd better get ready.'

'There's no time.' He took hold of her wrist and pulled her to her feet. 'Come on.'

'I have to fetch the bone figure.'

'We're late already.'

'It is an offering for the gods.'

Albar gritted his teeth, but Marna stood with her hands on her hips.

'You will have to be quick.'

Albar accompanied her to the village. The silence and empty tunnel gave Marna a feeling of being in a tomb. The folk who hadn't left early in the day had set off on their march to the stones. Marna thought she heard chanting in the distance. She entered her house and went to the dresser.

'It's not here,' she said.

'Can't you women remember where you put anything,' Albar said.

'It was on the dresser this morning.'

'It's not there now.'

'Somebody must have been here, moving things.'

'Like who?'

Marna puckered her lips.

What does it look like?' Albar asked.

'About this high,' Marna demonstrated with her fingers, 'made of whalebone. Wilmer carved it.'

'With holes at the top and bottom for hanging?'

'Yes, how did you know?'

'Because it is sitting beside your bed,' Albar pointed.

'That's impossible. I didn't leave it there.'

'Maybe your mother did.'

'She told me to put it on the dresser for safe-keeping.'

'She knows what you're like. You don't see anything unless it's in front of you.' Albar joked, but Marna knew he was annoyed at the delay.

Marna picked the figure up. There were tell-tale sticky finger marks. 'Boda must have been playing with it. He chews everything. I can't give it to the gods like this,' she wiped the figure on her tunic.

'What else do you have?'

Marna thought of Roben's black stone. 'Nothing,' she said.

'Then it will have to do.' Albar took hold of her arm and steered her out of the house.

'I need my shawl,' Marna protested.

'If you walk fast, you won't notice the wind.'

'It will be cold later.'

'Dance it off.'

Albar set a hefty pace. Marna was feeling woozy after her nap, but he didn't allow her to fall behind, beating his drum whenever she slowed. They caught the tail end of the march at the edge of the loch. Albar went ahead to take the lead. In the absence of Thork, he assumed the role of drum master. Marna stayed at the back, helping the older villagers, but she spotted Henjar keeping pace with Albar. He was reluctant to slow his march, but was forced to call a halt when Florel's stiff joints would take her no further.

'I knew we should have left her at home,' Albar muttered to the lad beside him.

'I tried to convince her, but gran hasn't missed a parade in thirty five years,' the boy answered.

Two of the men fashioned a stretcher from cloaks and carried her between them, with an arm around each of their necks.

Henjar had fallen behind. 'My feet are killing me too,' she grumbled. 'Who will carry me?'

Nobody volunteered.

'I'll take Boda,' Marna offered.

The torches were burnt down and threatening to flicker out by the time the parade arrived at Barnhouse. Thork,

Joannet and her bakers came to meet them.

'What kept you?' Thork demanded.

'It doesn't matter, we're here now,' Albar answered, glaring at Marna.

'Gather everyone together,' Thork ordered.

Joannet scurried off to carry out Thork's command. The villagers from Barnhouse stepped from their houses to greet the newcomers. Marna recognised the men from Smerquoy, by Wideford hill. They all looked the same, with their flattened noses, wide-set eyes and fat bellies. Thork found a mound to climb on. He banged his staff on the firm ground. Everyone crowded round.

'We have journeyed here from our villages to please our gods,' Thork announced. He waited for applause, but the others were too tired to raise more than a small cheer.

'Get on with it before the stew gets cold,' someone from Barnhouse called.

'We are not here to eat,' Thork said. This didn't go down well. There was mumbling among the assembled villagers. Marna knew her brother had prepared a longer speech. She had heard him practising when he thought she was asleep, but he decided it was wiser to take the heckler's advice and get on with it.

'It is time to lay our gifts on the altar.' He pointed to the stone circle. In the centre was a pile of stones with a flattened boulder balancing on top. It was no match for the

238

carved creations Jona set up for his sacrifices.

'I shall bring my gift first,' Thork continued. 'Three axes with fine flint heads from Ireland.' He swung his cloak back and drew the weapons from his belt. The others weren't as impressed as he hoped. He intended holding all three in one hand, but this wasn't possible and he had to lay his staff on the ground. Raising the axes aloft, he strode to the chosen spot and put them in the centre of the makeshift stone table, muttering a chant. He returned to claim his staff. 'Who will bring their gift next?'

Nobody moved. Thork repeated the question and Albar stepped forwards.

'I have brought my drum,' he said. Marna guessed he had been practising saying the words. He smiled at getting them in the right order, but didn't move towards the altar.

'Lay your gift on the altar,' Thork instructed.

'Won't I need it later?' Albar asked. Thork gave a sigh and Albar carried his drum to the altar. He hesitated before setting it down.

'I have brought a tooth,' Florel said. 'It was precious to me once, but I won't need it now.' She opened her palm to show a rotten molar that had fallen out during the journey when one of the stretcher bearers stumbled. Her grandson took it from her and placed it beside the axes.

There followed a slow trickle of villagers, laying their goods on the table; a few pots, a broken comb and berries.

Marna begrudged giving her beautiful figurine when she saw Henjar place Boda's half-chewed dummy on the table. She had a mind to keep it hidden and pick a handful of wild flowers for the gods, but she spotted Wilmer watching and placed the ornament on the stone.

'I'll miss you, little friend,' she patted the figure.

'Would the folk from Barnhouse bring their offerings,' Thork said, unhappy that no-one had offered goats or cattle for a blood sacrifice. Wilmer laid a bone bracelet on the table, which was still half empty. An old woman donated beads and a bone needle and the young men brought a carved stone ball with a chunk missing.

'Has anyone else brought anything?' Thork sounded desperate. 'A young calf or a sheep perhaps?'

The men from Wideford stood with their arms folded and their faces dark.

'I have pots of ale,' a voice rose from the back, 'but I fancy the ale is more suited for human bellies than for gods.'

The crowd gave a cheer worth hearing and people broke away to collect mugs. Realising he was losing his audience, Thork signalled to the musicians to play. Albar reached for his sticks before remembering his drum had been offered to the gods. When Thork turned away he sneaked over to recover it and began beating in tune with the others. Seth had his pipes and he played music to dance to. Walf took hold of a girl's hands and led her to a space away from the hustle of the crowd. He stamped his foot on the ground three times then began dancing a jig. With the ale and honey mead flowing, it didn't take long for the others to join in. Joannet and her helpers brought cakes, bannocks and pies, still warm from the hot stones. Fingers were burned as they reached for them.

Thork had chosen a good night. The threatening clouds had floated over the island without blessing the land with rain. The breeze had died down and the setting summer sun lit the sky with reds, oranges and purple. Marna stuffed herself with pies, drank ale and danced with men from Barnhouse she hardly knew.

'Decorate your arms,' a man covered in artwork from his bare toes to his bald head offered to carve patterns on her skin with his knife. The blade hadn't been cleaned from gutting fish. Marna thanked him, but refused.

During the evening, objects were surreptitiously removed from the offering stone. Marna spotted Wilmer replacing his bone bracelet with a wooden one. She was tempted to reclaim the little figurine, but every time she approached she could feel Thork's eyes upon her.

'Have more ale,' Wilmer offered her a tumbler.

'My head is spinning like a sycamore seed in the breeze,' Marna answered.

'Nothing wrong with that,' Wilmer grinned, but Marna

slid the cup away. 'Scones?'

'I'm full of bere bannocks.'

'You must try the honey cakes.'

'Later.'

'Here is something you won't refuse.' Wilmer brought his right hand forward with the fist closed and nodded for Marna to hold out her palm. When she did, he opened his hand to place the four inch high whalebone figurine onto it. Marna was about to say something, but he silenced her with a finger to his lips.

'Do not fear. The sun will rise tomorrow and rain will fall to grow the crops. The gods are not as peevish as your brother pretends. Now I shall go and ask your mother to dance while I am still steady on my feet.'

'She's been tapping her toes all night.'

Before Wilmer moved off, they heard a disturbance. A figure was staggering towards the stone circle, shouting oaths for the gods in the heaven to hear.

'I order you to stop this farce. Get away from the circle before it is defiled by your unbelief and evil.'

A few heads turned in the direction, but the music played on and the dancers twisted and twirled as before.

'Who is it?' Wilmer asked.

'I think it is Jona,' Marna said.

'What is he doing here? Where is Thork?' Wilmer looked left, right and behind him, like a hound in the long grass hearing its master's call.

'Get back to your houses,' Jona waved his arms,
'Before the gods show their anger.' He took a stride
towards a wooden plank that held the pies, but he had been
drinking or chewing on plants, and he staggered into it. He
thrust his arm out to knock the food to the ground.

'Hey, watch what you are doing,' Seth called.

Thork gripped his staff so tight his knuckles were
white. He signalled the musicians to stop playing. The
dancers came to a standstill and looked around. Thork lifted
the priest's staff above his head, puffed out his chest and
marched towards Jona.

'You have no right to be here,' Thork said. 'You have
angered the gods. You abandoned us in our need. I am head
priest. The gods have chosen me to serve them.'

'What right do you have to that staff? You stole it from
me,' Jona slurred. Thork beat the ground beside Jona with
the stick and the older man stumbled back. 'A staff does not
make you a priest,' Jona said once he recovered. 'The gods
did not choose you and they will not help you.'

'Watch what you are saying, old man,' Thork
advanced towards him, but Seth moved to hold him back.

'Don't waste your energy on him. Everyone can see he
is off his head.'

'You call me mad for speaking the truth?' Jona
laughed. 'My eyes are not blind and my tongue will not

remain silent.'

Thork tried to wave Jona away, but he had the crowd's interest. Encouraged, Jona continued, 'Why is Horen keen to have his twin daughters married? Any stranger will do. Any stranger who believes the babies they bear are from his loins.'

'What are you suggesting?' Horen's face was scarlet.

'Your daughters do not need husbands when they have a father like you.'

'This is outrageous.' Horen felt for the stone knife he carried in his belt, but his daughters pulled him away.

'The signs will show soon,' Jona warned. 'Two pregnancies cannot be put down to too many pies. Do you intend to claim the Irishman fathered them? He has returned home and cannot admit or deny it.'

'He doesn't know Finn is dead,' Marna muttered.

'Horen is not the only scar in the community,' Jona licked his lips. 'You allow a murderer into your homes. You are happy for this killer to eat your bread, drink your ale and corrupt your children.'

'What are you talking about?' Walf shouted.

'Don't you want revenge on the person who killed your brother Joel?' Jona said.

I thought he said Roben killed Joel. Marna thought the words, but Jona turned to glare at her with his reddened face and bulging eyes. He pointed a finger.

'I see the evil one here, a wolf dressed as a lamb.'

Marna trembled, but she felt a steady hand on her shoulder. 'Leave Marna alone,' Wilmer gave her shoulder a squeeze then marched to confront Jona. 'You are not welcome here.'

'Aye, get gone,' Seth said. 'We're not fools to be swayed by your drunken ramblings.'

'That is what you are, blind fools.' Jona spat at Seth's feet. 'Only fools refuse to remove the dressings from their eyes.' He tried to demonstrate the action, but lost his footing and slipped on the scrub. He managed to stay on his feet by grabbing at Seth's tunic. Seth shoved him and he fell. A howl of laughter rose from the crowd.

'A curse on you,' Jona swore. He raised himself to his knees and looked at the sky. The moon was glowing blood red. 'Let the gods hear my words. You are wrong to treat me as you do.' He got to his feet. 'I will be avenged.'

'Fine, you've had your say,' Thork moved forwards. 'Now it is time to bring your show to a close. Get gone, or we shall chase you out.' He signalled to Seth and Walf, who advanced towards Jona. He stared at the brothers for a moment until he realised he was no match for them then spat on the ground once more and turned away. 'Can't even raise a proper blood sacrifice,' he muttered as he staggered off. Marna watched until his figure disappeared over the small hill.

'Don't worry about him,' Wilmer said as she stood trembling while the others returned to their dancing. 'He has chewed too many dangerous plants. His mind doesn't know where it is. I doubt it is connected to his body. He's lucky Walf didn't set his hunting dogs on him.'

'I know. I would feel sorry for him if he didn't frighten me.' She looked around. 'Talking of hunting dogs, where is Pip?'

'He will be begging cakes with his doleful eyes or stealing them if that doesn't work. I don't know who taught him his manners,' Wilmer answered. 'Ah, there he is, over beside Henjar's young lad.'

Marna looked across to see Boda sitting cross-legged on the ground, guarded by the hound. There was nobody with him. Marna couldn't see Henjar or Lin. As she watched, Pip raised his head and howled.

'What's wrong?' Marna asked.

'I think the boy may be in trouble,' Wilmer answered.

'Boda,' Marna called as she ran across. He was lying on the ground with Pip standing over him. The dog allowed Marna to kneel and examine Boda. The boy's face was pale with a bluish tinge. There was saliva drooling from the side of his mouth. She felt inside and her fingers touched something hard.

'I think it's a stone. Boda must have tried to swallow it,' she said. 'It's stuck in his throat.' She wriggled her fingers, but the stone wouldn't budge. Boda didn't move. His body was cold.

'Over here quick, somebody help,' Wilmer cried. He lifted two rocks and hit them together like cymbals. When that failed he grabbed the nearest dancer. 'The boy can't breathe.' He pointed at Boda.

'What's that?' Albar asked. He signalled for the music to stop.

The revellers moved towards Marna and formed a ring round her and Boda. Henjar pushed her way to the front, with Albar beside her. She gave a cry, 'My baby.'

'I know what to do. Let me try,' Albar said. He gently raised the boy and felt for an area at the back of Boda's neck. With a swift tap he managed to dislodge the stone and it fell onto his outstretched palm. The boy still wasn't breathing. Albar opened his mouth and breathed his own air into Boda. Henjar wrapped her fingers round her hair and pulled out chunks as she looked on.

'Turn him on his side.'

'Slap his back.'

'Pull out his tongue.'

There was no shortage of advice from the on-lookers. Albar ignored them and continued breathing for the boy. He looked up at Henjar with a worried expression.

'Don't give up. My baby...' She bent down to stroke Boda's face. 'Oh.' Boda gave a splutter. 'He's alive.'

Albar pressed on the boy's chest to clear his airways. Boda's face became pinker and he cried. Albar picked him up, bounced him in his arms then gave him to Henjar.

'Are you all right, my baby? Mummy told you not to chew stones.' She turned to Albar. 'You were wonderful. You saved Boda's life.'

'It was nothing,' Albar blushed. 'We have Wilmer's dog to thank for spotting something was wrong in time.'

Henjar bent to stroke Pip with her free hand, then placed a kiss on Albar's cheeks. Thork had pushed his way to the front, but hadn't interfered while Albar worked. As the crowd cheered for Albar, he stepped forwards.

'The boy is fine now,' he said, 'But let this be a warning. The gods are not happy with the measly gifts. It is clear that a blood sacrifice is required.'

The crowd muttered. Some agreed with Thork, but most disapproved.

'If the gods are unhappy unless blood is spilt, I will fetch a calf,' Walf spoke up. 'I will not risk losing my nephew or another child through selfishness.'

The onlookers nodded and murmured their approval. Thork closed his eyes, as if communicating with the gods. He opened them suddenly and raised his arms to the sky. 'It is good. Bring your calf to the altar.'

Walf kept a small herd of cows near Barnhouse, claiming the land was better for them there. His friends knew it was an excuse to visit the area and a certain woman without his wife suspecting.

'I'll come with you, brother,' Seth volunteered.

'I don't need help to collar a calf.'

While the revellers waited, Thork recited the words of an ancient song, thanking the gods for their provision.

'Here he comes now,' a young lad interrupted the twenty second verse.

Thork was about to praise the gods for the summer berries and autumn nuts, but there was a commotion. Walf was struggling to pull a year old bull calf towards the stones. His arms were straddled round the beast's neck, but the calf was strong. Seth watched and laughed.

'You can collar a calf on your own, can you?'

'Bring the sacrifice to the altar,' Thork called. He instructed the crowd to follow him. 'I shall sacrifice the calf with one of the ceremonial flint axes.'

It occurred to Marna that the reason her brother wanted a sacrifice was to try out the axe heads.

'To the altar,' the cry went up. Albar picked up his drum and began beating it.

Marna followed the others to the pile of stones. Thork's face darkened.

'What's wrong?' Marna asked.

Thork gestured towards the make-shift table. Marna looked down. Few of the original offerings were left.

'Oh,' she covered her mouth. Not only had the worshippers reclaimed their own gifts, the largest of Thork's flint axes was gone.

Chapter 17

Thork pounded his fist on the stone altar, causing the remaining objects to bounce off. 'Who has taken the axe I offered to the god of hunting?'

'Not me.'

'I was nowhere near the table.'

'Perhaps it has blown on the ground.'

'Someone must have seen somebody lift it.' Thork peered round the group, sussing out guilty faces. 'The thief must come forwards now or risk severe punishment.'

'We were all occupied with poor Boda,' Wilmer answered from the back. 'Nobody was near the altar.'

'Somebody was.'

'Watch out!'

Walf's warning was crucial. He had lost his grip on the young bull and the animal was out of control. It tossed its head and pawed the ground, ready to charge. One of the girls gave a shriek. Terrified, the beast snorted and ran towards the noise. The girl screamed again. It was Nadea.

'Stand back.' Thork grabbed one of the remaining axes and pushed his way towards the bull. He thrust his arm at the animal, but his strike barely tickled the calf's hide as it fled past. Horen pulled his daughter away and the villagers parted, allowing the beast open access to the meadow and down to the loch. Walf tried to run after it, but he was no sprinter and gave up. He stood with his brother, panting as he watched the bull escape.

'Give us strength,' Thork flapped his arms. Seth gave an exaggerated sigh. Marna was pleased to see the calf wade into the shallow water at the edge of the loch and drink the fresh water.

'Call that a bull. You should see the cattle we keep on the hill,' one of the Wideford men jeered.

Walf's head was full of ale and he took offence at the remark. He gestured to Seth and they marched towards the men. Walf didn't know which of the men made the insult, so he threw a fist at the nearest man. He was also the smallest. The man wobbled and fell into his neighbour.

'Pick on someone your own size.' One of the Wideford men kneed Walf in the groin.

'That's my brother, you thug,' Seth pushed the man. The Wideford men were outnumbered. Some of the Barnhouse men decided to even up the match, but others supported Walf. They were all game for a fight.

'Not the celebration we planned. What do we do?' Albar whispered over-loudly to Thork. Marna was near her brother and overheard.

Thork wasn't watching the drunken brawl. He had his eyes on a band of men striding towards them. They wore their beards long, braided with coloured beads and their faces were painted blue. Several of them carried carved cattle horns. Marna was worried about the ones with axes.

'Who are they?' she asked.

'Priests from the Ness,' Albar said.

'They may be priests, but they think they are gods,' Thork added.

'What do they want?'

'To spoil our party.'

'You told them about the celebration, didn't you?' Albar said. 'You got their permission, right?'

'Our village helped build their new stone circle. My father was among the men who raised the guard stone fifteen summers back.'

'You mentioned that when you invited them to our sacrifice,' Albar sounded doubtful.

'The stones at Stenness have stood for more years than the priests at the Ness can recall. No-one has ownership of them. We can use them as we wish, just as the priests from the Ness can.'

'You didn't tell them,' Albar said. 'We are in big, big trouble.'

The men reached the edge of the stone circle. The leader gave a cry and the procession stopped. He turned to stare at the fight. Bodies were strewn across the ground and those standing were staggering into one another, throwing punches in the air. Thork strode to greet them.

'Welcome,' the leader raised his right hand, but his voice was cold. Thork raised his left hand in reply.

'I am Patro of the Ness,' the leader said.

'I remember you,' Marna mumbled.

Patro glared at her.

'I am Thork, priest to the villagers of Skara Brae,' Thork said, unperturbed by the newcomer's superior tone.

'Indeed? I was led to believe Jona was your priest.'

'Jona has problems…with his health,' Thork answered. 'I have assumed his position. We are here to make a sacrifice to the gods in celebration of the fact.'

'A sacrifice?' The leader looked again at the fight.

'The men from Wideford have had too much ale,' Albar answered.

'I wasn't addressing you, boy,' Patro sneered. He glanced at the unstained altar. 'We had word that a ceremony was taking place.'

'Who from?' Thork asked.

'From Jona - your head priest.'

'I am head priest of Skara Brae,' Thork re-iterated. Patro raised his painted eyebrow, neatly snipped into an inverted "v". 'Jona has lost his senses,' Thork continued. 'He has outcast himself from our community.'

'You, a priest?' one of Patro's followers laughed.

'I said head priest,' Thork answered, pushing his shoulders back. 'Albar is my assistant.'

'Weren't you two the drummers the last time you came here?' the man said.

'Ah, of course.' Patro snapped his fingers, as if he had been trying to place Thork. 'It is typical of your village to anoint a drum beater as priest. Next you'll be telling us the girl here is a priestess.' Patro encouraged his followers to mock. Marna felt her cheeks burn.

'Marna is my sister, but if she were a priestess, why would it concern you?'

Marna cringed at her brother's answer, but she was proud of him too.

'Everything concerns us,' Patro answered. 'You do not have permission to have your...'

While he decided on his words, he watched the tail end of the brawl. Henjar walked towards them gesturing to Marna. Patro glared from the men to Henjar

'... your *orgy*, here at our sacred stone circle.'

'The stone circle does not belong to you. I was instructed by the gods of the sea, land and sky to make an offering to them,' Thork stood his ground. 'What further permission do I need?'

Marna was shaking under her cloak. It wasn't wise to play games with the priests from the Ness.

'You call an axe head, third rate jewellery and burnt scones an offering?' Patro thrust his arm out to scatter the objects. 'Is that all the people of Skara Brae think the gods are worth?' Marna felt the figurine in the pocket of her tunic, but didn't bring it out.

'We have a yearling calf.' Thork said. He pointed to the loch, but Walf's young bull was no longer in sight.

'Enough,' Patro turned to his priests and instructed them to blow their horns. The noise rattled off the stones like the summer calls of the sea birds against the cliffs. The men stopped fighting and looked over with blooded faces. The spectators became aware of the new-comers and gathered round, faces filled with unspoken questions. The priests stopped playing. Patro raised his arms and his cloak blew out like a swan taking flight.

'Word has reached us at the Ness of the evil in your midst,' Patro shouted. His men repeated the word "evil" in low voices. 'There have been unexplained deaths, mysterious disappearances and a blight on your crops.'

'What disappearances? What blight?' Marna queried, but Patro ignored her.

'An offering is required. The gods demand blood, not broken pots and blunt knives.'

The other priests mumbled the word "blood", making a thrumming noise that Marna found unsettling.

'You shall follow us to the Ness, where preparations are being made for a proper sacrifice. Before noon tomorrow, the waters of the loch will run red with blood.'

His fellow priests gave a cheer, encouraging the villagers to join in. When they didn't, the priests stamped their feet, but it was only when they reached for axes in their belts that a few hurrahs were raised.

'I'm up for a feast of meat,' Horen said, pushing his daughters forwards. Nadea grabbed hold of the man next to her and dragged him with her. The revellers began to shuffle into a line behind Patro.

'None of you are fit to march to the Ness,' Thork argued. 'You will miss your footing in the dark and stagger into one of the lochs.'

'Don't expect us to pull you out,' Albar added.

'The corridor is safe,' Patro re-assured the gathering. 'Nollo shall beat the drum to guide the way.'

One of Patro's men stood to the front of the group. Marna hadn't noticed, but he had a drum slung over his neck. It was resting behind his back, but he drew it round and struck the surface with the palm of his hand.

'Ulla, ulla, matawulla,' Patro chanted something incomprehensible. His men blew their horns.

Thork raised his staff. He looked towards Marna hoping she would provide inspiration. She shrugged.

'Yabba wabba wolly,' Thork shouted.

The villagers from Skara Brae stared at him, but plumped on following Patro. They marched off to the beat of the drum leaving Thork, Alba and Marna.

'You can't beat a good ox roast,' Henjar said.

'Better go then,' one of the Wideford men scoffed.

'I need to find Boda,' her voice showed she was torn.

Lin was trotting at the back of the parade without the boy.

'He's with the Barnhouse girls,' Marna said.

'Wish we were,' another of the Wideford men said, pumping his arm.

There was little chance of the Barnhouse girls entertaining the drunken Wideford men and it wasn't long before they staggered off.

Realising the party was over, the families from Barnhouse trudged back to their homes. Wilmer waited, holding a sleepy Pip like a baby.

'I feel as tired as he is,' Marna confessed.

'You are welcome to stay with me,' Wilmer said.

Marna looked to Thork.

'I can find space for everyone,' Wilmer said.

Thork was still watching the procession straddle towards the Ness. Marna answered for him. 'Thank you. That would be kind.'

'I'm exhausted too,' Henjar agreed, 'Although I won't sleep. My nerves are tingling. It feels like I have toothache all over my body.'

'We can't have that,' Wilmer said with a smile. 'I have the very thing for tingling nerves: a warm herbal infusion, guaranteed to give a good night's sleep. I shall go and concoct beakers of it for all of you.'

'We wouldn't want to put you to any trouble,' Marna said. Henjar gave her a nudge.

'It is no problem. I make some for myself at night. There will be plenty to spare.'

Wilmer set Pip on the ground. The dog gave a whine and followed his master. Albar collected Boda from the girls and carried him to Wilmer's hut. Thork and Marna walked in silence, listening as Henjar prattled nonsense. Pip had reached the house first and growled at Thork as he bent to enter. Marna stroked the pup's head.

'There's nothing to fear from Thork,' she soothed. 'He is softer than a downy mattress.'

'I'll take Pip outside,' Wilmer led the dog away. When he returned he brought a bundle of skins borrowed from his neighbours. Marna arranged them while Wilmer brewed his sleeping draught.

'That one is for Henjar and Boda,' she tapped Thork's hand to stop him taking the largest skin.

Wilmer heard the squabble and came over. 'Henjar and Boda can have my cot. You can sleep in here with them, Marna. I'll fetch heather and you can lay the heavier skins over it. We men can sleep in my workshop.'

Thork and Albar went to the next room to prepare the floor. Henjar settled Boda and Marna laid out the skins. Wilmer returned to his brew.

'Ready,' he called after a short time. The others crowded round and Wilmer poured the amber liquid into five stone beakers. 'Careful, it's hot.'

'What's in it?' Thork asked, raising the beaker to his nose. 'It smells like poppy juice.'

'There are poppies in it, willow bark to ease the muscles, lavender from a southern trader and my own secret ingredient,' Wilmer answered.

'Honey, too,' Marna said, sipping the drink. It tasted like her mother's ale.

'I confess I have a sweet tooth,' Wilmer smiled.

Wilmer took their cups when they finished. He was keen to talk, but Thork made an excuse and retired to the next room. Marna stretched her arms and yawned. Henjar was sitting near Albar with her eyes closed, but Boda was full of energy. He half-crawled, half-toddled to the door.

'Pity you can't give Boda your potion,' Albar said.

'I fear it would be too strong for a babe, but I have the next best thing.' He moved to the wall dresser and brought out a hand-held harp. Sitting on a wooden bench, he settled the instrument in his arms and strummed the strings. Boda was fascinated by the sound. He reached up to touch the instrument. Wilmer allowed the infant to pluck a note, before beginning to play a soft melody.

'I know that tune,' Albar said. 'My mother sang words to it when I was small.'

'I was taught it from a minstrel. No doubt she passed through your village too on her travels. That was many years ago,' Wilmer said. His face showed he was recalling the woman with fondness.

Albar started singing. He had a rich, deep voice that filled the room, but was soothing to the ears.

'Don't stop,' Henjar said.

'Boda is resting,' Albar said. 'I'll put him to bed.'

'I think we had better leave you ladies,' Wilmer said. 'Have pleasant dreams and I shall see you in the morning. With luck the loch will provide fish for breakfast.'

'Not too early,' Marna murmured. She was curled in the skins and the brew was doing its job. Her eyes were heavy and she could feel her muscles relax. She was asleep before Henjar's snoring and Boda's hiccups could keep her awake.

The night passed with dreams of hot scones. Marna thought the rich smell of honey was another dream until Henjar gave her a shove.

'I thought you were going to sleep until evening,' Henjar bent to shout in her ear. Marna rolled over and Henjar pulled the skin she was hugging away from her. 'Get up lazy bones. Thork wants to find out what is happening at the Ness. Albar is going with him.'

'Doesn't mean we have to,' Marna grumbled.

'Yes it does.'

'Where is Wilmer?' Marna asked.

'Making breakfast. Can't you smell the honey?'

'Mmm, delicious.'

'He was whittling me a new comb, but the noise upset Boda. He's only grumpy because of his gums. Wilmer says honey is excellent for soothing teething pains.'

'Wilmer thinks honey is the answer to everything.'

'Don't be grumpy too,' Henjar said. 'I need to talk.'

'What about?'

'Albar.'

'What has he done?'

Henjar giggled. 'I won't tell you until you get up.'

Marna forced herself out of bed and straightened her hair. Henjar dragged her next door where Wilmer was talking to Thork. Albar was playing with Boda.

'Did you sleep well?' Wilmer asked.

'A little too well,' Thork answered. 'We should have left some time ago. It is almost noon.'

'You could have woken me,' Marna said.

'He would have if he'd been up,' Albar said.

'You will have time for sweet honey cakes before you leave,' Wilmer offered. 'They were made fresh this morning by my neighbour.'

'I've eaten enough bannocks to feed me until winter,' Thork said.

'I wasn't up early enough to fish,' Wilmer said ruefully.

'No matter, we should be leaving.'

Marna filled her pockets with a supply of cakes while

her brother looked for his coat. It was at the side of his makeshift bed and he reached to lift it.

'Ugh, what's this?'

There was a stain on Thork's coat that tinged his hand red and clung to his fingers.

'Horen's raspberry ale,' Albar said. 'You drank your fair share of it last night. It didn't all reach your gob.'

'And my head is suffering for it this morning,' Thork agreed. He rubbed his hand down his legging.

'A blast of autumn air will do you good,' Wilmer said.

The wind was certainly blasting as they set out. Marna struggled to keep in line. The fresh air made her hungry and she held her tummy to stop it rumbling.

'You sound like the cow that got away last night,' Albar laughed.

'It was a bull,' Thork reminded him.

'A baby bull,' Henjar added.

'It got the better of Walf,' Thork sulked. 'What do you say, Marna?'

Marna had taken a bite from a cake. The honey melted on her tongue and stuck to her lips. With her mouth glued up, she was unable to answer.

'I might as well talk to Boda,' Thork grumbled.

Marna's head was fuzzy and she dragged behind the others. They reached the rocky path that ran between the two lochs. The honey left a clawing taste in her mouth and she stopped beside one of the lochs.

'Wait a moment,' she called, but her voice was lost in the wind, or ignored. A growth of reeds bordered a half-moon shaped pool at the water's edge. Marna dipped her hand into the water to scoop up a mouthful. The water was red. She screamed and allowed the liquid to fall through her fingers into the loch. Her hand was stained scarlet. She lifted it to her nose to sniff. It smelt of blood.

The others heard her scream and stopped.

'What's up?' Albar called. Marna didn't answer. She was staring at her fingers. The colour had faded by the time the others reached her.

'What is it now?' Thork put his hands on his hips.

'The loch water – it's running with blood,' she pointed. 'That's what Patro said it would do.'

Chapter 18

'Patro,' Thork grunted at the mention of the priest. He touched a foot into the water. 'It seems fine to me.'

'You still have Wilmer's sleeping potion in your head,' Henjar teased.

'There's something in the water,' Albar squinted. 'Over there, among the reeds.'

'I see it too,' Henjar said.

Thork gave a sigh. 'Watch this for me.' He handed Marna his staff. 'But don't touch it.'

Marna was about to take the stick, but pulled her hand back at Thork's instruction. The staff fell to the ground.

'Idiot!' Thork picked it up.

'You told me not to touch it.'

'Could you two stop squabbling,' Henjar said.

Marna took the staff and Thork waded into the water. Henjar gave Albar a poke and he followed. They sank to their waists as they made their way towards the object. Marna half expected them to vanish under the water. Henjar held tight to Boda and made gasping noises.

'They've got something,' Henjar said.

There was splashing and cursing as the men dragged what they found towards the bank. Thork pulled himself out of the water first and heaved the find up onto the bank.

'Watch what you're doing,' Albar warned as Thork lost his grip and the object slid back, knocking Albar under the water. He righted himself with a splash at Thork.

Marna and Henjar jogged round to join the men, in time to stop their water fight. Between them they hauled the bundle out. It was larger than an adult swan and heavier. Marna helped Albar out of the water and they stood beside Thork looking at it.

'Aargh,' Henjar screamed, shielding her son's eyes.

Thork swore. It was a body, lying face down, just as Finn had been. Marna spat out the cake crumbs that rose from her stomach to her throat.

'We should see who it is,' Albar said.

Thork screwed his face. He nudged the body with his foot. It moved and he drew back.

'You'll have to lift it,' Albar said.

'Give me a hand then.'

Thork and Albar took hold of an arm and leg and jostled the corpse until it rolled over. Marna recognised Jona's red hair. Tangled among it and lodged deep in the skull of his forehead was an axe. Not any axe, but one of the flints she saw her brother place on the altar.

'The gods have their blood offering,' Albar said.

'This isn't the work of gods,' Thork said. 'It is the stolen axe. Some man did this.'

'Is he dead?' Henjar asked. Thork and Albar gave her a look.

'Yes,' Marna forced the word out.

Thork looked at Marna and his eyes rested on the staff. She offered it to him and he took it.

'But who would kill Jona?' Henjar said.

The other three stared at one another.

'I don't know,' Thork said.

'After his party piece at the stones last night, half the village would want to silence him,' Albar answered.

'He said he knew who murdered Roben,' Marna tried to remember Jona's words. 'He said it was someone living among us. Someone at the celebration.'

'Someone who would not wish Jona to divulge a name,' Albar added.

'But Marna,' Henjar looked aghast. 'He accused you.'

'I didn't kill him.' Marna couldn't believe her friends could think it, but they were looking at her strangely. Henjar took a step back and guarded Boda with her hand.

'Of course not,' Albar said, 'but you are good at finding bodies.'

Thork was staring at the corpse, trying to force it away by the power of his mind. 'What are we going to do? If we report to the Ness, the council there will detain us for days. Patro would love to put the blame on me. He hates anyone challenging his authority.'

'And it is your axe in Jona's skull,' Albar said.

'When the body is discovered, Patro will know we passed here. We can't keep it secret,' Marna calculated.

'They will want to question us,' Albar said.

'We could throw it back in the water,' Henjar suggested.

'Jona does not deserve that,' Thork answered before Marna and Albar could concur.

'What are we going to do?' Henjar fretted.

They bandied ideas around until Marna came up with a solution. 'Henjar and Albar can take Boda to the Ness and report what they've found, meanwhile...'

'Wait a moment, what have we found? I mean, what do we say we've found?' Albar asked.

'You stumbled on the body lying here.'

'We found a wet body lying on dry land. Nobody will believe that, especially since my tunic is soaking.'

'Say it was tangled in the reeds. You pulled it out, but didn't have the strength to carry it further,' Marna said.

'They will ask where Thork is.'

'Tell them Thork went to the tomb at Maeshowe. I went too if they ask about me, but I don't think they will.'

'Why would Thork go to Maeshowe?' Henjar asked. 'He isn't dead.'

'Not yet,' Thork muttered.

'He seeks spiritual guidance for his new role,' Marna explained.

'Oh.' Henjar stared at Thork with awe. Marna was about to tell her it was a story, but decided that would be too much for her friend to cope with.

'Can anyone think of a better plan?' Thork asked.

'Other than fleeing the island, no,' Albar answered.

Henjar sucked her bottom lip, but didn't speak.

'We'll go with Marna's idea then,' Thork decided.

Albar put his arm round Henjar. Marna crouched over the body. 'Wait.'

'What now?' Thork asked.

'I'm retrieving your axe.' She pulled at the handle, but the flint head was lodged in the bone. There was a crack and she let go.

'Everybody saw it was missing,' Albar said. 'They can't blame Thork.'

'Everybody saw Thork draw attention to the fact that it was missing,' Marna qualified. 'When people are afraid they come up with ludicrous theories. They might think Thork was making a show, so nobody would suspect him of murder when the body was found.'

'It would be easier to make sure nobody found the body,' Albar said. 'A heavy stone would ensure it lay at the bottom of the loch until the fish chomped enough away so that even his daughter wouldn't recognise him.'

'Sounds like you've thought it out,' Thork said.

'It's too complicated for me,' Henjar scratched her head. Boda began to cry.

'Whoever is carrying out these murders has thought

everything out. They aren't accidents,' Marna said.

'Albar is the killer?' Henjar pushed his arm away.

'No silly,' Marna hoped she didn't have to explain everything to Henjar again.

'The killer couldn't know Jona would be here,' Thork said.

'Jona wasn't known for keeping secrets. He told Patro about the ceremony.'

'Patro?' Henjar looked shocked and grabbed Albar's hand.

'If the killer knew Jona was going to the ceremony, why didn't he kill him before he threw his accusations around,' Thork argued.

'I don't know,' Marna admitted. Events of the previous night were coming back to her. 'Maybe the killer was taken by surprise at Jona's appearance. The axe was stolen afterwards, when everyone was attending to Boda.'

'You're saying the murderer deliberately made my baby choke?' Henjar cried. 'If he did, I'll…I'll…'

'Kill him?' Thork suggested.

'There was no-one with Boda when he choked,' Albar said, 'Except the dog.'

'Our murderer didn't stick a stone in Boda's mouth, but he took advantage of the situation. If it hadn't been Boda choking, he would have found another opportunity.'

'Like what?' Henjar asked.

'I don't know; start a fire with one of the torches or pick a fight with the Wideford men,' Marna guessed.

'You say "he",' Thork said. 'It might be a woman.'

'How could a woman thrust an axe into Jona's skull?' Albar said.

'Or overpower a man as strong as Finn,' Marna said.

'What about Finn?' Henjar was confused.

The others exchanged looks, but didn't answer.

'A woman could have had help,' Thork argued.

'I suppose so,' Marna conceded her brother had a point. 'What woman are you thinking of? Me?'

'No silly, take another look at the body.'

Marna looked, but had no idea what she was supposed to see. 'What is it?'

'On Jona's arm.'

Jona's arm was covered by the sleeve of his tunic and tangled in reeds. Marna moved closer. She reached to shift a strand of reed and gasped. With his wrists exposed, Marna saw the two deep puncture marks in the flesh.

'The wounds that were on Finn's leg,' Marna said.

'The sign of the evil one,' Thork said.

'Someone from our village is a devil?' Albar said.

'Not from our village,' Thork answered. 'Marna should ask Sempal about his house guest.'

'Erin?'

'If I'm not mistaken, these belong to her, don't they?'

Thork pointed to a mound of thick clover growing on the bank near the body. Lying among the flowers were Erin's pipes.

Chapter 19

Marna stooped to pick the pipes up. Her fingers tingled as she felt the wood. The painted figures seemed to dance and for a second she thought she heard Erin's laughter.

'I'll take them to her,' Marna said.

'Are you mad? That's evidence,' Albar said.

'Finding her pipes here doesn't mean she killed Jona. It seems too… obvious.'

'It means she was here,' Thork said. 'What was she doing?'

'Not thrusting an axe into Jona. Erin wasn't at the ceremony. She couldn't have taken your flint.'

'She could have been in disguise. She looks enough like a man without painting her face blue and hiding beneath a cloak,' Thork answered.

Marna recalled advising Sempal how to dress to attend the feast. He couldn't because of his leg, but Erin could. 'We can learn more by keeping her on our side,' she said.

'What if she is the killer?' Albar said.

'Who is in league with devils,' Thork added.

'I meant until we have more evidence,' Marna qualified.

'Fine, if you say so, sis. We'd better be off before Patro's priests make one of their patrols.'

'What about the axe?' Marna asked.

Thork gripped the handle with one hand. It came away

with one tug. He wiped the blade on his coat and secured it beneath his belt. 'The gods won't want it now.'

Albar and Henjar repeated what they were to say, making sure they agreed on the details, then they bade Thork and Marna goodbye.

'And good luck,' Thork said.

'Why did you say that?' Marna nagged as they watched their friends depart. 'Henjar will worry.'

They turned from the loch and retraced their path, passing the stone circle of Stenness. A group from Barnhouse were dismantling the altar. Wilmer was directing proceedings, but he didn't spot them and they didn't stop.

'We're near the sea. I should have brought my basket to collect seaweed,' Marna said.

'You would hardly have been thinking of seaweed when you left home, unless you have a gift you haven't told us about.'

Marna remembered what she had been thinking before Albar interrupted her. It wasn't about seaweed, but about talking to Jona. There was something she wanted to ask him, but although it played on her lips, she couldn't think what. She couldn't ask him now, but perhaps... Had he told her what she needed to know in a round about way? Why had he pointed to her at the ceremony?

'I'll take a walk on the cliff,' she decided. 'It will

clear my head.'

'Don't go near the edge. You drank beakers of ale last night.'

'No more than you.'

'My head is as clear as spring water. I shall go on to Orphir and find Caran.'

'We won't expect you home tonight then.'

Marna watched her brother stride off, using his staff as a walking stick. She waited a moment before taking her own path to the cliffs, hoping to find Sempal and Erin. It would be satisfying to probe Erin about her clandestine meetings with Jona in front of Sempal. She would have to tell the truth if she wanted her pipes back.

The wind was strong on the exposed cliff head. Marna was careful of her footing. She felt a shiver when she thought of what might have happened before, if Wilmer hadn't rescued her.

There had been no-one to grab Finn when he fell. Or had someone been there to give the fatal push?

Marna couldn't believe the Irish woman would push her brother over the cliff. If she caught Finn by surprise she could have unbalanced him, but her own brother? Thork was a good brother, but even if he treated her badly, Marna could never harm him. Families didn't do things like that, did they?

With thoughts crashing inside her skull like waves

against the rocks, Marna missed the path to the bay and reached the gorse bush that marked the turn for the village.

'Bother,' she clicked her tongue, contemplating leaving the meeting for another time, but the pipes in her pocket rubbed against her leg, eager to be re-united with their mistress. She turned back and increased her pace. When she reached the stream she gave a low call and was answered by the squawk of a gull. Sempal appeared from the cave and clambered over the rocks to join Marna.

'What's up? You look worried,' he said.

'Jona is dead.'

'What! How? Where? When? Who found him?'

'We did, this morning, in the water of Harray loch, near where it meets Stenness. He had an axe through his head. Thork's axe.' She grabbed Sempal's tunic. 'Jona was alive when he left the gathering last night.'

'You said "We" found him. Who are "we"?'

'Me, Thork, Albar and Henjar. Boda too, but he won't know what was going on. At least, I hope he won't.'

'What were you doing there?'

'Walking to the Ness from Barnhouse.' Marna realised Sempal was unaware of what happened at the feast. Erin hadn't reported back. 'It doesn't matter who found him. What matters is who killed him.'

'Calm down,' Sempal put an arm round her shoulder, but she drew away.

'There's something you should know,' Marna said. 'Where is Erin?'

'In the cave, sleeping. Why?'

'I found these on the bank of the loch, close to where we found Jona's body.' Marna reached in her pocket and brought out the pipes. Sempal looked at them without speaking. 'I need to speak with Erin,' Marna said.

'Erin had nothing to do with Jona's death,' Sempal said.

'Maybe not, but she either met him before he died or intended to meet with him and saw him in the water.'

'With your brother's axe in his skull,' Sempal reminded her. 'Maybe you want to warn Erin against telling the others what she saw.'

'Don't be ridiculous.'

'You accuse Erin of killing a man with twice her strength and yet I'm ridiculous for suggesting your brother might have. Perhaps you think it was the faerie folk.'

'We're friends. Let's not argue.'

Sempal sighed. 'Erin's tired. I don't want to wake her.'

'When did she get back? Was there blood on her clothes?'

'Enough.' Sempal turned to look out to sea. 'Erin has nothing to do with this. Her brother's death has been a shock. Don't you understand that?'

Marna glowered at Sempal. Thork's idea of someone

helping Erin didn't seem strange. 'Did you go with her to see Jona?' she asked.

Sempal gave a forced laugh. 'You suspect me. What sort of friend are you?'

'A good friend and I don't suspect you of anything. If you were with Erin, I would know she was innocent.'

'You have my word that Erin is innocent.'

Marna inclined her head, but didn't voice her agreement. Her gaze followed the dip of a wave. The foamy head galloped onto the pebbled beach with the sound of hooves.

'I'm glad we're not in your boat today,' Marna said.

Sempal chewed his lip.

'Can I ask you a question?' she said.

'You are going to, no matter what I say.'

'Where did Joel intend fishing, on the day he drowned?'

'How on earth am I meant to know that?'

'But you often went fishing with Joel.'

'What are you suggesting? We've been through this. I wasn't with Joel that afternoon. I wish I had been, but even the gods cannot turn back time.'

'You know where he liked to fish. Where would he have gone? Think, Sempal, it could be important.'

Sempal rubbed the stubble on his chin. 'It depended on the time of year and the tides. In the mornings he looked for flat fish in the waters near the shore. Henjar has a taste for flounders.'

'What about the afternoons?'

'He would fish for cod and bass further out. I don't like the deeper waters, even when the sea is calm. That's why I didn't go with him in the afternoons.'

Marna listened, but something niggled. 'He couldn't have gone too far out. It doesn't fit with events. Joel was gone long enough to sail towards the horizon, so why did his body float to shore so soon after the accident?'

'Joel was an experienced fisherman. He knew the waters close to home. He wouldn't have lost control of his boat there. Besides, he was a strong swimmer. If he fell in, he could reach land before the chill seeped into his bones.'

'Jona didn't think it was an accident.'

'Jona blamed Roben, but we know that can't be true,' Sempal said.

'Roben couldn't have been in the boat, but what if someone else was? Someone Joel trusted, but who was acting for Roben.'

'Joel trusted everybody, but Roben didn't have friends. Nobody would kill for him,' Sempal said.

'I saw somebody on the cliff after Joel's body was found. I thought it was you. He was wearing a blue cloak. A blue cloak…' Marna repeated. 'Just like the one Thork found in Jona's cave. Why didn't I think of that before?'

'You saw Jona on the cliff after Joel's death?'

'No, I would have recognised Jona, even from a distance. It was someone else.'

'With Jona's cloak?'

'Jona has, had, a red cloak. I dyed it for him. He must have found the other cloak.'

'So?'

'Maybe the killer knew he'd been seen and hid it.'

'You're not making sense, Marna. According to your argument, somebody was in the boat with Joel. He pushed Joel overboard, brought the boat to land, climbed up the cliff, saw you watching and threw a good cloak away for Jona to find.'

'There is a path up the cliff from the bay. The killer could have seen me. We were too far to identify each other, but I might recognise the cloak, if I saw it again.'

'Only you thought it was me.'

'At first.'

'Why should it matter that Jona found the cloak? Did you tell him you saw the killer wearing it?'

'No, but I think Jona knew who the cloak belonged to and worked out why it was thrown away,' Marna said. 'He said something about clues coming together. He knew enough to blackmail the murderer. That's why I need to speak with Erin.'

'You need to speak to me, do you?' Erin had a way of

creeping up and surprising people. Marna jumped.

'You look pale. You shouldn't be up,' Sempal moved to her side.

'I want to hear what Marna has to say,' Erin waved him aside.

'I found these,' Marna dangled the pipes in front of her. Erin snatched them and hugged them to her breasts. She caressed the wood. Marna expected her to lift them to her lips and play, but she hesitated.

'What have you done to them?' she accused.

'Nothing. Thork found them in the reeds at the loch.'

'Thork? Ah, your handsome brother who talks to the gods,' Erin said. 'They guided him to the spot.'

'The gods had nothing to do with it. Thork found your pipes beside Jona's body.'

Erin gasped and took a step back.

'Jona is dead, Erin,' Sempal said, reaching for her hand.

'Is he?' Erin bent to kiss the pipes. 'I can't say I am sorry. It is wrong to try and take by force what isn't freely offered. I called to the faerie folk for recompense. No doubt they had a hand in his death.'

'He had a human axe in his forehead.' Marna said.

'When did you last see Jona?' Sempal asked.

'That is no business of yours.'

'We think Jona was killed because he was

blackmailing a murderer. The man who killed your brother.'

'You said my brother's death was an accident.'

'If Jona told you anything, you could be in danger.'

Erin puckered her lips then raised her pipes to her mouth. They produced a screeching sound as the wet grass stuck in the tubes was blown out.

'I'm sorry, my beauties,' she whispered. 'Talk to me.'

Erin played a slow air. The music spoke to Marna of a strange, green land surrounded by sea - Ireland or some faerie kingdom. There were people dancing. Beautiful people with smooth skin, deep blue eyes and the fairest hair Marna could imagine. Their eyes held all the sadness of the world. It took a moment to realise Erin had stopped playing and was speaking in a low voice.

'Jona spoke of the language of the heavens. It sounded wonderful, speaking to the gods in their own tongue, knowing their innermost thoughts. I wanted to learn, so I sought Jona out after his fight with Thork. He was bleeding and I nursed him. He sent me to collect his staff, but it was gone. He went crazy, but I was able to soothe him. Later, he bragged that he was going to the stone circle, to your feast, to create mayhem.'

'How did he know about the feast?' Marna asked.

'I don't know. He wanted to ruin it because Thork took his staff,' Erin answered. 'He said he had important information for someone. Information they would prefer no-one knew. He didn't tell me who or what.'

'You met him yesterday. Before or after the feast?' Marna questioned.

'In the afternoon. He had been drinking and his aura was black. So black I couldn't see his lips when he kissed me. His breath tasted foul. Fearing for him, I went with him to the stones, but stayed by the loch to speak with the nymphs while he went to your ceremony. He came back raging and tried to have his way with me. When I refused he called me names and grabbed my arm. That's when I lost my pipes. I was crawling on the ground, searching for my children when he lowered himself onto me. He had chewed too many plants and was high on his own importance. I pushed him off and he was rolling on the ground like a frightened hedgehog when I kicked him in the balls. He may have fallen in the water, I didn't stay to find out, but I didn't put an axe in his skull.'

'Of course you didn't.' Sempal moved to put an arm round her, but she stepped away.

'I'm not saying I wouldn't have, if I'd had one.'

'You are sure Jona didn't mention names?' Marna probed. 'Before he went to the feast, or when he returned.'

'Several,' Erin gave a cruel laugh, 'Including your own.'

Chapter 20

Erin lifted her right palm to Marna's forehead. She paused with her finger inches away. Marna felt a tingling from them and nodded. Erin placed her palm against Marna's skin, brushing away her fringe of hair. Her hand was as icy as the sea water and the tips of her fingers rippled like the waves, drawing out thoughts.

Erin drew her hand away sharply, sending Marna stumbling back.

'The evil is among you. You would see it if you opened your eyes and closed your heart,' Erin said. 'You cannot trust your closest friend.'

'Henjar? Why, what has she done?'

Erin shrugged. 'I thought Ireland was wild, but it has nothing on this island.'

'If you don't like it, you can leave,' Marna muttered. From the look Erin gave her Marna knew she heard. 'I'm going for a stroll on the shore,' she said.

'You do that,' Erin answered. 'Talk to the Selkies. They can tell you what you need to see. Meanwhile, I shall play music on my pipes that will rip the eyes of my brother's killer from their sockets and send him to the next world cursing his mother for giving him birth.' She took hold of Sempal's hand. 'I have something to show you, darling.'

I wouldn't like to cross her, Marna thought as she

watched Erin lead Sempal back to the cave. Sempal would tire of her soon. Or just tire.

The tide was too far in to walk along the shore and she was forced onto the cliff path. There was time to think. The hand placing was Erin's way to gain attention and wasn't significant, but repeating what she knew helped organise her thoughts. Jona had found something to link the discarded blue cloak with Joel's death, she was sure. If she could discover what it was, then all they need do was find who the owner of the cloak was. It was good quality wool. Marna hadn't dyed it, but she was friends with the dyers in the nearby villages. Someone would recognise it.

She reached the turn off to the village, but her mind was turning events over and she decided to head further along the cliff path. She could see why the murderer would kill Jona, to keep him quiet. If the killer was in league with Roben over Joel's accident, a falling out about payment would explain his death, but what about Finn? His trading was over and he was heading home. And what made the weird marks on his and Jona's bodies?

Talk to the Selkies.

Why had Erin said that? The Selkies were sea spirits who took the form of seals.

Finn was a seasoned seaman. Had Henjar told him something about Joel's death that made him suspicious? Had he thought it unusual for Joel to drown so near the shore? Was he asking questions or was he in the wrong place at the wrong time?

She was no nearer a solution when she reached the bay where Jona had his cave. A cormorant dived into the water and surfaced with a fish in its beak. She admired the skill of the hunter. Thork was also a hunter. He and Sempal had combed the bay. If anything was to be found, Thork's sharp eyes would have uncovered it.

She kept to the path, skirting round the inlet, avoiding the terns. The coast line was made up of hundreds of small bays, and bays within bays. The next inlet along wasn't very accessible. The track down was strewn with loose rocks and thick roots exposed by the winds. Marna was about to bye-pass it, but cast her eye down first.

The tide was turning and she could see what looked like a driftwood branch on the shingle. It looked a fair-sized chunk and Marna knew it would be useful to the village. The weather was mild, excellent conditions for trading vessels to journey to their islands. She hoped a boat hadn't come to harm on the unfamiliar rocks. If it had there might be survivors in need of succour.

Marna picked her way down to the small beach, slipping on the shrub. She crunched across the pebbles towards the driftwood. It was a boat, deliberately pulled up from the sea. Marna spotted the tracks.

The people of Skara Brae were farmers, or hunters like

Thork. There weren't many brave enough to test themselves against the ocean. Joel had been one of the few with the skills. Perhaps, in time, he would have taught Boda. Jona warned against provoking the wrath of the sea gods, but Marna guessed that was because he was afraid.

Could it be what she was looking for? Joel's boat.

It was lying upside down, to prevent rain gathering inside. Marna tried to turn it, but she couldn't even lift the side off the sand. The bottom was covered in seaweed. Marna pulled it away, looking for an identifying mark. Joel had painted a picture of Henjar on the side of his boat. It didn't take long for Marna to uncover chipped paint on the wood. She rubbed away more of the algae and slime and traced round the marks.

It wasn't a shock. In her heart Marna had known it was Joel's boat. Jona must have found it and drawn it up the shore, but he hadn't told anyone of his find.

Had he discovered something in the boat?

Something he was using against the killer.

Her first thought was that he had found the cloak, but that wasn't possible. She had seen someone wearing it after Joel's body was found. She had seen it at the loch side too, when Jona had his vision.

Did Jona find something to make him suspect that his vision wasn't from the gods?

She snapped her fingers several times. There was

something she was missing. She tried again to prise the boat over, but after cracking three fingernails she gave up. She needed help. Thork had gone to Orphir and most of the villagers were still at the Ness.

Marna cursed her weakness as she strode across the shore. She needed to speak with Henjar. Erin was wrong about her. Her friend wasn't as bright as the others, but she was loyal. She might remember something she had said to Finn, something other than sweet nothings.

Too bad Henjar and Albar would be held by Patro at the Ness. Her mother was also there. She decided the best thing to do was return to the village and prepare the house for her mother and brother's return, perhaps even make bread. She could pick herbs to add to broth, in the hope of her mother making a pot on her return.

The best place to find the mint and water cress her mother enjoyed was near Skaill loch. Marna took the path inland. It was a pleasant afternoon, with the sun chasing the clouds out to sea. She sang as she skipped along, remembering the song Albar sang the previous night, but she couldn't catch the tune. It was difficult to sing cheerful songs with the vision of Jona's dead eyes staring at her. Another song came into her head, one she'd heard from a visiting trader. He came from a southern land where they poured scents on their dead and wrapped them in linen before encasing them in painted casings which were buried in tombs. The words were strange. The trader explained them using hand gestures, but Marna had her own interpretation. The dead had a message for the living, but the living were too busy with their lives to listen.

As she hummed the tune, she thought of Jona's message. Why had he come to the feast, yet kept his findings secret? She was sure his message was directed at someone in the crowd. They understood, but their reaction wasn't what Jona expected. She shivered as she saw Jona's hand pointing at her. Jona had been hallucinating. His hand wasn't straight.

Thork had been standing near her. It was his axe head in Jona's head. He could have slipped out of Wilmer's hut, made his way to the loch and confronted Jona.

She remembered the stains on his coat. He was quick to wipe them. What if they hadn't been ale, but blood?

Chapter 21

It was strange being in the house alone. Marna laid the gathered herbs on a woven mat to dry. She pounded grain heads into flour for the bread then used her wood drill to light a fire. The tinder lit first time.

'Ha,' Marna declared, but there was no-one to boast to. The fire burnt well, but the room was cold and she wrapped a skin round her shoulders. The fire cast a giant shadow from the bone figurine on the dresser. She watched it sway as she drifted off to sleep.

She was woken by the calls of the first villagers returning from the Ness the following morning and hurried to greet them. Their spirits from the feasting had been dashed by the news of Jona's death. Despite his recent behaviour, Jona was well-liked.

The priests at the Ness insisted on questioning everyone. Patro was reluctant to allow anyone to travel home, but despite its size, the Ness settlement was built for rituals not day-to-day living. Patro and a few of his priests and helpers stayed there permanently, but it was impossible for them to feed so many people without prior warning. The villagers had weapons and the priests feared a riot.

Everyone had their opinion. Marna heard her brother's name mentioned as a suspect, but also Horen, Sempal and the Irish witch.

'Marna, where have you been?' Seth called.

Everyone was asking questions.

'Did you know Jona was dead?

'Did you see his spirit at Maeshowe?'

'Maeshowe?' It took a moment for Marna to remember she was supposed to have been there with Thork.

'Where is Thork? Did you leave him in the cairn?'

'Has he received guidance from the spirits?'

She brushed the questions aside until one young man thought he was being funny when he quipped, 'You can sense things. Who will be next for an early grave?'

'There has been a fisherman, a fire-maker, a trader and a priest. I imagine the next victim will be a potter.'

The young man stopped laughing. He was known for his ability to throw and fire clay into attractive and useful forms. Marna smiled. 'Has anyone has seen Henjar?'

'She's with Albar. They weren't far behind,' the young man's companion answered.

'They may have rested in the long grass,' the potter said.

'Thank you.'

Marna left the villagers and followed the track towards the Ness. It wasn't long before she spotted Albar with Boda on his shoulders, followed by Henjar.

'I need your help,' she said, running up.

'Good morning to you too,' Albar answered.

'Sorry, but we don't have time. Henjar, can your

mother look after Boda?'

'She is a little way back,' Henjar said. 'It's her legs.'

Marna glanced down the road. She couldn't see Lin.

'What is this about?' Albar asked.

'We won't get into trouble, will we?' Henjar said. 'I've had enough of that. The priests threatened to throw Albar into a pit. They wanted to take Boda from me.'

'I need your help to lift something, that's all.'

'Something?' Albar asked.

Albar could be trusted to keep a secret, but Henjar had a loud mouth and quick tongue.

'Something heavy,' she said lamely.

'Women always want me for my body,' Albar grinned and Henjar prodded him in the ribs. The force sent him swaying across the path and Boda cried.

'Look what you've done,' Henjar chided, but Marna could tell she was teasing Albar.

'While we're waiting on your mother, there is something I need to ask,' Marna said to Henjar. 'It's about Finn.' She spoke in a whisper and made a gesture towards Albar. Henjar stopped, allowing Albar to walk ahead.

'What about Finn?' Henjar asked.

'Did he say anything to you before he died?'

'He could hardly say anything after he died, unless I'd been chewing salvia and chatting with the spirit world. Mind you, everybody else seems to be, so why not?'

Marna stared at her. 'Did he say anything or not?'

'He said a good number of silly things, most of which turned out to be false,' Henjar replied sharply.

'Did he say anything that might have led to his death?'

'Drinking too much, that's what led to his accident, or do you think the faerie folk were seeking revenge?'

'I think somebody was.'

Henjar sighed. 'He promised to get me a new bone comb as a token of his sincerity. They aren't cheap. Roben was lucky a whale beached on the shore when it did and Wilmer was willing to make one for me. Finn didn't say anything about seeing Horen's girls, if that's what you mean. He didn't promise them combs.'

'What about Erin? Did he mention her?'

'Only to say he was never sailing with her again. She brought a goat, two dogs, a cat and a mule on board with her. The cat jumped off before they set sail, but the others fouled the space and the mule brayed the entire voyage. Finn said if they had been at sea another night he would have thrown the mule overboard.'

'That's horrible,' Marna said.

'Listening to a mule is enough to sour the most patient of people, and for all his assets, Finn wasn't that.'

'I didn't see animals with the traders,' Marna said.

'Finn sold them when they landed. Erin was mad.'

'What are you two gabbing about?' Albar interrupted.

'Girl talk,' Marna and Henjar said together and laughed.

'Who were you talking to?' Henjar rounded on him. 'Don't deny it. I was keeping an eye on you.'

'Joannet. I saw her watching us. If I hadn't told her something she would have spread her own tale round the village. Your mother will be a while. Her joints are stiff and she is hitching a ride on the bread sledge. Joannet has agreed to mind Boda, unless you want me to help Marna on my own.'

Henjar pouted. She didn't like the thought of Joannet watching her son, but it was clear she didn't appreciate Marna being alone with Albar. She took Boda, kissed his forehead and marched towards Joannet.

'Ready,' she said, when she returned.

After the trek from the Ness, Henjar was not happy to be heading up the cliff path. She was trailing behind and panting before they reached the bay and Marna knew she would be useless when it came to lifting. The boat was there, untouched by nature or human hand. She was about to warn Henjar to take care on the rocky steps, but was surprised to see her friend rush towards the boat.

'That's "Sea Maid", Joel's boat,' Henjar clasped her mouth. Her face was pale. 'There's where he painted my portrait on the bow.' She stroked her hand over the wood.

'We need to get it righted,' Marna said. 'I think we'll

find a clue to what happened when Joel died.'

Henjar stepped back. 'Why must you remind me?'

'It's important.' Marna took her friend's arm. 'Think of Roben, Finn and Jona. You want their killer found.'

Henjar dug her toes into the sand without answering.

'We're here now,' Albar rolled up his sleeves. 'The sooner we do as Marna asks, the sooner we can get home.' He bent to dig at the sand, trying to get a finger-hold on the wooden rim. Marna helped, while Henjar watched.

'Aren't you giving us a hand?' Albar joked.

'Someone has to make sure you pull together.'

With a good deal of heaving and grunting, they managed to lift one side of the boat a few feet from the ground. It was heavier than Marna thought and even with Albar's muscles it seemed unlikely they could flip it over.

'Can you hold it up for a moment?' Marna asked. Albar spluttered a reply which sounded rude, but Marna took it as a 'yes.' She had spotted something blue caught on a splinter of wood beneath the boat's seat. After letting go, she waited to make sure Albar could balance the boat without dropping it on her head.

'Are you doing anything or not?' Albar complained. His knuckles were white and his cheeks purple.

Marna squashed low to crawl under the boat. She couldn't raise her head to see where the rag was, but her fingers felt the material and she tugged it. It was stuck tight.

There was a creak as Albar re-adjusted his grip.

'You're doing a brilliant job,' Henjar encouraged

Albar made an effort to raise the side of the boat higher. Marna reached for a stone and thrust the rough edge at the wood, cutting into the material.

'Fingers… slipping… Can't… hold…,' Albar puffed.

Henjar grabbed the side of the boat, but the weight was too great. 'Marna, come out.'

The wood groaned. Marna scrambled with hands and feet to edge her body out. The wood crashed to the beach, missing her outstretched left hand by an inch.

'Did you get what you were after?' Henjar asked.

Marna held a rag of blue thread, but Henjar wasn't watching. She was rubbing life into Albar's fingers.

'Thanks Albar,' Marna said.

'What about me? I helped too,' Henjar complained.

'Thank you, Henjar.' Marna gave her friend a hug.

'Don't I get a hug?' Albar said, but a look from Henjar set him right.

'It's only a scrap of cloth. The sea has drained it of colour. It can't tell us anything,' Albar said.

'It smells too,' Henjar added, holding her nose.

'Did Joel have a blue cloak?' Marna asked.

'No. He didn't like the colour. He said it reminded him of the sea.'

'That's weird for a fisherman to say,' Albar said.

'Is it? He was at sea all day. Why would he want to be reminded of it at home? Joel didn't take his cloak when he went fishing. It was a good cloak. I didn't want it smelling of fish and wasted by salt water.'

'This proves someone was in the boat with him on his final voyage,' Marna explained.

'Sempal has a blue cloak and he was in the boat that morning,' Henjar said.

'This isn't the same blue as Sempal's cloak,' Marna answered. 'I dyed his cloak for him using woad. Even after months of being washed by the tides, this scrap is different. I'm pretty sure it will match the cloak I have at home. The one Thork found in Jona's cave.'

'Jona killed my husband?' Henjar almost screamed. Albar moved to put an arm around her.

'No,' Marna said with a sigh. Henjar hadn't understood anything. 'It's complicated. I'll explain later.' She turned towards the bank.

'Where are you going?' Albar asked.

'There are questions I need to ask in the neighbouring villages. Thanks again for your help. Both of you.'

'You're leaving us here?' Henjar said.

'An empty shore, the sound of the sea, no Boda,' Albar smiled.

'If you put it that way…'

Marna left them as they settled behind a sand dune.

She hurried to the village and in to her house, fumbling among the skins in her cot to find the cloak.

'What are you up to? Her mother was home and re-arranging the pots Marna used the previous evening.

'Nothing,' Marna rescued the cloak from beneath a seal skin. 'Yes.' To her delight it was the same blue hue as the scrap she found on the boat. There was a rip at the bottom she could poke her fingers through.

'Do you want me to mend that?' her mother asked.

'No, it's perfect the way it is.'

Her mother made a face, but she was used to Marna's odd behaviour. 'Do you know where your brother is?'

'He was going to Orphir to see Caran. He should be back today,' Marna answered.

'If he's gone to see Caran he won't be back today or tomorrow,' her mother said. 'Still, it's one less stomach to fill. Whatever did you add to that bread you made? It tastes like one of your dyes.'

'I was crushing plants. Perhaps I didn't clean the pot well enough before grinding the grain.'

'You used my grain stone for crushing dyes,' her mother's voice was hard.

'Sorry, I didn't think.'

'That's your problem. You've got your mind on so many complicated matters, you fail to see what is obvious,' her mother chided. 'Where are you off to now? You're always in a rush.'

'I have to find... I need to ask...I won't be long.' Marna was out of the hut before her mother could say anything more. She knew the dyers in the region. One of them would recognise the dye. Even if they couldn't remember who the cloak was coloured for, it would narrow the culprit to an area.

Rosa was the dye maker in Barnhouse. She taught Marna and most of the dyers in the region. Whoever had produced the dye was a skilled crafts person. Rosa would know who.

As she jogged along, she wondered if her mother was right. Was something so obvious, she was missing it? A wind was blowing and it was drizzling with rain when she reached the meadow near Barnhouse. Wilmer was walking towards her with Pip at his heels and she gave a wave.

'Marna, what brings you here? There's nothing wrong is there?' Wilmer sounded concerned.

'I'm looking for Rosa. Is she at home?'

'Do you need help with a dye?' Wilmer saw the cloak in her hands. 'I don't think she is at home. I'm sure she said she was going to the loch to pick meadowsweet.' He took hold of Marna's hands. 'Your fingers are frozen and you are getting wet. Why don't you come in for a warm drink of honey mead, while you wait?'

'I'd love to, but I don't have time. I have to find Rosa.

You said she was by the loch?'

'Let me accompany you. I'm heading to the Ness with bracelets and charms. The loch is on my way.'

'Thank you,' Marna said, bending to stroke Pip. The dog gave a soft whine.

'Pip doesn't like rain, Wilmer said. 'He hates getting wet, as much as I do, but the priests won't wait for their trinkets.'

It was a short walk to the loch and Marna was keen to question Wilmer about the Ness.

'Who do they think was responsible for Jona's death?' she asked. Wilmer frowned.

'There are murmurs that your brother may have had something to do with it.'

'But that is ridiculous,' Marna raised her voice.

'Patro is annoyed with Thork. He doesn't like his authority being tested. It didn't help that Thork left before he could be questioned. Patro had his priests guard Maeshowe for hours.'

'Patro is a pigeon-head,' Marna scoffed.

Wilmer gave a chuckle. 'That he might be, but he has influence and power.'

'From the gods?'

'From men with stone axes and flint arrowheads.'

They reached the edge of the loch. Marna looked around. 'Rosa must be round the other side,' Marna said.

'Thank you for walking with me. I'd better let you get on with your business.'

'It was my pleasure. Can I ask what business you have with Rosa?' He stared again at the cloak, as if hoping it would catch in the breeze and be carried off.

'She is renowned as a dyer of blue pigments. I want to ask her about this cloak.'

'Oh?'

Marna held it up. The tear was plain to see.

'Where did you get that?' Wilmer asked.

'Jona found it. Look, there's a scrap torn from the bottom. This scrap,' she spoke quickly. 'It fits. I found it in Joel's boat. It's not Sempal's. It must belong to the person who killed him.'

'Slow down, Marna, you're ahead of me.' Wilmer moved closer, edging her towards the bank. 'Joel's death was an accident, surely?'

'No. Jona was right; there was someone in the boat with him. That person killed him. The same man who murdered Roben, Finn and Jona. Rosa will know who this cloak belongs to.'

'I'm sure she will. It's a good cloak.' Wilmer took the cloak from Marna and examined it. Before she could stop him, he crumpled it into a ball, raised it above his shoulder and tossed the bundle into the middle of the loch. Pip looked like he was about to retrieve it, but put one paw in the water and stepped back.

'Why did you do that?' Marna accused. 'Now we won't know...'

'It is for the best,' Wilmer smiled, but there was no sparkle in his eyes.

'You? No, you couldn't kill anyone.'

Erin had warned her not to trust a friend. Of course, Erin would have been referring to a man, not a woman.

'Couldn't I? Granted, Roben's death was an accident, but Joel's death was planned. Not by me though.'

'I don't understand.' Marna could feel herself being driven nearer the water's edge as Wilmer moved closer.

'Roben lusted after Henjar and I wanted the ability to make fire. I needed it. Our village was desperate after Hector's death. We had to rely on the whims of the priests from the Ness and pay them dearly in service or wait for the rare visits from Roben. I was horrified by Roben's proposal, at first, but then I saw that a sacrifice was needed.'

'A sacrifice? But you don't believe in gods.'

'I wasn't trusting to the gods. Roben and I made an agreement. I would ensure Joel had an 'accident' and Roben would teach me how to use the black stones. I persuaded Joel to take me out fishing. I'd been before, so he wasn't suspicious. Joel wanted to sail in search of cod, but I knew I would have to bring the boat home myself. I couldn't do that, miles out in a heavy sea.'

'You pushed Joel into the water?'

'We rounded the cliffs and I pointed at a shadow in the water. I think I said it was a porpoise. I knew he could swim to the shore if I pushed him overboard, so I whacked him on the head with one of his oars. I had been dreading it for days, but actually it was the ease of killing a man that scared me. I rowed the boat to a quiet bay, got out and pushed it back to sea. I calculated I could climb the cliff while everyone was attending to Joel's body.'

'You were the figure in blue I saw on the cliff.'

'Yes, I thought I saw somebody, but convinced myself it was nothing. A mistake, I know, but my biggest mistake was trusting Roben. The scoundrel denied there was a bargain and I could hardly call on the elders for justice. Fortunately, Rawdric appeared with his flints, so perhaps the gods were appeased.'

'So why did you kill Roben?'

'That was an accident, as I said. Roben hadn't paid me for the whale bone comb I made for Henjar. I was still angry from the incident with Joel and demanded he return it to me or I would take the matter to Patro at the Ness. That shook him. He came to Barnhouse shortly before Joel's burial. We argued, Roben got violent, I pushed him and he fell against a flagstone. Like I said, an accident, but no-one would have believed me. I would have been killed, or worse, sent to some tiny little island rock to scrape a living from the dirt.' He paused for Marna to give an opinion, but she could only gape at him in disbelief.

'There was a problem getting rid of the body,' Wilmer continued, as if confessing relieved him of his guilt. 'My house is large, but not to conceal a corpse. It came to me during a walk round the stones. Jona put great store by talking to his gods, so I persuaded him he had seen a vision by the loch. He came to Barnhouse in quite a state, demanding the men open Maeshowe. I dragged Roben's body there that night, before your parade arrived.'

Marna's feet were getting wet. The water was up to her ankles and Wilmer was forcing her in deeper. She couldn't get away. 'What did you do with the cloak?'

'Like I said, Roben's death was an accident and I hadn't planned for the fall out. I was careless. When I returned to Skara Brae as fire-maker, Jona invited me to stay in his house. He saw my cloak and associated it with his vision at the loch. When he stumbled across Joel's boat, well he wasn't stupid.'

'He said as much when we disturbed him with Erin,' Marna remembered.

'He was blackmailing me. When he came to the ceremony and accused me openly, I knew he had to die. Lucky that you were standing next to me and Jona's pointing was a little awry. It gave me time to act before the crowd realised who he meant.'

'You took the axe when Boda was choking.'

'Of course not. You saw how easy it was to take gifts from the table. I had nothing to do with the incident and I am glad no harm came to the boy.'

'You gave us the sleeping draught, pretending to take it too. When we were asleep you slipped out to kill Jona.'

'Yes, you are a smart girl. I took your brother's coat. You might have noticed the blood. Jona wasn't easy to fell. Thankfully Pip was with me to niggle at his wrists.'

'Those were the strange marks on the body.' Marna was up to her knees in loch water. Wilmer pressed closer. 'The same marks on Finn. Why did you kill him?'

'You can't guess? Not so clever then.' Wilmer put his hands on Marna's neck. 'I'm genuinely sorry I have to kill you. I thought we were friends.'

Marna couldn't tell if his regret was genuine or not as she struggled to wrest free from his grip. She could hear Pip barking from the shore. 'Don't do this. Let me help you.'

'It's too late for that, I'm afraid. Don't worry about your mother being alone. I can take care of her. We already have a relationship.'

It took a moment for Marna to realise what he was saying. 'You and my mother? In our house?'

'In Jona's house to be exact. After he left.'

'You poisoned my ale.'

'A small dose to keep you out of trouble. Pity it didn't work.' He pushed her nearer the water.

'Wait. Give me time to work out what Finn had to do with this,' Marna spluttered.

Wilmer hesitated then loosened his grip, but kept his hands rested on Marna's shoulders. 'Very well.'

'Henjar must have told Finn something about Joel.' It was a guess and Marna saw from Wilmer's expression she was on the wrong track. Fear made her mind work quickly. 'No, it was the comb.'

'Go on,' Wilmer was listening.

'I found it on the cliff edge before I spotted Finn's body, but lost it when we dragged the body behind Sempal's boat.'

'Ah, that explains it. I wondered how Finn's body could wash up where it did. I should have realised it had something to do with you and your simple friend.'

'Sempal isn't simple.'

'He does come up with stupidest notions, though. You told me about the comb. Pity you lost it.'

'It *was* Henjar's comb. The one Roben asked you to make,' Marna said. 'You tried to throw me off the scent whenever I mentioned it.'

'That comb was one of my best works. Roben hadn't paid me for it and I knew I could sell it to traders for a good price. I took it from his dead hand. '

'When Finn asked you for a comb, you sold him the same one?'

'I didn't know he would give it to Henjar. I thought it was a gift for his wife in Ireland.'

'When you found out it was for Henjar you panicked. She would have demanded to know how you got her comb.'

'I met Finn on the cliff top and asked to buy it back. He laughed. There was no way I could have beaten Finn in a struggle, but I was lucky Pip was with me. He may not be a hunter, but he is very protective. When Finn raised an arm, Pip jumped on him. Finn toppled over the edge without me having to give more than a nudge. I wasn't sorry to see him fall. The man was no good.'

'You are hardly one to judge.'

'I wish I'd never begun this miserable business and it isn't over. I can't trust you to keep your mouth shut.'

Marna felt Wilmer's honey breath as he leaned over with his hands on her neck. He forced her head into the water as she struggled to escape. She heard Pip howling and thought she saw a blurry figure on the bank. She was pushed under with her mouth open and her lungs filled with water. It was too late. She didn't have the strength to save herself.

Chapter 22

Marna thought of her drowning father. She could see his smiling face. The water lapped gently around them until there was a splash and a shout. It was more than a shout; it was high-pitched screaming. Marna felt she was trapped in a cave full of banshees. She tried to banish the noise and as she did she felt herself floating to the surface.

She choked out a mouthful of water and gulped for air. It took a moment to see the sky and sense the commotion.

Where was Wilmer?

She flailed with her hands and feet until she was standing upright in the loch. The chilly water grazed her thighs and her wet tunic dragged her down. She rubbed her eyes and as her vision became clear she saw the jeweller splashing in the water a little way out. A hand reached to grab her from behind and she screamed.

'Are you all right?'

It was the worried voice of Thork. She reached for his arm and he yanked her from the water. She collapsed on the reeds and lay there. Thork put his cloak around her.

'Wilmer is still in the water,' she said, sitting up. 'He can't swim.'

'Neither can his accursed mutt,' Thork spat. 'They can both drown.'

Thork was looking over the water. Marna forced herself to her feet and moved beside him. Wilmer had gathered Pip in his arms and held the dog's head above the water, but his legs were trapped and he was being pulled beneath the waves.

'Do something,' Marna said to Thork.

'He tried to kill you, Marna. His brute of a dog made a good job of eating my leg, before I kicked it into the loch. If they don't drown, I'll go in and finish the job.'

Marna looked away, but she could hear Wilmer's cries. He managed to clamber nearer the bank, but was being tugged under. The end of his cloak was tangled among the roots of the water plants and weighed him down. Panicking didn't help. He couldn't unfasten his cloak without letting go of Pip. The dog was howling. Marna hobbled to the bank and reached out her arms.

'Toss Pip to me,' she called. 'I'll look after him.'

Wilmer hesitated. A wave from the loch rippled over the dog's head before subsiding.

'I promise,' Marna's voice was hoarse, but Wilmer heard her and gave a lop-sided smile. He seemed to mouth the word 'friends' before forcing his arms above his drowning head. With an immense effort that stole his remaining strength, he thrust the dog towards the shore. Pip landed with a plop in the shallow water and Marna rushed to rescue him before his frantic paddling sent him back out to the middle of the loch. She picked the dog up and it licked her face as she rubbed the sodden fur with her brother's cloak. She looked over the water to show Wilmer the dog was safe, but there were only bubbles in the water where he had been.

'Good riddance,' Thork said. 'You should have let the mutt drown too.'

'Pip saved my life,' Marna said.

'How do you work that one out?'

'Wilmer stopped trying to drown me to save him.'

'I was the one who kicked the dog in the water, so I saved your life,' Thork protested.

'Thank you,' Marna put Pip down and gave her brother a hug. She suddenly felt exhausted and she was crying. She leaned into Thork's chest. 'I'm so glad you were here.'

'Come on, let's go home,' Thork said. 'I'll carry you if I have to.'

'I'm fine. Here Pip,' Marna called to the dog who had wandered to the edge of the water. He looked out and gave a whine. 'Sorry Pip. Your master is gone.'

'Aye, you have a new mistress now, whelp and you had better obey her,' Thork said, fingering his belt.

Pip gave a last sorry look and trotted towards Marna. She petted his forehead and stroked his ear.

Marna managed three steps before collapsing. She felt Thork lift her onto his shoulder and Pip nuzzle against her trailing arm before everything went dark.

She woke to the smell of bere bannocks being baked

on a hot stone. The warm, floury aroma wove its way around her. She rolled over and gave a soft moan.

'I think she's awake,' a voice said. It was a familiar voice.

'Mother?' Marna groaned.

'You're back with us.'

'About time too.'

The second voice was definitely Thork's. Marna opened her eyes. Her mother and brother were leaning over her bed. Memories of the cold loch swirled in her head. She could taste the murky water, although she struggled to remember what had happened. Thork had been there. Thork had rescued her. *From what?* Her head was bursting with questions.

'Careful or the bannocks will burn,' she said.

Her mother gave a laugh of relief. 'A breath away from death and all you are worried about are the bannocks.'

'I'm sorry about Wilmer,' she reached for her mother's hand. Her mother put her other hand on top of Marna's. She didn't answer, but Marna could see a tear.

'I'll go and fetch Sempal,' Thork said.

'You saved me,' Marna looked at her brother.

'I'm glad you remember that.'

'Where's Pip?' Marna sat up.

'The mutt is fine. He can't be trusted when there are bannocks around though. He can smell them from outside the village walls,' Thork answered.

'How long have I been sleeping?' Marna asked.

'Too long,' her mother answered, wiping her eye.

'Three days,' Thork said.

'Goodness,' Marna jumped up. 'There is so much to do.'

'I'll fetch Sempal,' her mother said to Thork. She removed the bannocks from the stone and set them high up on the dresser before leaving the hut.

'The men from Barnhouse pulled Wilmer's body from the loch,' Thork said, when his mother left. 'It has been laid out with Jona's. Wilmer was well respected. I didn't think anyone need know what happened. I let them think it was an accident. Wilmer couldn't swim and there was a swell on the loch.'

'The people here will want to know more.'

'I've persuaded the elders that the spirits of our ancestors spoke to me at Maeshowe. The gods are appeased and there will be no more trouble.'

'They believed you?'

'Aye, but no doubt they will still pester you for details. Meanwhile, Sempal has returned to the village a wiser man. He has accepted the role of fire-maker and storyteller. We plan to have an evening of tales tomorrow night.'

'What if I hadn't been awake? You wouldn't have gone ahead with a storytelling evening without me?'

'Here is Sempal now,' Thork managed to avoid answering.

Sempal had on a new tunic and cloak. His beard was trimmed into a triangle barely covering his chin. Marna spotted Pip followed him in. The dog's tail was visible from beneath Sempal's cloak.

'No you don't,' Thork bent to drag him out.

'Leave him, please,' Marna said. 'I'll make sure he stays away from the bannocks.' Pip lopped over and nestled beside her.

'She cares more about a lame dog than a ...' Thork began. Sempal frowned. 'I didn't mean... Sorry, I'll leave you two, three, together.'

'Where is Erin?' Marna asked when her brother left.

'Why do you ask?'

'Thork said you were back in the village. I'm not sure our village life would suit Erin.'

'Wilder than Ireland. That is exactly what would suit Erin. You mean you don't think Erin will suit our village.'

'She will liven the place up,' Marna said.

'She would, but she met a trader going to Shetland and decided to go with him,' Sempal said. 'Her words were "the faerie folk are calling me north".'

'There's no arguing with the faerie folk.'

'You don't believe in faerie folk,' Sempal said.

'She was right about Wilmer. His aura was fading. I

think she knew he was the killer.'

'Why didn't she say something?'

'Knowing Erin, she probably wanted to see us bumble our way to the answer.'

'It doesn't matter now. When will you be fit and out of bed? I have arranged a gathering of storytelling for tomorrow. The people want to know what happened.'

'I'm not sure I want to remember,' Marna said. 'Wilmer wasn't himself, not the kind man we knew. He saved my life on the cliff top.'

'Killing gets to people. Once you start, you can't stop. You don't have to tell everything the way it actually happened – especially not me making a fool of myself with Erin.'

Their conversation was interrupted by giggling. A group of young children had gathered in the doorway, peeking at Marna.

'You have admirers,' Sempal said. 'Everybody wants to see the new wise woman of the village.'

'Wise woman? I'm more like a stupid girl. If Thork hadn't been passing on his way back from Orphir I wouldn't be here.'

'Like I said, tales are based on the truth, but it's the way we tell them that makes the impact.'

'Thork will tell a good tale of how he saved me.'

'You won't be able to rely on Thork much longer.

When he marries Caran they are going to live in Orphir. Thork has been invited to be the priest there.'

'That is wonderful for both of them, but the village will be without a leader.'

Sempal cleared his throat. 'I'm one of the elders now and who needs a priest when we have a priestess?'

'A priestess? Me? Patro would never allow that.'

'It has nothing to do with him.'

'It would be good to see the look on his face,' Marna laughed as she imagined it. 'But I'm not strong enough to be a leader.'

'Henjar has Albar to look after her and Boda, so I'm free to be your protector.' Sempal moved to the dresser and took a bannock before returning to Marna's side.

'You protect me?' Marna took the bannock from him. She took a bite, but didn't have the appetite for it.

'The storyteller and the wise woman, I think we'd make the perfect pairing, don't you?' Sempal suggested.

'It has a ring to it, but don't forget Pip.' She offered the bannock to the dog and he snaffled it up. 'I would say; the storyteller, the wise woman and her trusty dog.'

'Let's hope we don't have too many more mysteries to solve.'

Marna and her friends' investigations continue in 'Evil in Eynhallow,' coming soon.

Evil in Eynhallow

Chapter 1

'Get off, you brutes,' Marna flapped her arms above her head, protecting her face from the warning swoops and spear-sharp beaks of the Arctic terns. Her flustering rocked the rowing boat she and Sempal were in.

'They are only guarding their nests and eggs, remember,' Sempal repeated the words Marna had said to him that morning. Her glare curbed his laughter. 'I guess we must be near the bay.' He wrenched the oars, sending Marna sprawling.

'Must you do that?' she complained.

'It would help if somebody gave me a hand with the rowing.'

'How can I? I need both arms to prevent us being

pecked alive.'

'I thought that was what he was here for.' Sempal nodded at the small dog cowering beside Marna's feet. It whimpered in response.

'Pip is afraid of the water,' Marna reminded him. 'You know his master drowned rescuing him from the loch.' She put a hand on Pip's head and he nestled closer.

'Good thing too,' Sempal replied. 'But that was last year. He can't still be upset.'

'You think because he's a dog, he doesn't suffer from traumatic incidents?'

'I didn't mean that.'

'Let's not talk about it.'

Marna had almost been drowned by the dog's master, Wilmer, in the "traumatic incident". The memory was raw.

Sempal steered the boat away from the cliff with the nesting terns, towards an inlet. It was the only safe landing spot on the island. Eynhallow lay between their island and the busy settlements on Rousay, and the current in the sound made it difficult to reach. This gave the islanders security from raiders, but it was a hindrance for trading. Marna had only been there once before, and Sempal never.

Marna peered over Sempal's hunched body to the shore. 'I can't see anyone. Are they expecting us?'

'I told Fara, the morning before she left, but she's growing as crazy as her father was. She is constantly doped out of her head, according to Gerk at any rate.'

'Gerk is the one who is the dope,' Marna defended her friend. 'I wouldn't pay attention to what he says. Fara is all right. Jona taught her what plants ease the burden of island life and I don't blame her for using them. Three of her cattle have stopped eating and are giving sour milk. Two of her neighbour's sheep have died and the problem is spreading. The islanders blame Fara.'

'Hopefully your mother's medicine can cure things.'

Marna felt for her bag at the bottom of the boat. The skin was damp, thanks to sea water seeping into the boat. 'Oh no, if the powder gets wet, it will be ruined.'

'If you sat still in the boat, the water wouldn't get in.'

Marna made a face, but clenched the bag to her chest

and sat as still as she could. She made cooing noises at Pip, to show Sempal she was annoyed with him, but it wasn't long before she wanted to speak.

'Did you talk with the traders from Wick?'

'I didn't get a chance. They had nothing we wanted, so they didn't wait. They were eager to press on to the Ness.'

'I didn't see them either,' Marna admitted, 'but Henjar mentioned there was a healer with them.'

'Oh, she said nothing to me.'

'No? Then why has your face turned bright pink, the way it does when you are telling tales?'

'It is the strain of rowing. How many of your mother's bere bannocks did you guzzle before we set off?'

'What did Henjar say about the healer?' Marna persisted.

'He has "magic" stones that can draw evil out of people and animals.'

'Evil?'

'That's what Henjar said. She may have misheard or

was using her over-active imagination. She has a thing about sickness and evil being linked.'

'That is ridiculous,' Marna leaned forwards and the boat wobbled again. 'Sorry.'

Sempal pulled the boat in to the bay and looked for a spot to land. The shore was deserted.

'Did she say what this healer was like?' Marna said.

'No.'

'You're lying again,' Marna slapped his knees. 'Henjar will have told you every detail. She has an eye for men.'

'I didn't say it was a man.'

'Oh.'

'But you're right. His name is Aiven and according to Henjar he's "not her type". Mind you, Albar was with her when she said that.'

'He's probably old and hairy,' Marna decided, 'Or bald and wrinkled. People believe anything old, bald men tell them. Even about magic stones.'

'Do I sense you are jealous of Aiven?'

'What is there to be jealous of? He sounds like a work-shy charlatan.'

'Just the sort they love at the Ness,' Sempal was enjoying winding Marna up. 'Patro and his cronies will no doubt be keen to have him stay for a while.'

Marna grunted. 'Keep your eyes on the water. You almost bumped into a rock.'

The water was shallow enough for them to step out and drag the boat, with Pip in it, up the pebbly beach to the bank. Sempal checked there was no damage to the hull before he secured it to a rock. 'You've been here before. Which way to the village?'

Marna looked round to get her bearings. 'I thought someone would come to greet us,' she said again. 'They must have spotted us approaching.'

'You don't know the way, do you?'

'It's been a while since I was here. Give me time.' Marna began to walk along the path worn in the bank towards the cliff. 'This way,' she called.

It hadn't rained for days and the ground was dry.

Marna took a step, caught her foot on a stone and slipped. She staggered several feet, trying to prevent herself falling, but tumbled to the ground and rolled over. Her head and foot hurt as she came to a halt. She lay face down on the grass, assessing her injuries.

'What are you laughing at?' she chided as she heard Sempal approach. 'Make yourself useful and give me a hand up.' She kept her head down, but lifted her arm. A hand with a strong grasp took hold of it.

'Are you all right?' the husky voice asked.

That definitely wasn't Sempal. She looked up to see a startling pair of hazel eyes watching her. 'Who are you?' she asked, none too civilly.

The eyes were connected to a handsome face, with chiseled cheekbones and chin. The man's dark hair was combed back and tied with a sinew. His beard was short and clean. The lips were smiling.

'My name is Aiven. Can I help you up or are you comfortable down there with the slugs?'

Marna let go of his hand with a jerk.

'Marna does her own thing,' Sempal explained as he joined the man.

'Ah, you are Marna. I have heard people speak of you. And you must be Sempal,' Aiven turned towards him. 'What is that you are carrying?'

'That, is my dog,' Marna answered. She got to her feet, rubbed her tunic then took Pip from Sempal. The dog covered her with drool as he licked her face.

Aiven made a face. 'Can't it walk?'

'Pip doesn't like the pebbles,' Sempal explained.

'He has a bad leg,' Marna added.

'Perhaps I can cure it,' Aiven said, reaching out to stroke Pip. Marna drew him away.

'He bites,' she warned.

'I've coped with worse.'

'Pip has already killed a man,' Sempal said.

Aiven made a sound from the side of his mouth in disbelief.

'A stranger to the islands,' Marna said, tickling Pip's ear.

'We have barely met, yet I sense you have a poor opinion of me,' Aiven rubbed his chin.

'I have heard people speak of you,' Marna was quick to reply. 'If you will excuse us, we have work here.'

'What sort of work?' Aiven moved to block Marna's way. Pip gave a soft growl, but nestled further in to Marna's chest.

'Healing,' Marna replied. 'I don't know how long you have been on Eynhallow, but you surely must have heard about the ailments of the cattle and sheep. My mother has prepared a potion...'

'Can I see it?' Aiven interrupted. Marna was reluctant to show him, but couldn't think of an excuse not to. She put Pip down and opened her bag, bringing out a lidded pot.

'May I?' Aiven raised his fingers towards the lid, but didn't open the pot until Marna nodded. He stuck his thumb in the mixture and removed a sample. After rubbing it between his fingers he lifted it to his nose.

'Dandelions, mint and ...what? Clam shells?'

Marna grabbed the lid and thrust it back on the pot.

'My mother is a well-known healer,' she said.

'I do not deny it,' Aiven said. 'Fortunately there is no need of her medicine. The cattle are well. I have cured them.'

'With your magic stones?' Marna jeered.

'My stones have power, yes, but the energy comes from the earth. The stones align the humours in the body and draw out what shouldn't be there.'

'And Fara's cows are now milking?'

'They would provide more milk if they had access to fresh water, but there is a shortage on the island.'

'Your stones can't make it rain?' Sempal said. Marna could tell Aiven didn't know if he was serious or mocking.

'No.'

Marna was tiring of the conversation. Someone as annoying as Aiven really shouldn't be so good-looking and charming. 'Fara is expecting us,' she said, moving past.

'You must be tired after your journey,' Aiven allowed. 'I'll escort you to the village.'

'I know the way,' Marna said.

'Well…' Sempal began, but a look from Marna stopped him.

'I'm heading there anyway,' Aiven answered. 'Would you like me to carry your dog for you?'

'Come Pip,' Marna strode ahead and beckoned to the dog. Pip rose and waddled after his mistress. Sempal and Aiven followed in silence. After five minutes she was lost. The island wasn't large and she should be able to see the village. She stopped and turned sharply. Sempal and Aiven halted in time to prevent a collision.

'I'm going the wrong way, amn't I?' she said.

'It's a circular island,' Aiven answered. 'I thought you were taking the scenic route.'

'Smarty.' Marna stomped round him and back along the track.

'Is she like this all the time?' Aiven asked Sempal.

'No, this is a good day,' she replied, without looking round. She heard Aiven laugh.

As they neared the village, Pip yelped and ran ahead. Marna called, but he disappeared behind a windswept beech hedge. He reappeared with a dead rat in his mouth.

'Put it down,' Marna ordered. Pip looked at her with large eyes.

'Better do as she says,' Aiven told the dog. Pip dropped the half-chewed rodent.

Sempal went on while Marna was dealing with Pip and he returned with Fara, who was carrying a baby, swaddled in skins. Marna moved to see the child.

'Is it a boy or a girl?' she asked Fara.

'A little girl. We call her Terese. I'm so glad you could come and see her.'

'She is beautiful,' Marna knew that was what Fara wanted to hear. 'At least my journey wasn't in vain. Aiven tells me the cattle are cured.'

'Yes. They have given good milk for two days and no more sheep have died. I'm sorry your mother's medicine was not needed, but it would be good if you could stay with us for a few days. I have a cloak I would like dyed and if Sempal doesn't mind, the villagers would welcome an evening of storytelling.'

'Don't get him started,' Marna pretended to be bored by Sempal's tales, although she loved hearing them.

'You are a storyteller?' Aiven asked.

'Sempal is the best storyteller on the islands,' Fara answered. 'Don't listen to Marna's teasing.'

They walked with Fara into the village. A number of villagers were about, busy at work, or gossip. Gerk invited them in to the house. Marna was about to step in when they heard a disturbance. It sounded like a woman wailing. Pip ran towards the noise with his tail in the air.

'You'd better catch him in case he bites someone,' Sempal whispered to Marna.

Aiven strode ahead of Marna. Most of the villagers were keen to find out what the trouble was. As Marna caught up, she saw an old woman kneeling on the ground. A girl was lying in front of her.

'What is the matter, Wandra?' a villager asked.

The woman tried to answer, but tears stifled her words. She scratched in the dust with her fingers.

'Is the girl ill?' Aiven asked. He reached in the pocket

of his tunic for his stones.

Marna bent down to take the girl's arm. It was cold to the touch and flopped in Marna's hand. Pip nudged beside Marna, sniffed the air and gave a low groan.

'Let me see,' Aiven knelt beside her, holding a stone in either hand.

'You won't need these,' Marna said. 'There is no life in her veins. Her lips are blue and her heart is still. It will take more than some magic stones to raise the dead.'

Thanks to Historic Scotland and The Ness Archaeological Dig for information used in this book.

Although considerable effort has been made to conform with historical opinion about the time, Maeshowe Murder is completely a work of fiction. Some license has been taken where information is uncertain.

Any resemblances to people alive or dead is purely co- incidental.

Printed in Great Britain
by Amazon

24592046R00188